Sand

and

Bone

Sand

and

Bone

D. Moonfire

Broken Typewriter Press • Cedar Rapids

Broken Typewriter Press
5001 1st Ave SE
Ste 105 #243
Cedar Rapids, IA 52402

Broken Typewriter Press
https://broken.typewriter.press/

ISBN 978-1-940509-25-9

Version 1.1.0

To Jenny and Jackie

A family split
years ago.
Sisters lost
but not forgotten.
An idle question.
Once again…
Reconnected.

Miwāfu

This novel is set in the Mifuno Desert where the native language is Miwāfu. Names in this language are significantly different from English, so here is a short guide on pronunciation and usage.

The biggest difference is that every name is gendered, which is identified by the accent on the penultimate syllable. There are three types of accents:

- *Grave* (as in hèru for stallion) is a tiny tick that goes down to the right. The grave accent indicates a masculine aspect, either in physical gender, size, or power. Names with grave accents either end in a lower pitch or the entire word is spoken in a lower tone.
- *Macron* (for example, hēru for colt) is a bar over the vowel. This is a neuter term, used for many gender-free words or expressions within the language. It is also used for mechanical devices, abstract concepts, and children —both human and beast. Macrons are spoken as a long vowel or drawing out the word just a beat longer than normal.

- *Acute* (héru for mare) is a tiny tick that goes to the upper right. The acute indicates feminine aspects of the word. It can represent control without power or precision. These words end on a high note or the entire word is spoken in a higher pitch.

The only instances where accents aren't used is adjectives or indication of ownership. So, if a valley is owned by the clan Shimusògo, it is known as Shimusogo Valley.

The names themselves are phonetic. A syllable is always from a consonant cluster to the vowel. For examples: Mi.wā.fu (IPA /mi.waː.ɸɯ/), Shi.mu.sò.go (/ɕi.mɯ.↓so.go/), and De.sò.chu (/de.↓so.tɕɯ/). The only exception is the letter "n" which is considered part of the syllable before it when not followed by a vowel. For example, ga.n.ré.ko (/ga.ŋ↑re.ko/) and ka.né.ko (/ka.↑ne.ko/).

Miwāfu has no capital letters, they are added to satisfy English conventions.

Previously

Sand and Ash started with Rutejìmo as an outsider to his own clan. After the events of *Sand and Blood*, he had been accepted as an adult of the clan but not universally welcomed. He found a courier route which he ran alone, and spent little time in Shimusogo Valley. In his hours alone he nursed a crush on Mikáryo—the night warrior who attacked him in the previous book, only to save him later.

Despite his avoidance of the valley, a young woman, Mapábyo, developed a crush of her own on him. The rest of the clan tried to subtly discourage Rutejìmo's fantasies for a woman he hadn't seen in a decade and encourage his attention on the girl, who they felt was a better choice for him as a life partner.

Things changed when Mapábyo went on her own rite of passage. When she survived, she emulated Rutejìmo—which revealed the animosity that had grown between him and his older brother, Desòchu. Desòchu treated Rutejìmo as a poison to the clan, mainly driven by Rutejìmo's inability to follow the same path as the others.

After Mapábyo's entrance into adulthood, the clan decided to strongly encourage a relationship between her and

Rutejìmo by their usual method: taking them into the desert and abandoning them to find love. This failed when they arrived at Wamifuko City where Rutejìmo met up with his decade-long crush, Mikáryo. Lost in his own fantasies, he abandoned his own people for days while rekindling his relationship with her. When it ended, she cast him out to go back to his life.

Sullen, he returned to his family only to be attacked by his brother and kicked out of the clan for a year. He quickly found that being without a clan was a death sentence in the desert and only Mapábyo, acting in direction violation of the clan elders, was able to save him as she caught up with him and protected him against the ostracization of being clan-less.

During this time, Rutejìmo was given various chores and tasks to complete, such as taking out garbage and burning corpses. The latter became more important as he learned the rituals of tending to the dead. Later, he would meet with another kojinōmi, a caretaker of the dead. He embraced his tasks as a comforter to the dying and the one who could handle the corpses.

The Shimusògo's goal of getting the two together finally succeeded when Rutejìmo fell for Mapábyo. They tried to avoid returning to Shimusogo Valley but were eventually forced back. Rutejìmo was still ignored as someone without a clan, which led to him almost killing himself and fleeing forever, only stopping when his friends skirted around disobeying the elders and encouraged him to stay through subtle behaviors.

Months later, Mapábyo and he were expecting their first child. Unfortunately, an accident caused her to lose her child to miscarriage and one of Rutejìmo's best friends died. In the process, Desòchu realized that his brother had his own path to follow, which was greatly different from the path of a warrior.

The rest of the year passed and Rutejìmo was finally allowed to return to the clan. His first words were to ask Mapábyo to marry him.

Chapter 1

Running Away

The clans understand the masculine powers of Tachìra and Chobìre. They have no subtlety compared to the feminine whispers of Mifúno.

—Korechyoki Baroshìko

A screech filled the air, radiating away from the sharp cliffs that surrounded Shimusogo Valley. Even ripped from a human's throat, the sound traveled further than a mere cry could ever match. It rolled along the sand dunes and past the short ridges of rocks peppering the desert around the valley.

Rutejìmo froze when the sound slammed into him. The screech demanded action, forcing him to focus on the cliffs that framed the home valley. The sound continued past him, but he heard it repeating in his head like a memory refusing to be forgotten. He clenched his hand, and the leather ball he was about to throw slipped from his palm and landed on the ground with a muted thud.

A rod—just over sixteen feet—from him, Mapábyo turned to look toward the valley. He could see her from the corner of his vision, her nearly black skin hard to miss against the brown sand. He wanted to look at her, but the screech pulled his attention to the valley where a crowd already gathered around a golden flame.

"J-Jìmo?" whispered Mapábyo. "What happened? Who called us?"

Rutejìmo couldn't tear his eyes away from the cliff. At the entrance of the valley, between the two large banners that declared the Shimusogo Clan's home, the fire continued to stretch up until it became a vortex of flames and wind. Tiny motes of light spun around it; if he were closer, he knew he would see translucent feathers. "Chimípu," he answered. Only the clan's warriors were capable of displaying such power, and all but Chimípu were out protecting the clan's couriers.

"Papa?" asked Kitòpi, Rutejìmo's son. The small voice of the five-year-old carried over the sands.

Rutejìmo forced himself to look away from the valley, struggling against the need to run home. His son was over a chain, sixty-six feet, away—holding his hands up while waiting for the ball. Unlike Rutejìmo and Mapábyo, he didn't seem affected by the screech still echoing in Rutejìmo's head.

Curious, Rutejìmo glanced over his shoulder to Mapábyo. His wife stood on her toes to look over the dunes to see into the valley. Her orange skirt fluttered in the breeze except where Piróma, their three-year-old daughter, clung to her leg. The little girl's black hair snapped in the wind, bouncing against the orange fabric. At the far end of her braid was a small metal ring that prevented it from flying up.

"We should go," Mapábyo said, "the others are already heading back."

Rutejìmo turned back to the valley. Coming in from all directions were the couriers of the clan. They all ran after translucent small birds, the manifestation of Shimusògo; the speed of their sprints kicking up long plumes of sand and dust.

Mapábyo took a step toward the valley. "Jìmo?" She used the shortened form of his name, a name only used among friends and family.

He hesitated as a different pressure arose in him. A command far more subtle than the screech. He shook his head and held his breath, straining to hear something over the breeze and shifting sands.

A flicker of movement shot out from the valley. His gaze caught it, and he watched as it sailed across the sands, leaving no footprints or dust behind. It was a shimusogo dépa, the small birds that the clan chased, but it moved far faster than the others. It covered the mile between Rutejìmo and the valley in a matter of seconds.

He spun as it passed, watching it sail across the sand. A prickle of fear surfaced as he felt magic gathering along the path the dépa took. With a gasp, he spun around. The small bird always ran just as fast as the runner who chased it, which meant that Chimípu would be passing soon. Stepping toward Mapábyo, he called out. "Get Tópi!"

Mapábyo frowned at Rutejìmo and clutched Piróma. "W-What!?"

"Shield Tópi! I can't get to him fast enough!" he yelled just as another translucent bird ran past him. He could feel the energy grip him, and he sprinted after it. He accelerated into a blur and covered the distance to Piróma in a heartbeat.

When he dropped to his knees to sweep up his daughter, Mapábyo was already gone in a cloud of sand. The wind of her passing whipped at his face until he bent over his daughter.

"R-Rutejìmo?" whispered his daughter, her soft voice loud in the space between his arms.

"Close your eyes," he commanded and pulled her tight to his bare chest.

She buried her face into the black curls that dusted his pectorals and sternum. Her tiny arms wrapped around his side and she clutched tight.

"Hold on," he whispered into her dark hair and held her tight. "She's going to—"

A woman sprinted past. She moved in a blur faster than his eyes could focus. She disappeared from sight before he could blink, leaving only an afterimage of golden flames behind. It was Chimípu, one of the clan's warriors and the fastest runner in the valley.

Rutejìmo tensed just as the wind of Chimípu's passing punched into him. Rocks and sand slashed into his back. The impact tore through flesh and gouged his shoulders and sides.

Piróma cried out and yanked her hands against his chest, trying to shield them more effectively. He saw blood welling up from many small scratches on her dark skin, abrasions from the sand blasting past them.

His stomach twisted with frustration.

Wind continued to slash past him, slicing through his trousers and leaving more cuts along his back and neck.

Rutejìmo grabbed Piróma's head and pressed his palms to her ears. "Wait for—"

The second blast struck in an ear-shattering crack. Unlike the first, which only cut his back and left him bloody, the second struck with the force of a steel hammer and the roar of the air being ripped apart. The sound burst across his vision, turning sound into agony and blindness. The force tore open his back, stripping furrows in his skin and ripping flesh.

As soon as it came, the wind faded. Rutejìmo shuddered as he lifted his head and stared at the desert behind his daughter. A shallow ravine had been scoured out of the desert, the force of the wind sucking it clear from the bedrock. A few miles away, the gouge in the desert continued through a field of rock and gravel. There was no sign Chimípu had slowed.

When blood began to drip down his back, he groaned.

Moments later, more dépas raced past them. All traveled slower than Chimípu's, but the flock of translucent spirits still sailed past in a wave of rippling power and translucent feathers.

A blast of wind struck him and he looked up as Mapábyo appeared next to him in a cloud of dust. The sand sailed past them before quickly settling in new patterns on the ground.

"Jìmo, I need to go with them," Mapábyo said as she slipped Kitòpi from her hip. She looked up again and pursed her lips.

Kitòpi brushed the sand from his face. Like his father, he wore no shirt while they were playing. He stepped away to peer at the ravine left by Chimípu's passing.

Air pressure rose rapidly, and then wind blasted past with the first of the runners. More of them quickly followed, each one kicking up winds that tugged at their clothes. Rutejìmo braced himself and watched as they passed, a sick feeling growing in his stomach. He saw brandished weapons and angry faces.

When the last one raced by, Mapábyo turned to Rutejìmo. "Where do you need to go? With us or back home?" She rested her hand on a fighting knife, one finger on the hilt and the other on the sheath.

Rutejìmo glanced down the path left by Chimípu and the others. He felt a tugging on his attention which drew him back to the valley. He bowed his head for a moment, then gestured to Kitòpi and Piróma. "I'll take them home."

Mapábyo slipped up to him, her slender body fitting in his arms. She kissed him on the lips. "I see you, Great Shimusogo Rutejìmo." Her whisper barely rose above the wind swirling a-round them. The phrase "I see you" had carried them through the darkest part of their lives and into the light of happiness.

He smiled and kissed her back. "I see you."

She stepped back as her own dépa raced behind her. She turned on her heels and sprinted away, accelerating out of sight as she chased after the others.

"M-Mama leaving?" asked Piróma in her high-pitched, delicate voice.

Kitòpi looked at Rutejìmo for a moment then said, "She's going to help the others."

Rutejìmo's skin crawled at the disappointed look his son gave him. He shook his head and held out his hands. "Come on, we need to go back."

Piróma rushed over to Rutejìmo, but Kitòpi sulked slowly after her. Rutejìmo scooped them both up and jogged toward the valley. A few steps later, a dépa of his own raced past, and he pushed himself to run after it. The world blurred as he accelerated faster than he could without Shimusògo. He reached the valley in minutes.

When he saw a crowd of teenagers, elders, and children, he came to a shuddering stop. They were gathered around two people on the ground. One of them, Rutejìmo's grandmother, cradled the body of a man, her long white hair draped over her shoulder and the heavy ring at the end swung with her movements.

Without taking his eyes off of the two on the ground, Rutejìmo knelt to release his children. They slipped away and he stood up. He said nothing, but the crowds parted around him as he walked up.

His grandmother was holding Bakóki, a courier who had come home that day. He lay on his back, his mouth gaping wide as he tried to breathe. An arrow stuck out of his chest, the broad head dripping a crimson pool beneath his torso. Where the shaft met ruined flesh, bright red bubbles formed and popped with every gasp.

Tejíko, Rutejìmo's grandmother, looked up as he approached. She said nothing, but her piercing green eyes focused sharply on him. Her yellow dress, one of her favorites, had been stained from throat to knee with Bakóki's blood.

Bakóki groaned and slumped forward, his dull eyes focusing on Rutejìmo.

Rutejìmo stood there and looked back at Bakóki. The rest of the world faded away until he could sense only two people. He let his own thoughts quiet with the rest of the world until he heard nothing but Bakóki's labored breathing and the whisper of sand rolling across the dunes.

The sounds of the desert grew louder. The wind blew across Bakóki and deposited swirls of golden grains across his face. It clung to his wounds and formed ragged lines along the ridges of blood-soaked fabric. A second breeze scattered more sand across his body.

Years ago, Rutejìmo learned the world gave the answers if he remained quiet. The requests came in subtle movement and gestures, a token left by his door or a tool resting in his path. Eventually, he learned that humans weren't the only source of knowledge.

More sand draped over Bakóki's body, settling into his wounds and hair. Rutejìmo watched as they rolled into the furrows of his clothes and the wrinkles of his skin. A few seconds later, a stronger wind blew more against his body.

When Rutejìmo saw a familiar pattern, he let out his breath in a quiet gasp. The same pattern had draped over countless bodies of the dead and dying, identifying the ones that he needed to tend to while others cared for those who would survive. He wasn't sure which spirit marked the bodies with sand. It couldn't be Tachìra, the sun spirit and source of Shimusògo's power. The sun spirit was more concerned with the glory of warriors and the endless fight against the clans of the night.

Rutejìmo believed Mifúno, the mother of the desert, spoke to him. It terrified him to think she did; there were hundreds of stories of fools who claimed to channel her power that ended in their death. The desert didn't suffer fools. Of the three great spirits, though, she was the only one who could mark the sand during daylight, moonlight, and the darkness when neither of the other spirits were in the sky.

The world around him came back into focus. He heard the ebbs of conversation around him, ripples of whispers and quiet words from those who couldn't race after Chimípu. Teenagers and children were too young, their minds not strong enough to see the ghostly birds or to understand the clan's powers. The elders were too weak to keep up with the clan's powers, nor could they survive a fight at the end of a run.

Rutejìmo glanced at his grandmother who looked back with a silent question. He shook his head and stepped back.

Tejíko's jaw tightened, and she clutched Bakóki tightly.

"Damn—" gasped Bakóki.

Silence shot through the crowds, all conversations stopping instantly as Bakóki choked out the words.

"—the moon...."

Bakóki's words finished in complete silence. Green eyes, the mark of the desert, rose to stare at Rutejìmo as he backed away. There were tears in the people who stared at him along with looks of despair and sadness.

No one said a word as Rutejìmo turned his back to his clan and walked into the valley. He wasn't running after the others, he wasn't going to fight. He needed to fulfill his other duty, the one that didn't come from Shimusògo or his clan, to serve the desert mother who had just claimed Bakóki.

Chapter 2

Cowardice

No death is too horrific for one who refuses to defend their clan.
—Jyobikofu Nishígi

Rutejìmo pushed aside the heavy blanket blocking the entrance to his home, a cave carved out of the side of the valley. He released it as he passed. The red fabric scraped along his shoulder, and he felt the embroidered bumps of his and Mapábyo's name before it slumped into place.

The sudden darkness blinded him. He held out his hand and ran his fingertips along the familiar stone wall to make his way to the back bedrooms. He stepped over piles of toys and dolls he forgot to have Kitòpi clean up the night before. Now, his duties for the dead would take him away for at least a day, if not longer.

By the time he reached the back rooms his eyes had adjusted to the dim light from the three glowing spheres hanging from the ceiling. The blue light cast the room into stark shadows that clawed up the walls covered in chalk and scribbles.

He stepped into the sleeping area and made his way to the far end of the bed. His knees bumped against the stone blocks underneath the thick pad he shared with his wife. He knelt and pulled out a wooden box. Standing, he set it on the bed.

Unlike most possessions, the box didn't have a name on it. Only a single, carved word adorned the top: "Ash." In a world where the clan was important, a single name was unheard of. But, to Rutejìmo, it signified everything about his duty to the dead.

The lid creaked when he opened it. On a pile of undyed clothes rested a hand-made book with the same name. Given to Rutejìmo by a woman he never heard speak, the book contained the rituals he would need; the silent words to speak and the proper way of tending to the dying, and the rituals to perform for the dead.

Sadness gripped his heart as he set the book aside and pulled out the top set of clothes. There were no colors in the white fabric, nor had it been embroidered or decorated. Simple white colors to represent someone who took on the mantle of death. The same colors he had worn when he was ostracized for betraying the Shimusògo.

He stripped quickly and tossed his clothes in a basket for laundry. The cool air of the cave washed over him, sinking into his skin. He shivered before grabbing the fabric. A few moments later, he wore white.

"Papa?" Kitòpi watched from the entrance of the cave.

Rutejìmo almost looked at his son, but stopped himself. When wearing white, he chose to step outside of society. The adults of the clan knew to look away and not to speak to him. He was dead in their eyes while he wore white.

Children, on the other hand, didn't understand the subtle ways, and it wasn't the clan's nature to explain things, only demonstrate. He let out his breath and kept his eyes averted.

Mapábyo had sheltered Kitòpi and Piróma from seeing their father in white, but she had to serve her clan just as much as he had to serve Bakóki.

Rutejìmo listened for a moment, then winced inwardly. He didn't expect Kitòpi to follow him, nor did he expect his son to stand in the entrance blocking Rutejìmo's departure.

Kitòpi whispered, "Why are you a coward?"

Rutejìmo jerked at the accusing words. He had heard them countless times whispered in the communal areas of the valley and out among the other clans. He knew that Kitòpi had heard it from someone else, but to hear the words in his son's voice punched him in the chest and gripped his heart tightly.

"Why did you come here instead of going with Mama?" asked his son.

Next to Kitòpi, Rutejìmo heard Piróma's footsteps as she joined her brother.

Lifting his head to look at the ceiling, Rutejìmo struggled with his options. To demonstrate he was among the dead, he couldn't talk or touch them. He couldn't explain what he did, or his reasons, without betraying the ritual that started as soon as he pulled on white.

Kitòpi stepped forward. "You're weak and slow, right? Is that why you run away?"

Each word struck Rutejìmo, and he fought back the tears. He was the slowest of the clan. He didn't have Chimípu's stamina or even Mapábyo's strength. But, he was also the only one who could touch the dead, a calling he treasured as much as his wife and children.

"Boy," a new voice said from the other room, "who are you talking to?"

Kitòpi's bare feet, less than a yard from Rutejìmo, scuffed as he turned away from Rutejìmo. "Pidòhu?"

"Great Tateshyuso Pidòhu," corrected Pidòhu. He used the polite form of his name, which included the name of his clan spirit, Tateshyúso. Pidòhu lived in the valley with the Shimusògo as one of its guardians. His clan spirit had the same relationship with Shimusògo. "And I'll ask again, who are you talking to?"

"Papa. I was asking why he was—"

"Your papa isn't in here." Pidòhu's soft voice grew louder as he approached.

"He's right there!"

"I do not see him."

Kitòpi let out an exasperated grunt. "You aren't looking, he's right—"

"Boy!"

Rutejìmo bowed his head at the sharp tone, silently thanking Pidòhu for helping without forcing Rutejìmo to break out of his role.

Kitòpi stepped back, closer to Rutejìmo.

"Boy!" yelled Pidòhu.

"He's right—"

"Great Shimusogo Rutejìmo is not here. You don't see him." Silence.

"This is the way it is. Your papa is dead right now—"

"But—"

Pidòhu continued smoothly. "—and the living cannot see the dead. Only the dying can see them. Are you dying?"

"No."

"Then your papa isn't here. Bakóki needs him."

"I-Is," Piróma's voice rose as she whispered, "Bakóki dying?"

For a long moment, there was silence. Rutejìmo held his breath, fearing that Pidòhu had come to say that the courier had passed on.

"I cannot see him. Come over here."

Rutejìmo heard Pidòhu draw Kitòpi away. Grateful, Rutejìmo stepped across the room and headed for the door, his head bowed. When he saw Piróma's feet still in the entrance, he froze.

Piróma stood there, unmoving.

"Ròma? Come over here, please."

With a swift movement, Piróma knelt in front of Rutejìmo. He tried to look away, but her piercing green eyes caught his own.

"Girl!" yelled Pidòhu.

Rutejìmo's breath froze in his throat. He could see the curiosity in her eyes, and a solemn quietness that startled him. She didn't smile or frown, only looked at him for a heartbeat before standing up. The stuffed animal in her hand, a red leather dépa, swung around her hip as she stepped away from Rutejìmo and pressed her back against the arch between the two caves.

He let out his breath and tried to calm his rapidly beating heart. The sight of her curious gaze swam in his thoughts as he hurried past her and out of the cave. He needed to return before Bakóki passed on.

Chapter 3

Exhaustion

Rituals and names dominate every waking moment of the barbarians' lives.
—Pikin Bar, *Superiority of Blood*

Smelling of smoke and incense, Rutejìmo staggered home in the early evening of the next day. He had walked naked across the desert since sunrise, and his skin burned from exposure. A high-pitched ringing echoed in his ears, and he struggled to keep his eyes focused through the haze that settled into his thoughts. When he could focus his mind, he pictured the flames of the funeral pyre flashing before him.

The transition back to the living required a purification ritual that strained the mind and body. When he first read the ritual, it sounded simple enough: strip down and start walking at the moment the sun rises above the horizon, and follow it until it sets. It required going a day without food or water, dangerous in the desert.

Performing the ritual was an entirely different experience. The book didn't speak of the agony of sunstroke, the fear of brigands and sandstorms, or even the struggle to keep walking when the sun bore down and skin burned. He had done the ritual for five years, and each time it left him barely able to stand.

He groaned and focused on the sun. Only a finger's width remained above the horizon, and he was still a league away. He forced himself not to despair and kept planting one foot in front of the other. His bare feet crunched on the gravel field, but he didn't feel the sharp edges through the thick callouses of his soles.

A wave of dizziness slammed into him. His vision blurred, and the ringing intensified. He tried to force his foot to step forward, but his sole refused to leave the ground. The effort to move twisted his hip, and his legs collapsed.

He struck the earth with his knees. Agony shot up his thighs and spine to explode in the back of his eyes with a flash of light. The ringing became a high-pitched whine, and the world spun violently around him.

With a groan, he pitched forward. He couldn't stop himself from landing face-first. The sharp rocks cut into his face and chest. He groaned into the gravel. He tried to get his hands underneath him, but his limbs refused to move.

He shuddered and exhaled, trying to concentrate through the pain tearing at his thoughts. His breath kicked up dust in a small eddy that caught the last of the sunlight. He pawed helplessly in an attempt to stand up, but his body was too weak to do more than shove pebbles around.

Rutejìmo sagged into the ground, heedless of the rocks that cut into his face and pierced his thighs. He could smell blood in the air, a coppery smell that burned the back of his throat.

He considered remaining there until the vultures picked his bones, but images of his family rose through the pain and fading light. He groaned and scraped his fingers through the rocks. As soon as he could, he balled his hands into fists and forced them into the gravel. He pushed himself up, ignoring the rock cutting into his knuckles and the shuddering that coursed through him.

It took all his strength to pull one knee underneath his chest. The cracked skin dug through the rocks, the chalky scrape of stone on stone. He gasped and forced his other knee beneath him. At the same time, he pushed himself up until he could slump back on his knees and shins, balancing more by his weight holding him in place than the slack muscles of his body.

Panting, he opened his eyes. It was dark out except for the band of red lining the horizon and a burning light streaking toward him. He focused on the golden light as it left a trail of sparkling motes behind it. Chimípu was the only one in the valley that night who could use magic after the sun set. Everyone else was limited by Shimusògo's power, which came from the sun spirit. When the sun set, the magic fled all the clans of the day and left them as powerless as children.

She came to a stop in front of him, and the wind of her running buffeted his face, peppering his abused body with debris, but it quickly died down with a rustle as rocks bounced off the ground.

Chimípu rested one hand on her hip and held her other out for him. A halo of golden flames and translucent feathers lit her dark skin. It coursed along her reddish hair and set it waving. Her eyes glittered in the light and looked almost inhuman.

She stepped forward and slipped her arm around his waist. "I've got you." The flames continued to rise off her body, but the fire didn't burn him. Instead, it filled him with the same euphoria he felt when he ran. The power of Shimusògo.

Rutejìmo groaned and leaned into her. Even though she was slender, her body was hard as rock. She lifted him smoothly to his feet and bore him as if he weighed nothing. The knife strapped to her hip thumped against his naked thigh.

She held him tight and aimed toward Shimusogo Valley. "The hardest part is always waiting for sunset. Some of us, like your wife, struggle more than others."

He nodded, but said nothing. He concentrated on walking the best he could, even though he knew that Chimípu would never let him fall.

They walked in silence. He pretended that she didn't hear his gasps and grunts. It didn't matter that Chimípu had seen him at his worst, he had to do his best to keep up with greatest warrior he knew.

"We managed to save Nifùni and Byochína. Nifùni got some nasty bruises and cuts. Byochína needed stitches and will have a few scars to carry to her grave, but otherwise both will survive. We lost most of the money they were carrying. They used a shadow dancer to run away," her voice tensed, "and I couldn't catch him. Bastard outran me."

Rutejìmo glanced at her and saw the tension in her jaw.

Chimípu let out her breath. It sparkled with the flames that rolled off her body. "Tejíko is going to have a vote tomorrow night, when you recover. We need to find another clan to courier for. Otherwise we won't have enough to pay for the valley's supplies."

"Any," he took a deep breath, "possibilities? We're already running for most of the surrounding clans."

"A few chances for more business, but your brother mentioned the biggest. The Kosòbyo are looking for couriers."

He stumbled. "Kosòbyo? They are on the opposite side of the Mifuno Desert. Why would they want us?"

Chimípu veered to guide Rutejìmo around a sharp-edge hole between two rocks. She wasn't even breathing hard compared to Rutejìmo's panting. After a few rods of walking, she answered. "I guess when you are the most powerful clan under Tachìra, your business covers all of Mifúno. They have allies everywhere the sun touches and even a few places where the moon hides." She pulled a face.

Rutejìmo chuckled. "I also have friends where the moon hides." As a kojinōmi, he tended the dead for all clans, not only the ones who followed Tachìra but also the ones who gained power from Tachìra's nemesis and rival, Chobìre.

"You're not Kosòbyo." She turned to smile at him. "You are the little brother to most of the desert around here."

He stopped. "Only to you, Great Shimusogo Chimípu."

Chimípu pulled her arm away, hovering near him until he regained his balance. Brushing the hair from her face, she looked him over and nodded. Stepping next to him, she gestured toward the valley. "Come on, little brother. Your wife and children are holding dinner for you. And I was invited."

Only two people called him "little brother," Chimípu and Rutejìmo's older brother Desòchu. Normally, not being called by his name was an insult. But from them, it was a term of affection only spoken in private.

Glad for her presence, he headed home knowing that she would catch him if he fell.

Chapter 4

The Morning Before

The kojinōmi are the caretakers of the dying. They walk next to those who pass between the two worlds to ensure their souls reach Mifúno's breast.
　　　　　　　—Tedoku Nuchikomu Machikimu Garènu (Act 1, Scene 2)

Even in the depths of his family cave, Rutejìmo knew the moment the sun rose above the horizon. The delicate tickle of power started at the tips of his toes and fingers before quickly coursing along his veins and bones. It reached his heart and blossomed into a euphoric wave of pleasure that quickened his breath and heart.

Across the valley, all the adults would be waking up in the same manner. They were all part of Shimusògo's clan, and the dépa's power came from the sun spirit, Tachìra.

Mapábyo let out a soft coo. She made the same sound every morning, and he never tired of hearing it. Rutejìmo rolled on his side and swept his leg forward, burrowing through the blankets until his shin thudded against the hard muscles of her leg. After so many years of sprinting across the desert, both of their legs were solid as rock.

She let out a happy moan and backed up against him until her buttocks nestled against the crook formed by his hips.

"Good morning, my shikāfu." Shikāfu once described the longing Rutejìmo had for another woman but now it labeled the love he felt for Mapábyo.

He lifted his head and propped himself on his elbow. Leaning over her, he slipped his hand around her waist, trailed his fingers up until he cupped one of her breasts. A moment later, he found her nipple and teased it into hardness.

Mapábyo tilted her head back and he kissed her. "You better hurry," she said with a bump of her buttocks, "before the little ones—"

"Papa!" Kitòpi's cry only gave him a heartbeat of warning before he came crashing down on Rutejìmo's thighs.

Disappointed at the interruption, Rutejìmo rolled away.

Kitòpi crawled over Rutejìmo's rolling body. His hands and feet jammed into Rutejìmo's softer parts, bringing thuds of pain as Kitòpi fumbled blindly over the blankets and into the valley between his parents. He wedged himself between them, one knee against Rutejìmo's stomach and, judging from the soft grunt, the other against his mother.

Rutejìmo groaned from the ache of being jabbed. "You know, Tópi, there is a glow light on the table by the arch."

"No," Kitòpi grunted, "I'm good. Just... there!" His foot nailed Rutejìmo in the groin.

Rutejìmo groaned and blinked away the sparks floating before his eyes.

The clicking of a travel light filled the room. Rutejìmo lifted his head and looked toward his feet. A blue glow spread out from Piróma's tiny fingers. It lit her face before spearing out the space between her digits. The light came from a glass sphere with a crystal hanging inside it. A clockwork mechanism tapped against the crystal and, through a process Rutejìmo didn't understand, caused the translucent piece of mineral to glow. She shook it twice before setting it on the blankets.

Piróma stared at Rutejìmo, her eyes glittering, and patted the bed questioningly.

Rutejìmo smiled and held out his hand. "Come on."

She grabbed the blankets and hauled herself up. When she stood on the bed, her nightgown fluttered back to her ankles. It was red, one of Shimusògo's colors, but in the blue light, it was black as night. Only her eyes were lit up, giving him the impression of her being a cat. With a giggle, she crawled over Mapábyo's and Rutejìmo's legs and thumped into the gap between their bodies.

In a matter of seconds, Rutejìmo was on the edge of the bed and holding squirming children instead of his wife. He laughed and exhaled hard and sloppily into Kitòpi's neck.

Kitòpi let out an exasperated cry and tried to wiggle away, but he was trapped in the bed. "Papa!"

Mapábyo cleared her throat. "No roughhousing. I'm not falling out of the bed—again."

"Yes, Mama," said Kitòpi.

Piróma nodded but then jammed her finger into Kitòpi's side. When her brother squealed, she slipped into the gap between him and Mapábyo.

Rutejìmo sighed happily and hugged Kitòpi tightly. "Have a good night?"

"No," Kitòpi sighed before he turned to his father. "Why do you have to leave this morning? Why can't you stay?"

"Well," Rutejìmo started, "we have a job to do. The clan wants me and your mother to be among the six who are going to Kosobyo City."

"Because we need money?"

"That's right." Rutejìmo kissed Kitòpi on the forehead.

Kitòpi squirmed and pulled away. "But, why you? I heard Nifùni saying you would slow everyone down."

Rutejìmo froze for a moment in the sudden wash of regret and memories. "I know, I am slower than—"

Piróma interrupted him. "Aren't you always the slowest?"

Rutejìmo thought for a moment before he responded. "Everyone is good at something. I may not be the fastest runner there is, but do you really think anyone could keep up with Chimípu?"

"No…." whispered Piróma.

"Mípu is really fast," said Kitòpi excitedly, "she's," he swung his hands and accidentally smacked Piróma, "whoosh and she's gone!"

Piróma jerked slightly at the impact and then looked at her brother. After a moment, she returned her attention back to her mother.

Mapábyo giggled. "Not even Desòchu can run that fast. If those two are going to the valley by themselves, then the one slowing her down would be Desòchu. We all run at different speeds, some faster and some slower. Part of being in the clan is that we run as fast as the slowest and we never leave anyone behind."

Piróma lifted her head. "Then why aren't Hyonèku and Kiríshi going?"

Rutejìmo waggled his finger. "You know they don't like being called by their full names."

"Or," added Mapábyo, "just use grandpapa and grandmama." She winked at Rutejìmo.

"Sorry, Rutejìmo," whispered Piróma, "I keep forgetting."

Leaning over Kitòpi, Rutejìmo kissed his daughter. "It's okay, little one." He didn't correct her.

Kitòpi squirmed and Rutejìmo bore down, pinning Kitòpi to the bed for a few seconds with his weight before returning to the edge.

"Papa!"

"You were there, it was comfortable." Rutejìmo made a show of leaning on him, "I could go right back to sleep if you stopped moving."

Kitòpi squirmed harder.

Mapábyo yawned and let out a sigh. "We should be getting up. We have a long run ahead of us."

"Yeah, yeah." Rutejìmo stretched and crawled out of bed. He wore a loose pair of sleeping trousers and a thin shirt. Outside of the blankets, the cool air of the cave prickled his skin and he shivered.

"Papa, why do you have to leave? Why can't you stay in the valley?"

Rutejìmo looked back at his son. Kitòpi sat on the edge of the bed with Piróma next to him. They swung their feet off the edge as they stared at him.

He turned and swept them both into a tight hug. "Because it is what I need to do."

Kitòpi asked, "Why can't grandpapa and grandmama go instead? They can't handle mama's mail route, can they?"

Mapábyo laughed and crawled on the bed to hug all three of them. "That mail route was grandpapa's route before I was born. In fact, they rescued my blood parents on it, back when I was Ròma's age."

"So," Piróma twisted in her mother's grip, "they can handle it?"

"Between the two of them, they will speed along the roads, and no one will ever lay a finger on them. They are safer on that route than anywhere else in the desert."

"Then why aren't they going to the Kosòbyo's?"

"Because," Kiríshi said from the entrance of the door, "I can barely get you four out of bed in the morning." She grinned and slapped the side of the archway.

"Grandmama!"

"Kiríshi!"

Both children ran to the edge of the bed and jumped for Kiríshi.

She caught them and staggered back. "Oof! You are getting big." She stood up and smiled at Mapábyo and Rutejìmo. "Hurry up, you two. We are holding breakfast for you."

"Yes, Great Shimusogo Kiríshi," Rutejìmo said with a grin.

"Yes, Mama," added Mapábyo.

Kiríshi gave Mapábyo a mock glare before dragging both children out of the room. "Come on, let's get you two dressed and out in the sun. We have to say prayers to Tachìra before..." Her voice faded around the corner.

Rutejìmo watched the lights from the children's cave flash with their movement. His thoughts turned darker as their questions echoed in his head.

Mapábyo came around and hugged him. "It doesn't matter if it takes us longer to get there."

"Two weeks more is a long time." Reflexively, he wrapped his arms around her body.

"Two more weeks is nothing when I'm with you."

"I know, but he's right."

"And so were you. We all have different skills. You may not be the fastest, but it was a unanimous vote to bring you along for a reason. You are brave, wonderful, and a good father. No one doesn't want you to go."

Rutejìmo chuckled dryly. "Nearly unanimous. Nifùni voted against it."

"Shut up, Jìmo." She continued after pulling him tight to her body. "You never give up, no matter how much the world grinds you down. When anyone else would have given up, you kept on running forward."

He relented and leaned into her, resting his head on hers.

"You are also kojinōmi. You see things differently than anyone else. And, we may need that out there."

"One would hope we won't encounter the dead on this trip."

"I'd rather have you there and never need you to don whites." She lifted her head to look at him. "You run your own path. And I will follow you anywhere, you know that? Because I see you. And I will never stop."

He closed his eyes and kissed her, enjoying the feel of her soft lips against his own. "I see you," he said.

"And I," snapped Kiríshi, "hear both of you stalling. Get dressed and outside!"

Rutejìmo lifted his head but didn't look at Mapábyo's mother. He smiled broadly before he said, "Yes, Great Shimusogo Kiríshi."

Chapter 5

Halfway There

One can be told a tale endless times, but it doesn't make it true. Experience it once, and it will be learned forever.

—Desert proverb

Spinning on one foot, Rutejìmo ducked underneath Nifùni's stick. He didn't move fast enough, and the wood clipped the top of his skull. Even though they were sparring, Nifùni's blow rang Rutejìmo's ears. He lost his momentum and dropped to a knee, wincing as the pain shot up his leg. Desperate to avoid a second strike, he thrust his tazágu up. The steel weapon had no edge and only a sharp tip. It whistled through the air before he brought it to a halt where he expected the blow to come from.

No impact ran through his hand. No blow smacked him in the back or side.

Rutejìmo looked up, his eyes coming into focus.

Nifùni had stepped back to bring his stick into a parry position. The younger man, in his mid-twenties, had a mask of rage on his face. He stepped back and shook his head violently. The strands of his black hair clung to the recent wound that cut a line from his forehead to his cheek. Even after two weeks, the cut hadn't fully healed from when the robber's attack.

From a rock a few yards away, Desòchu grunted. "What's wrong, Nifùni?"

Stepping back, Nifùni swung his stick haphazardly at Rutejìmo before tossing it aside. "No... no more. I'm not fighting against anyone who has a real weapon."

Desòchu stood up from a wide rock and brushed off his orange trousers. He had stripped off his shirt after they made camp. The lines of his pectorals and abdomen were well-defined and covered in scars from years of fighting, the gray hair curled between the scars flowing with his movements. His left arm had a scar that ran from his thumb to his shoulder, and more lines crisscrossed his stomach, shoulders, and neck.

He jumped off the rock, and his bare feet crunched in the sand. He strolled over to where Rutejìmo and Nifùni were sparring. "Why not? We all need practice."

Nifùni gestured angrily at Rutejìmo. "Why does he get to fight with a real weapon, and I get... I'm fighting with a stick from one of the sand-cursed tents! He could kill me with that... that thing!"

Desòchu shook his head. "No, you are in more danger of getting bit by sand flies than Jìmo hurting you."

Rutejìmo straightened up and wiped the sweat from his brow. His tazágu shook in his grip. Unlike the reds and oranges the entire clan wore, the leather of his weapon had been dyed black and blue by its original owner. Rutejìmo had engraved a Shimusògo name along the length of the blade when he first blooded it, but the rest of the weapon came from another clan, one that gained power from the moon instead of the sun.

"That's a lethal weapon!"

"Yes," said Desòchu, "but he's also been using it for fifteen years."

Nifùni snorted and gestured at Rutejìmo. His shirt clung to his sweat-soaked chest, and he peeled it off with the movement. "And he hasn't killed anyone in all that time. All he does is run away whenever someone even says a strong word! He's a moon-bleached, sand-damned coward who can barely keep his bladder under control, much less swing a weapon!"

From a few rods away, the other clan members looked up. Mapábyo knelt by the fire and stirred a small pot of food. Chimípu sat next to her while she cooked thin strips of meat with an alchemical flame.

The third was Byochína, the other courier attacked a few weeks before. She only wore a white band over her breasts and a pair of orange shorts, making the fading cuts and scars along her bare arms more visible. Her back still glistened with sweat from her high-speed sprint around their campsite after they stopped.

The others, except for Rutejìmo and Chimípu, were also sweaty from their exercises after the clan stopped for the night. One by one, they took the opportunity to circle around the campsite and run as fast as they could. Even Mapábyo, who had paced Rutejìmo for five years, needed a half hour to let it all out.

Rutejìmo was the only one who didn't need to run, since he spent the entire day racing at his fastest and pushing his furthest limits.

Even though Chimípu also took her chance to run, she wasn't exhausted or even sweaty. She could easily run ten times Rutejìmo's speed without breathing hard. He didn't even think she knew her own limits, and she had done feats of magic greater than any other warrior of the Shimusògo.

Rutejìmo felt the familiar burn of jealousy and pushed it down. He would never be a hero or legend. He turned away and looked at his brother.

Desòchu stretched, his muscles rippling, as he stopped next to Rutejìmo. "Well, little brother, think you still need to spar? Even if," he shot a glance at Nifùni, "you aren't going to actually hurt me?"

Breath quickening with the anticipation of sparring his warrior brother, Rutejìmo nodded. He adjusted his grip on his weapon. There wasn't much danger of hurting Desòchu. The tazágu only had a single sharp point; otherwise, it was smooth metal—a weapon designed for precise strokes and parrying. An ideal defensive weapon for Rutejìmo, who had never taken a life and hated violence.

Desòchu stepped forward and attacked. His primary weapon was a long dagger but Rutejìmo had sparred against it many times over the years, and they were both used to its length.

Rutejìmo parried with his weapon. The impact of the blow caused his weapon to ring out.

After a brief pause, Desòchu grinned and attacked again. The strikes quickly became a steady rhythm of impacts that shook Rutejìmo's arm.

Rutejìmo managed to keep up with his brother, but his body shook with the effort. At first, he only fell back from some strikes, but soon he was at full retreat. Sand and rocks kicked up around them with their movements and they broke out of the rod-length circle that marked the normal sparring area.

A translucent feather sailed across Rutejìmo's face with one of Desòchu's attacks. The blows came faster and then suddenly broke from the rhythm. Rutejìmo fought back a whimper as he twisted his body to dodge as much as he parried. Sweat burned his eyes in a matter of seconds. One wide sweep almost caught his ankles, but Rutejìmo jumped over it and rolled to the side. He came up in a fighting stance against the rocks.

Desòchu didn't give him a chance to catch his breath.

Rutejìmo let out a cry and parried with all his might. He met each blow with the limits of his strength. The impacts tore up his arm and reminded him that he had spent the last eight hours running at his limit. Exhaustion tore at his body, and the air wheezed from his throat, but he kept fighting back.

With a snarl, Desòchu's body exploded into golden flames. The slashes became streaked with gold and light.

Somehow Rutejìmo managed to keep up, though his strength rapidly dissipated. He missed one blow and his brother's knife scored a line along his arm. Rutejìmo screamed out and swung back, fighting against the agony of the cut that sliced into him.

Desòchu continued to rain attacks on him, the flash of his weapon becoming a burning blade that shattered the rock behind Rutejìmo and left a trail of feathers and fire behind.

Rutejìmo doggedly parried even as more of Desòchu's attacks got through.

And then, Desòchu's attacks suddenly stopped. The sharp point of Rutejìmo's tazágu swung at his brother's bare throat.

Panic exploded inside Rutejìmo. He reversed his swing. His muscles screamed out in agony as he wrenched his body around. He felt muscles tearing and the sweat-soaked grip of his weapon threatening to slip from his hands. He turned and slammed himself into the rock behind him. His tazágu slipped from his hand. He quickly joined it as he slumped to the ground.

Rutejìmo let out a sob, his body trembling from his exhaustion and the horror of almost hurting someone flashing through his mind. It didn't matter if it was his brother or a stranger, the idea of taking a life brought a violent twisting in his gut.

As the sob burst out of his throat, he slumped forward.

"And that," Desòchu said calmly, "is why I trust him. Do you have a problem with this, courier?"

Rutejìmo looked up to see Desòchu glaring at Nifùni. The use of a label instead of a name was a quiet insult.

Nifùni's face twisted into a scowl. His sweat ran along the furrows along his brow. "He's your brother."

Desòchu held up his weapon to show Rutejìmo's blood dripping down the length. "I don't hold back. And neither does Rutejìmo." Desòchu frowned and stepped forward. "I once made the same mistake you make now. I took Great Shimusogo Rutejìmo's reluctance to be cowardice. I told myself for years that he was weak and helpless. But you know what he did to change that?"

"What?" Nifùni glance at Rutejìmo, his eyes narrowed in anger.

"He died. For a year, he was dead to me—"

Rutejìmo's spiritual death was for the entire clan, but he didn't correct his brother.

Desòchu took another step forward. "And then I saw what he had become. He is stronger than I thought, than any of us thought. He carries a burden that we don't understand and he does it with silence, not violence."

Planting his hand on the rock, Rutejìmo forced himself to his feet. When he regained his balance, he left a bloody smear on the rock. For a long moment, he stared at the hand-print before stepping away from the rock and turning back to his brother who was still talking.

"And if I ever hear you call him a coward again—"

"Desòchu!" snapped Chimípu, interrupting him. She stood near the food. One hand rested on her own sword.

Desòchu looked at her and then sighed. He stepped back with a growl. "Just watch him, Nifùni. You'll see it. We all do at some point."

He looked at Rutejìmo with a silent question.

Rutejìmo pressed a hand against a sharp cut on the side of his arm and nodded.

Desòchu took a step and then disappeared in a burst of wind. Dust pulled after him, creating a cloud that sucked along the trail of his passing.

Rutejìmo closed his eyes as the wind peppered his aching body with sand and small rocks. He felt the sharp burning of his cuts, thankful for Desòchu's skill at fighting. The slashes were shallow and superficial, enough to draw blood without leaving serious injuries. It still hurt, and he fought against the urge to whimper.

When the wind died down, Rutejìmo opened his eyes. Nifùni was storming away, and Mapábyo approached with a roll of bandages.

"I see you," she whispered.

"I see you."

She pressed him against the rock and kissed him fiercely. "And you," she whispered, "are a sand-damned idiot for letting yourself get hurt when we still have a week of running until we get to Kosobyo Valley."

He chuckled and kissed her back, wrapping his arms around her waist. "Yes, but I had to show him that I wasn't a coward."

Mapábyo broke the kiss and stared into Rutejìmo's face. "This isn't the way to show it. You demonstrate it every day, every night. You show it when you come back from tending the dead and when you always run at your limit. Nifùni will see it, sooner or later."

Rutejìmo nodded, but it wasn't Nifùni's accusation that played in his head. It was Kitòpi's single question echoing endlessly, asking if he was a coward.

Chapter 6

Kosobyo City

The jewel of the desert, Kosobyo City is the grandest and most civilized of all barbaric locales.

—Kardin Gunterman, *The Sands in Sixty Months*

Rutejìmo's only experience with larger cities was Wamifuko City, the nearest to Shimusogo Valley. The mountain city had a smell that had burned itself into Rutejìmo's memories, a dank scent of rot and shit. He expected the same from Kosobyo City. In the weeks of running, he painted an image of their destination in the back of his mind. He could see it surrounded by tall stone walls with guards every few chains. And he had no doubt the stench would be overpowering.

Lost in thought, he almost ran past the others when they stopped at the top of the ridge. Only when Mapábyo called to him did he realize his mistake. To stop, he dug his feet into the ground, but his soles didn't break the rocky ground as normal. Instead, he skittered for a moment before pitching forward.

The ground rushed up to him, but then a blast of wind caught him. Strong hands, Chimípu's and Desòchu's, caught him before he hit.

"Pay attention, little brother," chided Chimípu.

Gasping for breath, Rutejìmo managed to get back to his feet with only his dignity injured. He stood up and looked at the others. "Why did we..." His voice trailed off when Nifùni gestured angrily for him to turn around.

Mapábyo giggled and did the same, but with a smile instead of a scowl.

Rutejìmo's breathing grew deeper as he turned around and got his first look at Kosobyo City. It wasn't anything like he imagined. There were no walls, only rows of stone houses and paths radiating from the center of the city. His mouth opened in shock as he tried to take in the sight. It was easily leagues across, with neat lines of roads and alleys. Almost all the buildings were built from a pale, yellow rock, but colorful murals across the front were visible even from this distance. The roofs were a flurry of reds, yellows, and greens.

In the center of the city, the buildings reached higher than Rutejìmo had ever seen. The tallest looked to be over ten stories, judging from the banks of windows. It was easily double the highest building in Wamifuko City. The murals continued even up the larger buildings with the Kosòbyo colors—gold and green and white—predominately visible.

Rutejìmo gulped and looked back at the rest of his clan. He didn't know what to say, and the sensation of being overwhelmed loomed close. To his surprise, almost everyone stared at the city in the same shock.

"It's beautiful," whispered Mapábyo.

"It's huge," said Nifùni with a growl. He gestured down to where the buildings broke up into larger estates and farms. "There are no guards, no gates. How can they protect a place this large?"

"How," said Mapábyo in a stunned voice, "do we find the Kosòbyo in there?"

Desòchu grunted and pointed to the tall buildings. "Follow the colors and the taller buildings. The best bet is to find some rooms for the night first. And then use the last few hours of the day to find out where to go."

After a moment, everyone nodded with agreement. There were looks of trepidation and fear.

Rutejìmo felt the same inside his own heart. He turned further away from the city to ease the discomfort building inside him. It was too large and too neat for his tastes.

He scanned the horizon, but when he saw two wisps of smoke, he froze. One was white and the other yellow. In a perfect world, the colors would be white and gold, the colors of death, but the familiar spiral of colors told volumes. Someone was dying and they needed help.

He glanced down at his feet and held his breath. He calmed his thoughts and watched the dust that rolled between his feet. It clung to his bare feet and traced the ridges of his hardened toes.

Another breeze rolled around his thighs, adding more dust and rocks to the sun-baked rock. The wind stopped suddenly and the dust settled.

Rutejìmo stared at the familiar pattern. The desert needed him to answer. He looked back up, focusing on the rapidly dissipating smoke. With a sigh, he knelt and swung his pack from his shoulder. Sweat dripped down his face as he dug into the bag and pulled out a set of white clothes.

"Jìmo?" Chimípu said next to him.

"I'm needed." He gestured with his chin toward the smoke.

Mapábyo gasped and spun around. He watched her scan the horizon, saw her shoulders slump when she stopped. Slowly, she turned around with a hurt look. "Do you have to?"

He stripped off his shirt to answer, the silence already draping over his thoughts. Even as he tugged the rough white fabric over his head, he felt her sadness and it echoed in his own heart.

"Pábyo?" Desòchu said as he came around. Rutejìmo knew that he wouldn't be looking at his brother. "If you need to go somewhere, we'll leave a message at the board by that well."

Rutejìmo glanced at where Desòchu pointed. It was one of the closest fountains, and there was always a message board near them. Desòchu's directions were not for Mapábyo, but to tell Rutejìmo where to go. When Rutejìmo donned white, they couldn't see him, and he couldn't respond, but they could communicate in other ways.

Mapábyo, tears in her eyes, shook her head. She turned to face Desòchu directly. "No, I'll come with you."

As one, the rest of his clan turned their backs on Rutejìmo. Without looking at him, the others turned and raced into the city.

He finished dressing and stood up. He reached down and picked up his pack; he had started taking a bag with him when he tended the dead while away from a city. The hilt of his weapon stuck out of one side.

The rest of the Shimusògo had already disappeared into the crowds funneling into the streets, but he could still see a few clouds of dust marking their path.

With a heavy heart, he turned away from the city and ran for the smoke.

Chapter 7

Broken Silence

No one knows what organizes the kojinōmi, only that one is there when someone dies.

—*Whispers of the Desert* (Act 2)

The steady drum of Rutejìmo's feet against the solid ground was almost peaceful. He chased Shimusògo as he always did, the dépa sprinted a few rods in front of him no matter how fast he pushed himself. Rutejìmo didn't feel an urgency to race, only a need to approach the smoke, so he ran at a comfortable pace that would carry him just under thirty miles in an hour.

His feet always struck solid ground. One of the powers of the Shimusògo clan solidified shifting sands and rolling rocks before his foot came down. As soon as he ran past, it crumbled back into sand in time for the wind of Rutejìmo's passing to rip it from the ground and send it flying in the air. Even at his relatively sluggish speed, the plume of sand and dust stretched a mile back on a still day.

Alone, he could lose himself in the euphoria of running. The power of Shimusògo was a pulse of pleasure and at the same time an ache, while running for hours at a time. But, for

Rutejìmo, it was always a struggle. And as his run stretched into an hour, his thoughts turned inward.

As much as he couldn't admit it in front of the other Shimu-sògo, Rutejìmo was thankful for being pulled away from Kosobyo City. Even his brief view of the city disturbed him. Cities needed walls for protection, not wide open rows of endless buildings. He couldn't imagine how the Kosòbyo protected their homes with so many exposed entrances. The only thing he could imagine was that no one would ever risk destruction by going against one of the most powerful clans in the desert. The Kosòbyo were known for their grudges.

Given the size of the powerful clan, Rutejìmo hadn't expected a call from the desert. There were other kojinōmi. No doubt there were at least a few in the Kosòbyo.

Even though he had only met one other kojinōmi in five years, the *Book of Ash* indicated they gravitated to places they were needed. In a city as large as Kosobyo City, there had to be those who needed someone to hold their hand while they died or to tend to the bodies after it happened. Why had the desert called on him so far from home?

Lost in thought, he blasted past a figure without realizing it, only catching a flash of white in the corner of his eye. With a gasp, Rutejìmo dug his feet into the ground. His sole cut through the solid rock, and he decelerated rapidly. Jumping to the side, he shot out in a wide circle to come around and chase after the figure walking away.

He reached the figure quickly, and he jammed his feet back into the ground to stop. His passing left a deep furrow in the ground, the impact of rock shattering underneath his feet nothing more than a tug and scrape against his hardened soles.

Rutejìmo remained crouched on the ground and held his breath. The wind that followed him blew over his body, peppering his back with rocks and sand. It slowed in a choking cloud before raining down. Moments later, he stood in a teardrop-shape of upturned sand and rocks.

It was a young man with pale brown skin and no hair. He drank from a skin when Rutejìmo stopped and he turned with the skin still held in his hand. He wore a white tunic and trousers. The rough fabric was almost identical to Rutejìmo's outfit.

The young man looked surprised. "Kojinōmi?"

Rutejìmo nodded and then stepped back in surprise. For five years, Rutejìmo had remained nearly silent when he took on the mantle of white. When he raised his voice, he was beaten until he learned not to make a noise. But the stranger had spoken at full volume, as if they were talking in a room together.

A frown crossed the other man's face. "I haven't seen you before."

Rutejìmo shook his head.

"Can't talk?"

Rutejìmo shook his head again, unwilling to break his own silence despite the kojinōmi speaking to him.

The other man turned and headed toward Rutejìmo. The frown deepened for a moment, then he stopped with a scoff. "You are one of those provincial types, aren't you? Live out in the desert somewhere near Tachìra's asshole?"

Uncomfortable, Rutejìmo didn't respond.

"Well, you can ignore that smoke," the young man gestured toward Rutejìmo's destination.

Rutejìmo glanced over his shoulder at the dual columns of colored smoke rising. They were close, less than a mile, but the kojinōmi was walking in the wrong direction.

"No one to save, just a bunch of Chobìre scum. And even the rest of them won't be needing help in a few hours. As soon as the moon sets, they won't last seconds."

Chobìre was the name of the moon spirit and Tachìra's rival. Legend had it that the two spirits fought for the affections of Mifúno, the desert, but neither ever took her hand. Instead, the clans who gained their power from the moon and sun fought just as the spirits did—but the mortals' battles frequently ended in blood and death.

Rutejìmo stroked the hilt of his tazágu. Unlike the rest of the Shimusògo who wore orange and red, his weapon was decorated in black and blue, the colors of a night clan. A woman in his past had given it to him before she disappeared into the night with one of Rutejìmo's former clan mates.

"Don't bother, kojinōmi. Your sand-blasted, sun-burned traditions won't help you here. You probably still do the purification rituals. Walking naked across the desert?" At Rutejìmo's hesitant nod, the young man scoffed. "Those ways are dead, Mifúno hasn't abandoned any of us when we gave up those rites."

A prickle of discomfort ran along Rutejìmo's body. The casual words were nothing like the rituals in the *Book of Ash*. He could still remember the old woman who gave him the book, right before she stripped naked and headed out on her own purification. He never saw the wild-haired woman again, but her silent lessons had carried him for half a decade.

The kojinōmi scoffed again. "Go on, waste your time. Maybe you'll end up dead like those night scum." He turned, drained his skin, and headed back toward Kosobyo City.

Rutejìmo didn't need to look at his feet to feel the wind blowing around his toes. If the young kojinōmi's words were any indication, he knew why Mifúno called Rutejìmo and not the others. Despite following a clan of the sun, Rutejìmo served everyone who needed it, night or day. He was never given a choice, nor wanted one. If it wasn't for the clans of both sides, he would have died in the desert years ago.

Turning on his heels, he raced away from the other kojinōmi.

Less than ten minutes later, he came up to a crowd of warriors circling around a gray and green wagon. The wagon stood in the middle of an empty space about a chain across. Outside, forming a ring, were at least three different clans wearing bright colors. A horse clan whooping and circling made up the outer ring. They all had short wooden bows in their hands, and their horses wavered like heat, slipping between the others easily despite the large bulk.

The other two clans were foot warriors. One carried a curved sword and the other appeared to favor a wide-bladed spear. Most of their weapons were out and brandished, but they made no effort to approach closer to the wagon.

As he walked, Rutejìmo focused on the painted wagon. The clan name, Nyobichóhi, was clearly painted on the side but two of the letters were speared with red-feathered arrows. There was also a smear of red along the wood. Ripples of green circled the wagon, moving like a cloud of noxious fumes that moved against the breeze that blew the sand.

Rutejìmo lifted his head to confirm that Chobìre was still in the sky. He was, but the moon was only a pale disk of white partially obscured by the horizon. In less than an hour, it would be out of sight and the clan in the wagon would lose all of their powers.

He didn't need the wind blowing against his back to know he was needed. He let out his breath and started toward the crowds. He focused his eyes on the ground and trusted that he would walk straight. It was how he approached a crowd while wearing white.

The noise of horses and talking grew louder as he covered the last few chains to the edge of the crowd. People stepped away from him, creating a path through the din. He knew that most of the warriors were aware of him, poised in case he simply pretended to be a kojinōmi. If he drew a weapon or became a threat, they would cut him down before he took a breath. But, as long as he remained silent and unobtrusive, they would ignore him.

The crowds continued to peel away from him. He walked slowly and steadily while being careful to keep his hand away from his weapon.

Conversations quieted but didn't die away. He could hear the whispers and murmurs as he passed. The muscles in his back tightened as he continued through the crowd of strangers, wondering if there were other differences with the clans in the northern desert.

When he saw feet blocking his path, he almost slammed into someone. With a soft gasp, he froze and stared down at the ground. He couldn't interact with the living, the warriors, but normally they stepped out of the way.

The man blocking Rutejìmo spoke. "Where do you think you're going?"

Rutejìmo tensed. It sounded like the man was talking directly to Rutejìmo. Rutejìmo wanted to look up and confirm it, but he couldn't. That would require him to interact with the man in front of him.

"Hey, Tsupòbi," called one of the warriors to the side, "who are you talking to?"

Tsupòbi snorted. "No one. Just a stupid ghost without the sense to get out of the sun."

Laughter rippled around Tsupòbi and Rutejìmo.

Rutejìmo stepped to the side.

Tsupòbi's blue and gold boots moved to block Rutejìmo.

More laughter around him.

"No, there aren't any ghosts needed here," said Tsupòbi.

The wind rolled over Rutejìmo's feet, kicking up more sand. Stream-
ers of grains rolled around Tsupòbi's feet as it headed toward the wagon. Rutejìmo felt a sparkling sensation pouring down his spine before it spread out through his body. The pressure to

approach the wagon increased and he knew that someone was about to die.

The world seemed to fade away until there was nothing but Rutejìmo and the wind. He watched the familiar patterns roll across the sand.

"Go away, ghost."

And then Rutejìmo could sense Tsupòbi. The man was before him, visible in Rutejìmo's mind as clearly as if he had looked up. He saw a middle-aged man with a shaggy beard and broad shoulders. He wielded a curved scimitar and had a short knife on his back.

Rutejìmo's heart began to beat faster. He was seeing something he had never seen before.

As if to respond, his toes and soles tingled. Before he could inhale, the sensation crawled up his legs and spine, spreading out across his skin. Whispers tickled his senses, the inaudible words of the desert just outside of his comprehension.

The wind increased behind Rutejìmo, and it buffeted his back. He watched as it swirled around him, painting more patterns around his feet but not around the warrior blocking him. The sand didn't touch or even bounce off of Tsupòbi, as if the man didn't exist anymore.

Rutejìmo tried to push his senses out. To his surprise, he could sense the others. They were lifting their hands or turning their backs against the wind that peppered them. Rutejìmo could feel how the sand bounced on their faces and arms, how it lodged into the folds of their fabric. There were no patterns of death, but they still responded to the desert.

A flash of insight slammed into Rutejìmo. The desert no longer acknowledged Tsupòbi existed.

Rutejìmo lifted his gaze. He took in each part of the man before him, from the sword on his side and the clan name proudly displayed along his belt and clothes.

As he dragged his gaze up, the wind rose to a howl. It swirled around Rutejìmo, depositing sand against his face and skin. It stuck to the sweat that glistened on his dark skin and clung to his hair. He could feel more of it shifting into his clothes and lodging against the sensitive parts of his flesh.

The man before him remained untouched by the sand and wind.

Rutejìmo finally brought his stare directly into Tsupòbi's eyes. He had never stared at anyone in public before, and the very act terrified Rutejìmo. He waited to be cut down but no blows came.

Tsupòbi stepped back and raised his weapon. Sweat sparkled on the warrior's brow when his face twisted into a mask of rage. The killing edge of the sword glowed with an inner light. It wasn't flame, but it wavered in the air around the warrior and sparkled along the name engraved along the metal.

A thousand options flashed through Rutejìmo's head as he stared at the glowing weapon. He could pull his own weapon and parry—he was good enough to survive at least a few seconds, but then the other warriors would easily overpower him. He could dodge out of the way, either to run or to charge forward.

And then an option he had never considered: he could speak. Right before he had become a kojinōmi, he learned that the dead never spoke to the living. It was beaten into him and he almost lost his life when he broke the silence. Now, after five years, he had forgotten that it was even a possibility. As he considered it, he felt a tingling boil up inside him, driving him to react and respond.

The warrior's blade came down in a high, overhead blow. It left a streak of golden fire behind it.

Rutejìmo opened his mouth and the wind died instantly, plunging the world into silence. In the brutal quiet, his words carried clearly across the crowds. "You are dead to her."

Tsupòbi tried to abort his swing, but the glowing blade came down. It caught Rutejìmo's shoulder, slicing through skin before bouncing off the bone. The warrior dropped his weapon and the blade cut another deep gouge out of Rutejìmo's flesh before falling to the ground.

Pain ripped through Rutejìmo's senses and it took all his effort not to cry out from the agony.

Tsupòbi panted frantically and his face was pale. "Y-You can't speak! You aren't allowed to!"

Rutejìmo said nothing. Hot blood rolled down his chest and back, soaking through the sand before slowing.

Turning to the surrounding warriors, the man cried out. "He can't talk! He can't say that!" There was desperation and fear in his voice, the same feeling echoed in Rutejìmo's heart.

Rutejìmo turned and followed Tsupòbi's gaze. As he did, he saw the flashes of fear in the surrounding warriors before they quickly looked away. A strange feeling filled Rutejìmo as he circled around, watching as the warriors were the ones to look away from him.

When he came around again, Rutejìmo found that the only one willing to look into his face was the man who tried to block him. Tsupòbi stood shaking in front of Rutejìmo, his hand clenching empty air.

"Y-You can't talk," he said in a broken whisper.

Rutejìmo took a deep breath and spoke the words he finally heard in the silence. "She will never welcome you into her arms, and you will die alone and forgotten." The words came rushing out, half formed by the whispers in his head but he filled in the gaps. "There is no clan under sun and moon that will ever welcome you again. You are—"

"No!" The warrior staggered back. "No, you aren't allowed—"

"—dead to Mifúno forevermore." The final words burst out of Rutejìmo's mouth. He felt power rush out of him, leaving him drained and shaking.

In the silence, no one moved.

Tsupòbi looked around. "Please? Someone?"

Rutejìmo followed his gaze again, his thoughts dull from the sudden emptiness inside him. He felt as if he had run for ten hours solid, but the exhaustion came from only a few words that had broken a man.

Only a few feet away, the nearest warrior turned around so his back was facing Rutejìmo and the dead man. Rutejìmo saw sweat pouring down Tsupòbi's face and fear in his eyes. The other warriors joined suit, turning away in a wave of movement that rippled through all the warriors.

The world spun around Rutejìmo as he watched their response. He had never had any force speak through him. The overwhelming sense of power quickly faded but it left behind only terror that he had done something forbidden.

As he stood there, the rest of the bystanders turned their backs on them. Even the horses turned away. In a moment, no one looked at Tsupòbi, the former warrior who had just been cast from society.

The rush turned to sadness as Rutejìmo regarded the former clan member. When Rutejìmo was declared dead, it was only for a year. But for the man before him it would be for the rest of his life. No clan, night or day, would talk to him. He couldn't find shelter at any oasis or in the cities. The news of his spiritual death would travel faster than he could, and soon he would be alone and abandoned. Just like Rutejìmo was five years ago, but for the rest of his life.

"W-What do I do?" Tsupòbi dropped to his knees, his voice cracking. "What?"

Rutejìmo stepped forward and the warrior flinched. With a sigh, Rutejìmo rested one hand on his shoulder. "Be silent,"

Rutejìmo whispered, "and learn to watch. Find a city and remain there. There is no more salvation in the desert for you. No oasis will shelter you. As long as you are dead to the sands, none of the living can look at you. If you force them to acknowledge your presence, they will kill you."

"I have nowhere to go."

"The city. There are other banyosiōu there. They will help you, if you help them."

Rutejìmo had received no such help when his tribe had cast him away. He spoke from experience, and he couldn't help but remember almost dying of dehydration in the middle of the desert as he chased after Mapábyo.

Tears ran down the man's face. He shook his head. "I-I can't."

"Then you will truly die." Rutejìmo let his hands slide off the shaking man's shoulder and stepped past him.

This time, no one stopped him as he crossed the distance to the lone wagon. The noxious cloud dissipated in front of him, blown away by a breeze that rolled past him. As he approached the back, the door cracked open and an older woman peeked out from the crack. Her one visible green eye widened and she opened the door.

At the sight of her surprised face, Rutejìmo glanced over his shoulder. The surrounding warriors were walking and riding away. All the anger and hatred of the mob had faded with Rutejìmo's words.

The old woman hesitated for a moment before opening the door to let him in. He walked up the wooden steps and inside.

The travel wagon could have comfortably fit seven; instead, a dozen crowded within. The stench of blood and death filled the cramped quarters.

Rutejìmo ignored everyone but a young girl on the floor. A pool of blood surrounded her as she clutched her stomach. Blood oozed from a sword cut that sliced her from her right hip to the bottom of her ribs of her left side. Coils of her intestines bulged around her fingers, and one loop was caught on her thumb.

She looked up at him with glistening eyes. "I-I'm scared." Her voice was a broken whisper.

The rest of the wagon emptied as Rutejìmo knelt in the blood and drew her close. Her skin was cold, and her blood colder. He rested his cheek against hers. He said nothing, he never needed to.

"Can y-you help me?" she whimpered and dug her fingers into her stomach. "I-It hurts. It hurts so much and it won't stop. All I did was try to greet him... and... and then he cut me."

Rutejìmo rested one hand on her stomach, not to hold her insides in but to cradle her hand. In her shimmering eyes, he saw his reflection. His eyes had turned gold and white, the color of death. He shuddered and closed them, resting his chin against her forehead.

He didn't have to say anything.

A moment later, she began to whisper. The words weren't important to him, but they were to her. She apologized to him for stealing her brother's dagger and praying to be born into one of the sun clans. She told him of her dreams and fantasies, the places she wanted to go. She let go of the things holding her to the world, the weight heaped on her young shoulders. Between the tears, she spoke until her voice faded in a choking gasp.

Moments later, she died in his arms.

When Rutejìmo looked up with tears in his own eyes, a stack of perfumed wood sat inside the wagon, along with some small trinkets of gold and white, gifts for the kojinōmi who would guide the fallen girl's soul to Mifúno's breast.

Chapter 8

Alone

The books of *Ash* are eclectic collections of barbaric rituals and death records passed for centuries among the desert clans. While initially destroyed by more reasonable folks, they quickly became a tool for measuring the slow progression of civilization among the barbarians.

—Bandor Turin, *Words of the Dead*

The little girl's confessions echoed in Rutejìmo's head in a quiet symphony as he wrote in his book. The hand-bound collections of pages creaked under his hand, the leather thong strained to hold the almost fifty pages of tightly-spaced writing. Over the years, he had added a dozen pages to the collection. It wouldn't be too long before the binding couldn't handle the additional pages, but he thought he had a few more years left before that happened.

Even with his additional pages, he didn't have room to write down any of the stories he had heard over the years. He wanted to detail the joys of the little girl's death, such as the choked story about how she had stolen her brother's toy when he wasn't looking. He had also wanted to write the horrors, like one man's confession for killing his sister. Each one was precious and important. Time would erase their stories and a part of Rutejìmo died every time he forgot one.

He could barely see the page underneath his hand. The dim light of the coming dawn provided only enough illumination to identify that he was writing on the page and his lettering didn't overlap with the line above it. One single line to condense a little girl's life to a simple phrase wasn't enough. After the name of her clan and how she died, there wasn't much left to describe her.

Rutejìmo wanted to write more. Years ago, he tried to, but there were simply too many stories to document. He ran out of paper and time long before the tales ran out.

Realizing his thoughts had become dark, he pried his mind away from the lost stories. But before he could find a happy memory, an image welled up of the young kojinōmi he had met from the day before.

Rutejìmo never learned his name or clan, but the young man had shown him a different aspect of the kojinōmi that Rutejìmo didn't know was possible. The revelations of his words and behavior felt profoundly uncomfortable. The idea that he, or any kojinōmi, could choose not to care for the dying went against everything he understood. Death struck everyone and therefore Rutejìmo, as a kojinōmi, should tend to everyone.

There were other disturbing things that the brief encounter revealed. For five years, he had faithfully performed the purification ritual even though it was the most exhausting part of his duties. The day of walking naked in the sun had left him burned completely and aching from his feet to his head. He hated it, but it was part of being a kojinōmi, or at least he thought it was.

Rutejìmo sighed and paged through the book with his small fingers, peering at the barely visible lines in hopes of having some answer. He knew he wouldn't find it from the book any more than he could ask the desert directly. It didn't stop him from looking.

A flicker of light caught his attention, halting his dark thoughts. He lifted his head to look toward the remains of the bonfire. Over the night, it had burned to the ground leaving nothing but a circle of black ash and a few cracked fragments of bone. Near the center, he spotted part of the girl's hip sticking up. A single spark lit on the tip of the shattered remains of a thigh bone.

His breath halted in his chest as he stared at it.

It started to dim.

A brief wind gave the spark life once again and it wavered in the ripples of heat.

Rutejìmo had seen the same thing many times. He felt it around him, a pressure gathering as if the desert itself was waiting for the last of the girl's spirit to fade away.

The ember faded again and darkness crowded close.

He kept himself still, feeling there was a mote of the girl's spirit remaining.

A breeze wafted over the sand, kicking up swirls of dark ash in a spiral that quickly faded.

The spark flared for the briefest moment, a tiny burst of life, before it was swallowed by the dark.

The tension around him snapped, and he felt his lungs work again. Wiping a tear from his eye, he bowed deeply to the ash and silently mouthed a prayer to Mifúno, the desert spirit and the mother of all spirits. When he finished, he set his book into his bag. Then, he stood up, his back to the ash, and stripped.

It only took a minute to remove and fold his clothes. He set them down by his bag. When he turned back around, the circle of ash and the girl's bones were gone. There was nothing to mark the place of her burning, other than the memories recorded in Rutejìmo's head and the notes in his book.

The desert worked silently and subtly. He never saw the sands swallow the ash, but the signs of the flames were always gone when he looked back. Not as visceral as the power Shimusògo gave him, it always left Rutejìmo in awe of the desert's power.

He bowed again, thanking Mifúno by mouthing the words.

There was no response from the wind.

He turned back around and picked up his bags. The white clothes had disappeared when he wasn't looking. He had seen it a hundred times now, but like the ash, it left him stunned that things could change so quickly when his back was turned.

Then, naked as the day he was born and carrying his bag, he started to walk toward the sun just as it peeked over the horizon. He had no destination or goal, only to walk toward the light. The only time Rutejìmo would stop would be when Tachìra held right above him for the few seconds of perfect harmony and then he would turn around and follow it back across the desert.

Despite what the other kojinōmi said, Rutejìmo felt he must do the ritual, no matter what.

————— Chapter 9 —————

Greatness

There is no greater honor than culling the mindless herds that walk in Ta-chìra's light.

—Chitori Basamìto, *Queen of the South*

Hours of walking sapped Rutejìmo's strength. He was exhausted, dehydrated, and starving. Every time he picked up his foot, it left a bloody footprint on the sand, and his leg shook. He had sliced open his foot just after noon, but he couldn't stop until the sun set below the horizon.

Only a few minutes remained before the sun disappeared. He could feel Tachìra's power flaring and the despair of knowing his magic, like most of the day clan's, would fade away in an instant. He wouldn't even have a few seconds of Shimusògo's power to speed his way across the sand. No, when he finished his ritual, the only thing left was to keep walking.

When the sun finally set, the last remnants of his energy faded, and he stumbled. He held out his hands for balance and managed to avoid plummeting to the ground. Groaning, the first sound he made since he started, he caught himself and straightened up. His foot throbbed but he shoved it into the heated sand and forced himself to take another step.

He walked less than a chain before stopping. Kneeling heavily on the sand, he pulled out his non-white clothes. The bright reds and oranges of Shimusògo were nearly invisible in the fading light.

"I thought all the old ways had died."

Rutejìmo jumped and bit back a scream. He looked around, but couldn't find the man who spoke.

A chuckle came from his right and Rutejìmo glanced in the direction of the sound. His eye caught a flicker of movement and a line of sparkling blue light. He attempted to clear his throat, which had long since sealed shut from dehydration. Only a rasp escaped his cracked lips.

The line spread out, as if a paper-thin man had turned to the side, unfolding into view and swelling out into three dimensions. Seconds later, the stranger gained the look of a solid figure instead of a shifting painting.

He appeared to be in his fifties, with two quivers of arrows at his side and a heavy bow over his shoulder. His clothes were dark green and black, colors of the night, and his weapons matched both in style and coloration.

"Ah," the man bowed. His white beard had been neatly braided down his chest, and the tip of it brushed the ground. "Forgive me, I was looking for someone and didn't want to be seen."

The man pulled out a flask and handed it to Rutejìmo.

Rutejìmo took it gratefully and sipped, afraid it was alcoholic. When he only tasted metallic water, he took a long gulp and sighed with pleasure as the ache in his throat faded. After a few seconds, he drank another gulp and then handed it back.

"No, please, finish when you can."

Still kneeling, Rutejìmo bowed. "Thank you. I'm Rutejìmo, and I speak for Shimusògo." It was the traditional greeting in the desert, though rarely did conversations between the night and day clans start peacefully.

The old man jerked and his eyes widened. "I am... surprised." He shook his head and then bowed. "Forgive me. I am Fidochìma, and I speak for Foteramàsu. I ask for forgiveness in not introducing myself. I was not expecting to exchange civilities."

Rutejìmo smiled, remembering Mikáryo, who he had once lusted after despite her dark clan. "A woman I once knew told me that, in the desert, there are some things not worth fighting for." He grinned. "Well, that wasn't exactly what she said, but it was a long time ago."

Fidochìma nodded. "She is a wise woman, though not with popular beliefs."

Rutejìmo shrugged.

The older man stroked his beard. "And where are you going, Great Shimusogo Rutejìmo? To Kosobyo City?"

"Yes, Great Foteramasu Fido... chìma."

Fidochìma chuckled. "It is a mouthful, isn't it? Would you be willing to call me simply Fidochìma? There is no greatness out here either."

Rutejìmo bowed. "A wise man, though not with popular beliefs," he said mimicking Fidochìma's tone.

For a long moment, both men looked at each other. Then Fidochìma burst into laughter. "I can see why you are comfortable with the dark. If you don't mind, Rutejìmo, I would be honored to escort you to the city... or as close as my kind is encouraged to visit."

"I would be honored."

"Though, it may be a more enjoyable walk if you were to put some clothes on."

Rutejìmo ducked his head to hide his smile. "Good idea."

He pulled his shirt over his head and yanked it into place. When he managed to clear his head, Fidochìma had dropped a bundle of white clothes on the ground next to him. They would be pristine and unworn, a gift to the kojinōmi.

Without hesitation, Rutejìmo stood up, finished dressing, and packed the white clothes in his bag. He had learned not to ask why people knew that he needed them or where they came from. Like everything else with the dead, it was not spoken about. Only performed in silence and without fanfare.

Rutejìmo groaned as he stood up. To his surprise, Fidochìma came up and slipped an arm around his waist to hold his balance. Rutejìmo looked at him.

The old man gave him a sly smile. "In the desert...."

Rutejìmo smiled and let the older man guide him.

They walked in silence for over a half hour. Fidochìma smelled of smoke and ozone. His outfit was crisp and sharp, almost like the thinness of his appearance. But, with one arm over his shoulders, Rutejìmo could feel none of the two-dimensional appearance.

Finally, Rutejìmo broke the silence. "Who were you looking for?"

"A man," came the curt reply.

A brief breeze tickled Rutejìmo's face. An image flashed through his mind, of the warrior who stood in his way, Tsupòbi. The memory was startling clear, and Rutejìmo paled with the intensity of details that slammed into him.

Fidochìma hesitated. He leaned over and peered into Rutejìmo's face. "Do you know which man I'm hunting?"

Rutejìmo picked his words carefully. "No, but I know of a man who one may wish to hunt."

"The man I'm hunting," Fidochìma's voice grew tense, "killed someone dear to me. A granddaughter of a daughter."

The image of the girl bubbled up and faded. The image of Tsupòbi came back, this time of the haunted look on his face and the horror as he tried to realize what had happened. The memory scared Rutejìmo even though he had spent an entire day thinking about it. He didn't know he was capable of declaring someone dead to the desert, but Mifúno had somehow backed his proclamation.

"He deserves the same," Fidochìma said, his eyes sparkling in the dim light.

Rutejìmo closed his eyes and shook his head. "That man is already dead."

"How?"

Rutejìmo said nothing. He didn't want to think about it if he could, nor did he ever want to say those words again. Even if he did, he didn't talk about the dead.

"Please, Rutejìmo, I need to know. There are very few of us in the shadow of Kosòbyo and even one death risks everything for us." Fidochìma pulled away and turned Rutejìmo. "How did this man die?"

Unable to say the words, Rutejìmo looked helplessly at him.

Fidochìma stepped back, his face glistening with tears. "I thought... I thought you were a friend of the night."

"I am," whispered Rutejìmo.

"Why can't you—" Fidochìma waved to the darkness around them "—tell me? Out here where no one is listening?"

"Because she is listening."

"She is dead!"

"No," Rutejìmo said carefully, "not your granddaughter of a daughter. She is in Mifúno's arms. And, I can't explain why this man is dead and why there is no reason for revenge, but I promise you, on... on..." He couldn't promise on Mifúno's name. He didn't have the right. "I swear, that man is dead."

Fidochìma shook his head. "No, I'm sorry. I can't accept that."

"I can't stop you, Great Foteramasu Fidochìma, but I wish I could." Rutejìmo returned the flask with a bow.

The older man retrieved it and then bowed curtly in return. He gripped his bow and turned to the side. His body flattened until there was nothing but a line in the darkness. And then even that faded.

"No, Rutejìmo," came his fading voice, "there is no greatness in the desert. Not for the night."

Chapter 10

Westerners

"And what do you ask of me?" asked Tachìra of Kosòbyo. The feathered snake lifted himself as the blood dripped down his side. "Only to stand by your side and fight until the end of days." Tachìra bowed to his greatest warrior. "Then you will be the first."

—Kosobyo Mitáki, *Legend of Kosòbyo*

Rutejìmo walked alone in the dark.

His destination glowed before him, a swelling of light and flame that brightened the horizon as if it was day. He could hear the din of people from Kosobyo City, even from across the sands.

The sheer expanse of Kosobyo City terrified him. Too large, too bright, and too alive, it didn't resemble anything he had seen during the day, and to have the entire city lit up at night was more than he could imagine. The wealth of the city was evident, even miles away. The road he followed had been paved in wide stones. They didn't shift under his feet, and the edges had long since been polished by countless feet and wheels.

He passed a small, fortified building made of the same stone as the road. Three guards sat on stools outside the door.

All of them wore red and gold with a clan name that Rutejìmo didn't recognize, but the building had Kosòbyo's colors and name engraved on the side.

The guards stared at him, but made no effort to stop or talk to him.

Rutejìmo looked at them curiously. The nearest guard gripped his sword and Rutejìmo forced his eyes back toward the city. He had passed two other guard buildings on the walk toward the city and had been met with the same attitude.

The road he followed would bring him to the western side of the city, one of the sides that typically welcomed Tachìra's clan. The northern and southern were entrances for Chobìre's chosen, though he suspected that with Kosòbyo's influence and from Fidochìma's comments, there were very few of the night clan in the shadows of the city.

Kosòbyo, one of the most powerful of the day clans, had been in the desert from the beginning. The stories told that the feathered serpent was Tachìra's fiercest ally, and their city reflected the clan's reputation and influence.

With exhaustion plucking at his senses and his vision blurred, Rutejìmo let his mind drift as he continued down the road. The slow impacts of his bare feet smacking on the rocks was soothing, but when he lifted his foot, he felt the last of the drying blood peeling from the warm stones.

He reached the peak of a hill and realized the light had played a trick on him. He thought the brightness meant he was only a few chains away. But, standing on the ridge, he saw all of Kosobyo City spread out before him. The blocks and buildings were arranged in letters that spelled out Kosòbyo. Each symbol appeared to have been designed so there was no question who owned the city.

Individual districts—he didn't know their names—were lit by different colors. The nearest had blue and yellow lights but one of the northern parts was completely red-tinted. Further along, green flames lined the streets of what appeared to be the grandiose part of the city, which was filled with tall buildings and decorated with statues and murals. The center of the green light district had a palace easily five stories tall with a massive snake head rising from the top.

"Drown me in sands," whispered Rutejìmo. The pain of walking and his exhaustion momentarily faded as he stared at the city. There was something about seeing the name of a clan in buildings and light that outshone his imagination. The clan was powerful, and they knew it. They didn't need any walls to guard the city; they were strong enough to fight anyone who dared to invade their lands.

Stunned, he stumbled forward before regaining his pace. He wanted to see the city up close.

An hour later, he walked among the towering buildings. The two-story buildings felt like canyon walls on both sides of him, sheer edges lined with glass windows and frail-looking iron balconies. On the ground level, the windows were much larger and gave tantalizing glimpses of the homes and stores inside.

The streetlights had dimmed in the time it took for him to walk into the city. He was in no danger of tripping on a hidden ridge of the paving stones that made up the roads, or the boards of the wooden walks on both sides of the street. Unlike the flickering, humming lights of home, the glow of these lights steadily covered every surface in tinted color.

Rutejìmo realized his mouth had dropped open. He closed it with a snap and tried to orient himself. From a distance, it looked like it was only a few blocks from the edge, but being caught in the narrow channels of the street confused him, and he lost his path to the message board.

Laughter drew his attention. He looked up to see a small group of people coming out of a bar. They were dressed in yellows and blues, but the outfits were strange. Instead of a shirt and trousers, they wore unusual jackets and strange hats that looked like miniature barrels. The women had donned dresses with hooped skirts and hats that were a cacophony of feathers and jewels.

Rutejìmo considered finding someone else to ask for help, but the last few groups were dressed in a similar fashion. No one wore the simple skirts, dresses, or shirts that he had grown up with. He worried his lip and crossed the street toward a couple. When he was a rod away, he bowed. "Excuse me, could I please—"

"What is this?" said one of the women. "Did something come crawling out of the desert? A little bird? You better be careful, there are snakes in this town."

The scorn in her voice scraped along Rutejìmo's ego and pride, but he kept his voice calm. "I'm lost. Could you please direct me to the nearest message board?"

"No," came the response, followed by laughter. They pushed past him and headed down the street.

Rutejìmo watched them for a moment and felt very alone. He ducked his head and walked in the opposite direction. He still didn't know where he was going, but he didn't like the growing feeling of discomfort.

Twenty minutes later, he was swaying with the effort to keep walking. His hand dripped with blood from when he tripped over his own feet and struck a stone wall. He could barely keep his head straight. He slumped against the wall for a moment to clear his head, but then he had to fight the urge to fall to the ground and sleep.

A pair of white boots stopped in front of him. They were sturdy and streaked with dust.

Rutejìmo started and then forced his head up to the stranger. His eyes refused to focus on the green and white blob for a moment. He frowned and peered forward until it finally came into focus. It was a woman in her mid-twenties wearing Kosòbyo's colors. Her dark skin looked almost black in the blue light above them. Even her hair was in an unfamiliar style. Instead of being straight and loose, it had been tied into neat rows that looked like furrows on a field.

"Excuse me," she spoke with a faint eastern accent, "you can't stay here."

"I'm... sorry. I'm tired. I'm Rutejìmo, and I speak for Shimusògo."

The woman frowned. "You speak for...?" And then a smile crossed her lips, and her green eyes narrowed for a second.

Rutejìmo groaned and steeled himself for another insult.

"You are from the west, aren't you?"

He nodded, his throat burning from the effort of speaking.

"We don't talk like that around here."

Rutejìmo stifled a yawn. "I'm sorry, Great Kosobyo..."

The woman gestured with her finger for Rutejìmo to pull himself from the wall. Her outfit, a long length of cloth wrapped around her body, shivered with her movement. "We don't speak like that either."

"How... I don't know." Despair rose up. "I'm so lost." He fought back a sob. "This town is too big."

She helped him stand on his feet. "Come on, where are you heading?"

"The message board?"

"Which one?"

"I..." He stumbled. "I don't remember anymore. I thought I did, but when I got here, I got lost. There was a large fountain, and I could see it while coming up the western road."

She pulled him against her. Her body was warm but solid under his weight. He could feel the play of muscles and the power of someone who fought, but she had no scars or marks of battle. Everything inside him said that she was a warrior, but a slender one with no obvious weapon. "I know the place. It's about ten blocks, do you think you can make it?"

Rutejìmo yawned a little longer than he needed to and then sighed. "I don't stop. I never stop."

She chuckled.

Slumped against her, Rutejìmo noticed she had a circular badge on her breast. It said Kosobyo Dimóryo along with a pair of words he didn't understand.

"I'm married, Rutejìmo. There is no reason to stare."

Rutejìmo looked up, frightened and embarrassed. "No, sorry. I mean, I never saw something like that before." He gestured to the badge.

"Don't you have guards in your town?"

"Not in the valley, but in Wamifuko City. But, they don't have markings like that."

She tapped her badge. "We have a much bigger city here, with almost a thousand warriors working."

"A... thousand... warriors?"

"How many does your clan have?"

"Four." He felt more alien than ever.

"There is almost a quarter million residents in this town. I suspect you have a lot less."

"Less than a hundred."

She tapped her badge again. "This just means I'm a... street guard, second rank."

"What does that mean?"

"It means I'm going to help you find the rest of your clan."

"Oh, thank you."

They walked a few blocks in silence.

"Why are you so tired, Rutejìmo?"

"I... had to do something, and I ended up far from the city."

"What?"

He said nothing.

"Does your clan know about it?"

He nodded. "It's what I do. No matter where I go."

"Why are you in town?"

"We desire a contract with Kosòbyo. We're couriers."

"Couriers? Oh, yes, I remember we had a call for them in the western areas. You run or ride?"

Rutejìmo started to feel uncomfortable with the questions, but he answered. "Run. Bird spirit."

"I was going to ask that next," said Dimóryo.

"Why?"

"My job is to protect the city and the clan. Knowing who's here is just part of that. Don't worry, I'm not going to take you to jail or anything. See?" She pointed with her free hand down the street.

At the end of the street, five massive message boards stood with about a rod of walking space between them. Papers fluttered along the wood, and he could see more of it piled underneath the boards in heaps of white and cream.

Rutejìmo stumbled. "That's big."

"It's a big city, but you'll get used to it."

"I don't think I could."

She held him tight as she guided him down the street. He felt no weapon on her, but the tight body and precision of her movements indicated skill and training. He guessed she was comparable in abilities to Desòchu but probably not as strong as Chimípu. She was a warrior and just as strange as the city around him.

A few minutes later, she deposited him next to the nearest message board. Stepping back, she ran her hands along her long black hair to pull it over her shoulder. Her right hand sparkled with three golden rings. "You said your clan was Shi…"

"Shimusògo."

"Let me see if they left you a message."

He watched her walk down the boards. Years ago, he would have been interested in her, but after having his heart ripped out by Mikáryo and handed back by Mapábyo, he just pushed the thought aside and concentrated on remaining awake.

"Jìmo!"

Rutejìmo jerked and thumped his head against the board. He had somehow slid down into a pile of papers. A long line of drool marked his chest and hand. He groaned and looked up as his brother stepped up.

Desòchu let out a sigh and knelt in front of him. "You look like shit someone ran through."

"I feel like one of Chobìre's shits." Rutejìmo groaned and let his brother haul him to his feet. "I'm sorry, I feel... fell asleep."

"For close to twenty minutes," Dimóryo said cheerfully as she stepped up to them. She flipped a tight braid from her shoulder. Rutejìmo noticed that the braid continued from the rows in her hair. "Don't worry, I was watching over him."

Desòchu shoved his hand around Rutejìmo's waist and held him up. "Thank you, Great Kosòbyo."

Dimóryo grinned. "Westerners. You have such a quaint way of speaking."

"It's what we do," said Desòchu with a smile that was only slightly forced. "At least until it's time to sleep."

"I thought you didn't stop." Her eyes never wavered from Desòchu.

Desòchu glanced down at Rutejìmo and smiled. "No, only one of us will never stop. The rest of us are still learning how to keep up."

She looked pointedly at Rutejìmo before turning back. Rutejìmo watched as her eyes flickered over Desòchu, pausing only briefly on his weapons before tracing up his chest back to his face. "It doesn't look like it from here."

Desòchu bristled, and his hand balled into a fist.

Rutejìmo rested a hand on him, struggling to keep his head up.

His brother turned back and nodded. When he looked back at her, he was smiling again. "It takes a while to see it." He hefted Rutejìmo up. "Come on, you need some sleep and time with your wife."

"Good luck, Shimusògo."

"And to you, Great Kosobyo...." Desòchu paused.

Rutejìmo whispered her name to his brother.

Desòchu bowed to her. "Great Kosobyo Dimóryo."

She laughed and turned around. "Westerners."

Chapter 11

Recovering

At first blush, infidelity is simple. Get caught and die. However, sex with the warrior caste is considered a non-event. Since there is no chance of producing a child, it isn't considered a betrayal of the marriage.
—Kandor Rusinmar, *The Sacrificial Wolves of the Desert*

Rutejìmo walked hand in hand with Mapábyo. The exhaustion from his purification ritual still plucked at his senses, but sleep and a full meal had helped him recover his energies. Even his recent injuries, including the cut in his shoulder, had already started to scab over and no longer throbbed.

He wasn't fully recovered, but he wanted to see some of Kosobyo City's wonders before heading back to the inn for lunch and a nap.

During the day, the city blossomed with people. All of them wore different outfits, some of them fantastic. There were hats and cloaks and high boots that weren't practical for running across the sand. As if they cared more about appearance than a skill and a trade. After growing up with practical outfits, the fashion disturbed him in a way he couldn't explain. He found himself frowning at clothes as much as he stared in awe at the more fantastic mechanical devices rolling down the road or chugging away in alleyways. Even the hair styles looked foreign, with more colors than the pervasive black scattered with browns, reds, and blues. There were greens and purples mixed in, colors that could not possibly happen naturally.

"There are so many people out here," Mapábyo whispered. "I don't know how they know each other."

On his other side, Chimípu pulled a roasted lizard out of her mouth. "They don't. Just a city filled with strangers."

"There are too many people." On the opposite side of the warrior, Nifùni looked through a list of Shimusògo they were to buy gifts for. Couriers traditionally brought small knickknacks back home when traveling far away. None of them had been so far across the desert before and the prizes from the city would be treasured. It also meant that they needed to purchase for the entire clan instead of only close family and friends.

Mapábyo leaned her head on Rutejìmo's shoulder. "I like it better when I know everyone's name."

"Said the courier who has a new representative every few months," came Chimípu's wry response.

Mapábyo giggled. "I know everyone though. And they know me, every oasis and village."

Rutejìmo smiled. He kissed the top of Mapábyo's head. Her friendliness had saved his life once when he stumbled into an oasis in the middle of the night, and he never regretted her actions.

Chimípu ran her hand through her reddish hair before biting the head off the lizard with a crunch. "This is what big cities are like."

"Not Wamifuko City," said Mapábyo.

"You've been doing the mail run for ten years—do you know everyone there?"

Mapábyo's silence was an answer.

Chimípu sighed and rotated the stick to work on the crispy feet. The look on her face faded to reflect the discomfort that

Rutejìmo felt. Kosobyo City was too big for desert folk like his clan.

He looked at the glass-fronted stores they were passing. A specialized store was rare for him, and he couldn't imagine how much business anyone needed in order to have a place dedicated to selling only perfume, much less the three they had passed in the last twenty minutes.

When he spotted a bookstore, he tapped Mapábyo's hand. "How about a book of poems for Pidòhu?"

Mapábyo smiled broadly, kissed his shoulder, and pulled away to head into the store. They had already bought gifts for almost everyone in the valley except for Pidòhu and Kitòpi.

Chimípu glanced at Rutejìmo. "How are you holding up?"

Rutejìmo saw Nifùni glare at him but he forced himself to focus on Chimípu. "I'll live, but... maybe an hour more?"

Chimípu stepped closer until they were only a foot apart. Her question was silent, but just as obvious. She wanted to know of any troubles when he answered Mifúno's call.

He hesitated to answer, thinking back to how he had seen a man's power be ripped from his body as he was sentenced to a life without the desert's blessing. A prickle of sweat danced on his brow. He took a deep breath and lied with a slow shake of his head.

She nodded and stepped back. She turned to look at Nifùni, who had his back to them. With a shake of her hand, she gestured down the street. "I want to get something special for Dòhu, would you wait with Fùni here for Pábyo?"

Rutejìmo grunted and stepped on the opposite side of the door from Nifùni.

"Thank you, little brother," she whispered before heading down the street. Her lithe body disappeared in the crowds in a matter of seconds.

Nifùni sighed loudly. "Why are you little brother to her?"

Rutejìmo leaned against the glass, but didn't look at Nifùni. "Just something we say."

"You don't deserve her affection."

Rutejìmo said nothing.

"All you do is run away."

Closing his eyes for a second, Rutejìmo counted to three before opening them. Across the street, in the opposing store, he could see someone stretching some sort of candy on a hook before they began to braid it. He wondered what it would taste like.

"You're a moon-damned coward. They should have never brought you along."

Rutejìmo sighed and shrugged. "I don't have an answer, Great Shimusogo Nifùni. The clan elders obviously thought I would be needed."

"And the second you see the city, you run off."

"I had to answer that call."

"This isn't your place. You aren't a... you don't do that... thing on this side of Mifúno."

"Actually," said Dimóryo in an amused voice, "I was going to say the same thing."

Both Shimusògo jumped at her sudden appearance.

Rutejìmo tilted his head as the Kosòbyo warrior stepped up between them. In the sunlight, she looked different than the night before. Her age appeared to be in the lower twenties, with a narrow face and skin the same dark brown as the candy in the store across the street. She had no obvious weapons, but the fabric wrapped around her body moved like armored cloth. He spotted a few strands of golden thread in the stiff fabric. The last time Rutejìmo had seen armor like that, Mikáryo pulled it over her body before she tossed him aside.

Memories bubbled up of his first shikāfu, his first longing love, but he couldn't remember what her face looked like anymore. Five years of marriage had dulled the memories of his first love.

Nifùni cleared his throat. He was straightening his shirt and a blush darkened his cheeks. Rutejìmo smiled to himself, he could almost see the younger man puffing up to impress the warrior.

Dimóryo glanced at him. "I'm Kosobyo Dimóryo."

"I-I'm," stammered Nifùni, "Nif... Shimusogo Nifùni."

Her eyes flickered along his body and her smile grew a little wider. "Are you a kojinōmi also?"

Nifùni's face paled. "No. No!"

"A courier? A runner?"

"Yes, one of the fastest."

Rutejìmo fought back the smile. He didn't need to ruin any chance Nifùni had with the warrior. If she was anything like every other warrior he knew, she would be a safe person to spend a night with; the clan spirits gave warriors more power-ful abilities, but the blessing came with a price—they lost their ability to have children.

Dimóryo tugged on one braid before favoring Nifùni with another smile. Rutejìmo noticed that her knuckles were callo-used and scarred, a detail he failed to catch the night before.

She turned back to Rutejìmo, and Nifùni's smile dropped. "You didn't say you were a kojinōmi, Rutejìmo."

Ice ran down Rutejìmo's spine. "It isn't something we talk a-bout."

"It may be in the west, but here, we like to know these things. There are only six kojinōmi in the city, and they are... rather protective of their services. We had a report that you...." Her voice trailed off as she appeared to struggle with the word.

Rutejìmo wanted to duck back into the store, but he held his ground. "I answer to the call. I don't have a choice."

Her green eyes sparkled as she looked over him. "And there is only one of you?"

"There are six of the Shimusògo in town, but only one... like me." He couldn't bring himself to say kojinōmi even knowing it was acceptable. Too many years of not speaking about what he did stilled his voice.

She dug into the folds of her armored fabric before pulling out a notebook. With a brass pen, she wrote something before ripping it off and handing it to Rutejìmo. "You've been requested to present yourself to the other kojinōmi at this address in three nights."

Rutejìmo took the paper, it was an address. "What time?"

Dimóryo frowned. "For dinner, isn't that when you always do those things?"

He shrugged to hide his confusion and looked at the unfamiliar address again.

"Well," she continued, "as soon as the sun sets, they'll expect you there. By yourself, I guess, but I don't know your rituals. I'm not privy to the priests of the dead."

The door next to Rutejìmo creaked open, and Mapábyo came out carrying two small, hand-bound books. "Jìmo, I found the most beautiful...." Her voice trailed off as she looked at the warrior in front her.

Dimóryo turned to look at her but her gaze lingered on Rutejìmo for a second. She bowed. "Well met, wife of Rutejìmo, I am Kosòbyo... wait, I am Dimóryo, and I speak for Kosòbyo," she said with only a hint of mocking in her voice.

Mapábyo's almost black skin darkened even further. She bowed in return. "I am Shimusogo Mapábyo." She straightened and shot a glance at Rutejìmo. "Is there something wrong?"

From her look, he knew there would be more personal questions when they were alone. Then, he looked back at the Kosòbyo warrior. He mentioned he was married, but never told Dimóryo much about Mapábyo.

"No," Dimóryo said, "not yet. Last night I helped Rutejìmo find the other member of your clan and asked some questions.

He was not as forthcoming with answers as I hoped, so I had to pry into your business. Please forgive me, I take my job of protecting the clan against all threats seriously."

Nifùni spoke up. "I-I would have answered."

Dimóryo said, "Thank you. It would have been easier if you were there."

Nifùni blushed and sank back against the wall.

Mapábyo took a step closer to Rutejìmo until her arm brushed his. "Is there anything we can help you with, Great Kosobyo Dimóryo?"

The warrior smiled again. "I love the way you westerners speak. No, I'm just glad that Rutejìmo returned to you safely." She bowed deeply and then again to Nifùni before turning and walking away.

All three of them watched her until she disappeared. Then Mapábyo turned to Rutejìmo. "And how does she know you're married?"

Rutejìmo blushed and held out his hand for the books. "She thought I was interested in her."

"You," snapped Mapábyo, "are not allowed to have another shikāfu." She tapped him on the chest with two fingers.

He leaned over and kissed her forehead. "You are my only flame. Besides," he grinned, "I think Nifùni is far more interested in her."

Nifùni shoved himself from the wall. "If she would notice me." He stormed away, shoving through the crowd going in the opposite direction.

Rutejìmo groaned.

"He is on a wire, isn't he?"

With a nod, he said, "Yes. He was telling me I'm a coward when she came up."

"You aren't one."

"Tópi said the same thing before we left."

"At least Tópi has the excuse of being a child. Nifùni is only acting like one." Mapábyo's voice was tense.

Rutejìmo plucked the top book from her hand and opened it. The words looked different for a moment, then he realized the arrangement was different than he was used to reading, there were too many glyphs instead of markers. But, it was still a book of poems, one of Pidòhu's passions. He bobbed his head in approval. "Dòhu will love it."

Mapábyo kissed him. "I hope so." She kissed him again. "But, right now, the inn room is empty, and," her smile grew more sultry, "I think you need a nap."

Rutejìmo looked at her. As he stared into her bright eyes, he felt himself growing warmer. With a grin, he slipped his hand around her waist and kissed her. "I am tired, my shikāfu."

— Chapter 12 —

The Offer

Age carries more weight than wisdom.

—Kosòbyo proverb

Rutejìmo hummed to himself as he walked along the paved road. A few hours with Mapábyo had brightened his mood, and he still enjoyed the afterglow that pulsed in his veins. He knew part of her passion was to remind him of their marriage and jealousy over the Kosòbyo warrior, but it didn't matter to him. He had sworn his love for Mapábyo and there was no force that would ever turn him away.

Around him, the streets were crowded with folk walking and drinking and talking. It was an hour after sunset, but the press of desert folk only diminished slightly since the street-lights had turned on.

He slowed down at a brightly-lit bar and peered inside. The press of people made it hard, but after a few minutes, he didn't see Nifùni and moved on. The younger man hadn't returned to the inn by sundown and everyone was out looking for him.

At first, he wondered if a festival was going on, but then it quickly became apparent these crowds were normal on all nights in the city, a far cry from the silence he grew up with. At home, when the sun went down, everyone retreated to their home caves. Now that he had seen how they did things here, he realized neither was wrong, simply the nature of the valley and the city, two different worlds in the same desert.

Rutejìmo didn't know how to approach Nifùni. There was anger in the younger man's heart, but it was the same hatred that so many of the younger clan members had. Very few of them understood how Rutejìmo stood between two worlds, a courier of Shimusògo and a kojinōmi. The passing between his two duties was exhausting and unforgiving, but he couldn't turn his back on either.

He always wondered if his slowness at running and his unwillingness to take a life were somehow connected with his services to the dead.

At the end of the block, he waited for a large mechanical spider to walk down the street. Made of brass, it shook the ground with every step. Unlike the massive scorpions that he had seen crossing the desert, the spider was his height and about twice the length of a wagon. The driver sat behind the ruby eyes, with one leg on each side of the neck. She kept her back straight while she rested one hand on the steering rod. Her hair appeared to be tucked into a low, circular hat. A pair of crossed daggers were sheathed on her back, the pommels matching the red eyes of the spider and the sheaths matching her yellow and white outfit.

On the back of the spider, there was a cradle of some sort with a man lounging inside it. He looked younger than the driver but wore the same colors she did. He waved at some of the people on the street but did nothing else.

Rutejìmo watched them pass. He wondered about the couple. She looked like a warrior of some sort, and he obviously wasn't. She appeared to be serving him, which was the opposite of everything Rutejìmo grew up with. Warriors served the clan, but not by carting an individual around.

Shrugging, he crossed the street and headed for the next bar. It was a larger one that ran the entire length of the block, about two chains, and he had to push himself inside to inspect it.

There was a heavily muscled man inside the door, watching the bar. He looked at Rutejìmo and then gestured toward the back.

Rutejìmo bowed. "Thank you." He didn't know how to address the man, he wasn't familiar with the clan colors and he didn't appear to have the name embroidered on his outfit like most of the Shimusògo did.

Following the gesture, he padded through the room. His bare feet contrasted to everyone else who wore shoes and boots. He wrapped his arms over his chest as he ducked toward the further room.

He found Nifùni in the quieter section of the public house. He sat at a small table, talking to a woman who wore a heavy cloak despite the heat of the room.

Rutejìmo hesitated, wondering if Nifùni was trying to find some company for the night. He was an adult, and none of the others would stop him. He started to turn away, but a gut feeling stopped him from leaving. He turned back just as a woman with a tray of food came walking up behind him. Muttering an apology, he ducked against a post to let her pass.

He watched Nifùni and the woman for a moment. The longer he looked, the less it felt like an attempt at an amorous encounter. She kept looking up and around her before ducking her head down. He caught a glimpse of light brown hair underneath her cloak and a flash of gold around her throat.

Nifùni was also nervous. Rutejìmo could tell by the way he was twisting his palm around his other wrist and the rapid tapping of his left foot.

The sense of wrongness rose. It was different than Mifúno's call but just as pressing. He cleared his throat and pushed away from the post to cross the room.

When Nifùni looked up at Rutejìmo, his expression dropped. "What are you doing here?"

Rutejìmo hesitated for a moment, then sat down. "You didn't return to the inn. We were worried about you."

"I'm fine, go away."

Rutejìmo glanced at the woman. Underneath the cloak, he saw a few lines around her eyes and wrinkles along her hands. He guessed her to be about his age, near thirty. "I'm sorry to interrupt."

The woman shook her head. "No, we were almost done. Are you also a courier?"

He nodded in response.

"Is Nifùni really the fastest?"

Rutejìmo glanced at Nifùni who looked back pleadingly. He started to agree, if anything to give Nifùni a chance, but the wrongness continued to rise in his throat. He felt the sensation hovering in his mind and pulsing in his veins. Something disturbed him, but he couldn't put a word on it. To stall, he muttered, "He's much faster than me."

"Thank the sands." The woman dug into her cloak and then pulled out a thick roll of paper money and a cylindrical case. The case was made of bone and heavily carved with scenes of snakes. It was as thick as Rutejìmo's wrist and a foot in length. He had seen thousands of them; they were used to deliver contracts and private messages. Just like many which had passed over his palms during his adult life as a courier.

She tucked the case in the crook of her elbow and peeled bills from the roll of money. To Rutejìmo's surprise, they were thousand pyābi notes.

When she had pulled off twenty and was still moving, Rutejìmo held up his hand. "Wait."

"Not now, Jìmo!" snapped Nifùni.

The woman froze.

Rutejìmo glared at Nifùni. "You negotiated a contract?"

"Yes, I did. It's just a delivery, nothing more."

"That—," Rutejìmo gestured to the twenty thousand pyābi on the table, "—is not 'just' a contract. No one pays twenty thousand for—"

"I-I can pay sixty more," said the woman. She held out the rest of the money.

Rutejìmo froze as the ice sank into his stomach. He shivered as he looked at her. "Eighty thousand for a delivery? To where?"

"To Wami-fuko City."

Rutejìmo's discomfort grew at her stumbling over the name. He felt the tension squeezing down on his chest, a pressure to respond. "What is in there?"

Nifùni reached out for Rutejìmo. "You can't ask—"

Rutejìmo yanked back. He could feel his voice growing more tense but he had to keep speaking. "No one pays that much for a simple delivery. That is what you pay for someone risking their life. So, I have to ask, what is in that case?"

"J-Just a message."

"To who?"

"The Wamifūko." She held out her shaking hands with the roll of bills rolling in her palm. "Please, just take it. I'll give you everything."

The desperation in her voice warred with the feeling in his gut. Everything told him to walk away, to leave her alone. But, he also wanted to help.

Nifùni's chair scraped on the floor as he moved closer. "Jìmo," he whispered, "that's over a hundred thousand pyābi! That would pay for the year! It makes up for the money we lost!"

Rutejìmo clenched his jaw, looking at the money in her palm. He knew how much the clan needed it. It was enough to make the clan comfortable. They could afford to even purchase new machines and magic for the clan valley.

He looked into her eyes, a swirling green, and the sorrow and desperation on her shadowed face plucked at his heart. He wanted to help her, a desperation that arose to grip his thoughts.

Rutejìmo almost said yes, but then he drew away. "Who are you?"

She inhaled sharply, and her hand slumped to the table. She glanced over her shoulder, and he saw a flash of a green and gold snake tattooed on her cheek. "No one," she whispered when she turned back. "Please, Great... Shim... Rutejìmo. I promise you, it's just a message."

Her eyes drew him in, tugging at his resistance. The bright green swam across his vision and seeped into his thoughts. He could deliver a simple message; no one would have to know.

His mouth opened without him thinking. He could feel the words bubbling out, but he drew back. Clearing his throat, he forced his thoughts to focus on her snake tattoo instead of her eyes.

"No." It was the hardest word he could ever speak.

"What!?" Nifùni slapped on the table as he stood up. "It's a hundred thousand pyābi!"

Rutejìmo glared at him. "And now everyone in this room knows."

Nifùni paled and looked around at everyone staring at him. Slowly, he sank back into his chair.

Rutejìmo kept watching him. "And in this case, I speak for Shimusògo." He matched glares with Nifùni.

Nifùni's jaw tightened and a muscle jumped with his anger. "You can't speak for Shimusògo."

"I can," announced Rutejìmo. He turned back to her. "I'm sorry, but if you want to hire the Shimusògo for services, please come to the Pochiryo Inn tomorrow morning. We will be glad to listen to you then, but I feel you need to explain the job in more detail before—"

"Please, I don't have time."

Rutejìmo nearly looked at her eyes and forced himself to focus on her tattoo. "No, we need a majority to accept this type of job. The others will be willing to listen, but at the moment, we are scattered—" He pointedly looked at Nifùni, "—across the town looking for one of ours."

Nifùni's face was a mask of rage. His lips quivered as he glared daggers at Rutejìmo.

Rutejìmo turned back. "Please understand, Great...." His voice trailed off as he tried to identify her clan. Normally, one would announce their clan, but she was obviously hiding. The only hint of her colors was the tattoo on her cheek. He could see green and gold in the hidden depths. His eyes dropped down to her hand. There was another tattoo on the back of her palm, another snake. There was only one clan who used green and gold with a snake, the Kosòbyo.

He lifted his attention back to hers. "We are willing to work with you, but neither Nifùni or I can accept this contract tonight."

She stood up. "I-I'm sorry, I have to leave then." She clutched the money and case in her hand as she stumbled toward a door in the back.

Rutejìmo felt a moment of relief when she disappeared out of sight.

"You are a moon-damned coward!" screamed Nifùni.

Around them, conversations halted instantly.

Nifùni stood up and shoved Rutejìmo back.

The chair creaked loudly as Rutejìmo tried to regain his balance. He managed to keep his feet, but it tilted over, clattering loudly in the sudden silence as Rutejìmo straightened.

Rutejìmo held up his hands. "Nifùni—"

"No! You are a coward! That could have set us up for the year! And you tossed it aside because you can't handle—"

As Nifùni screamed, Rutejìmo saw the muscular man at the door walking toward them.

"—a little challenge. It was just a simple, sand-damned delivery. We've done them every day of our sand-damned lives." Nifùni flailed at Rutejìmo, his fingers sailing inches away from Rutejìmo's shirt.

Rutejìmo gestured for Nifùni to calm down. "Let's go back and talk about this. Please, we need—"

Nifùni bellowed at the top of his lungs. "You are a sand-damned, moon-dazed coward whose own children are disgusted by you. You can't handle—"

The muscular man stopped next to him and crossed his arms. A golden flame coursed along his body, tracing the ridges of his muscles, and glinting off the piercings that marked his face and ears.

As Nifùni continued to rant, Rutejìmo turned to the man and bowed apologetically. "I'm sorry, please forgive my clan. I do not wish to interrupt your celebrations." He turned and walked out of the bar.

The muscular man walked past, his left hand balling into a fist.

Nifùni screamed after him. "Again! You are leaving again—" His voice stopped with a thud. The sound of air escaping his lungs filled the silence of the bar.

Rutejìmo closed his eyes tightly to fight back the tears. He should have never abandoned his clan, but Nifùni was no longer listening.

He stopped outside. A few seconds later, Nifùni came flying out the door to land in an ungainly heap on the ground.

Nifùni scrambled to his feet. "Coward! You idiotic, festering pile of shit smeared on—"

There was a blast of air and then Desòchu stood next to Rutejìmo. Around them, the street lights flared brilliantly. One burst into flames and another cracked loudly.

Rutejìmo fought the tears. He shook his head firmly. He didn't want Desòchu to stop the fight, but it was obvious that Nifùni didn't respect Rutejìmo's decision as an elder. "I'm sorry, but we have to talk about this."

"Talk about what?" asked Desòchu.

"A job!" snapped Nifùni, "A hundred thousand pyābi job that this rotted corpse of a man turned down because he was too afraid to risk his own life. It was a simple message. Just a simple, sand-damned message!"

Rutejìmo wanted to scream back, to yell something. Struggling, he turned to his brother. "I wanted to say yes."

"Then why didn't you?"

"Because I wanted to say yes despite what my heart was telling me. No one delivers a—"

"Don't give your side of the story, you castrated sack of horse shit!"

Desòchu stared at Rutejìmo for a long time.

Rutejìmo wiped the tears threatening to fall. "I'm sorry, Great Shimusogo Desòchu. I couldn't accept it without talking to the others."

Desòchu nodded twice. "Then let's talk."

"Of course," snapped Nifùni, "you'd take his side. You are his damned brother, you—"

Desòchu's punch caught Nifùni across the jaw, spinning the courier three times before he collapsed to the ground. The flash of golden light that followed the punch arced to the nearest streetlight which also burst into flames.

Something inside the bar exploded and there were screams of outrage.

The muscular bouncer stepped out of the door, his face twisted in a scowl.

With another sigh, Desòchu shook his head. "Let me pay for the damages."

Nifùni sat up, holding his jaw.

"And then, we are all going back to the inn."

Chapter 13

Voting

As if age could prevent the horrors already seen, decisions among a clan are made through the opinion of years.

—Heyojyunashi Gutèmo

Naked, Rutejìmo entered the shared inn room and tossed his towel on his sleeping mat. He started to throw his bathing bag after it but stopped when Mapábyo stood up from one of the beds. He smiled and held it out for her, along with the key to get into the bathing area.

She kissed him and trailed her fingers along his arm before grabbing both and heading out.

Feeling playful, he stepped back out of the room to watch her bare ass as she walked down the hall.

Mapábyo stopped at the door, blew him a kiss, and then unlocked it.

"You know," said Byochína from where she was dressing in the corner, "you could enjoy some privacy if you both went in at the same time."

"Yeah, but then neither would get cleaned," said Desòchu.

Chimípu snickered. She was finishing pulling on a red skirt hemmed in orange. Her bare legs, hard and solid as any Shimu-sògo runner, flexed with her movements.

A blush grew on Rutejìmo's cheeks. He and Mapábyo were the only married couple on the trip, and it led to teasing. He grabbed his trousers and began to dress.

The only one not laughing was Nifùni who sat in another corner, his clothes wrinkled on his body and a scowl on his face. His left cheek had a dark shadow from where Desòchu punched him.

Rutejìmo kept his eyes averted from the younger man and dressed quickly. He picked a pair of orange trousers and a white button-down shirt, one of his favorite outfits, but far plainer than anything the city folk wore outside. He had brought three tops and two trousers, which was enough for most trips.

Desòchu finished and sat down. He dug into his pack and pulled out a wallet with the clan's money.

"How much?" asked Chimípu.

After a moment of counting, Desòchu sighed. "Maybe three days at most. This city is expensive."

"At least we have the shopping done."

He nodded. "Except for Tòpi and Róma."

Rutejìmo spoke up. "Pábyo and I got Róma a hair comb."

"Jìmo," Chimípu said as she walked around him. "You're her papa. Those gifts don't count. I say we get her a book."

Nifùni scoffed.

"Poetry?" asked Byochína before she pulled her shirt down over her chest. Her hair, long and black, fanned out along the fabric before cascading down.

Chimípu shook her head. "No, Pidòhu lets her read his. How about one of those travel books I saw? They have pictures of the city in them, and they are made by a machine instead of hand-written. I bet she'd like those. She seems like a girl who would like to travel."

"How can you tell?" Byochína tugged her shirt into place. "She doesn't talk right."

Rutejìmo felt a prickle of defensiveness. "She talks."

"Yes, like an adult," said Byochína. "She's the only three-year-old that calls her papa by his name."

"And yet," added Desòchu, "we make all teenagers use their parent's names instead of mama and papa. She's just advanced for her age."

Byochína glanced at Rutejìmo and then back to Desòchu. "She's creepy. She doesn't blink enough and I always get the feeling that she's seeing something more than just me."

Chimípu said, "No, she just follows a different path." She smiled at him. "She's like Jìmo."

Rutejìmo smiled back, still blushing.

"Who's like Jìmo?" asked Mapábyo as she came in. Her body dripped with water and she smelled of soap and honey.

Rutejìmo breathed in and enjoyed her scent. "Róma."

"I agree, she's like her papa." Mapábyo tossed her towel and the bathing supplies on Rutejìmo's bag before she dressed herself. She was the last of the Shimusògo to use the washing area. He watched the water dripping off the bird tattoo on her breast and smiled.

Desòchu stood up. "Good thing we are talking to the Kosòbyo tomorrow. I don't think we can afford many more nights. Hopefully, they will give us an advance."

Nifùni raised his head, glared at Rutejìmo, and then said, "Rutejìmo has to present himself to the kojinōmi in three days."

The room grew still.

"We," Desòchu said, "don't talk about that."

"Why not?" asked Nifùni. "They talk about it on the streets without whispering."

"They aren't us. There are things that we don't talk about even among ourselves. It is the Shimusogo Way."

Rutejìmo hated when his brother spoke of the Shimusogo Way, but warriors were responsible for keeping the clan's traditions. He ducked his head, unwilling to participate in the looming fight.

The silence stretched awkwardly, punctuated only by the rustle of clothes.

Desòchu cleared his throat. "If we have to stay that long, we can manage another night but it will be tight. Today, we'll see if we can find a quick job or two. Just enough to cover the room."

Nifùni snarled and glared at Rutejìmo. "We would have had another job, if the coward didn't turn it down."

A muscle in Mapábyo's back tightened. After a heartbeat, she set down her brush with enough force that the end table shook.

Chimípu turned. "What?"

Nifùni waved his hand at Rutejìmo. "He turned down a job. It was a good one too, a simple delivery; but he was too much of a—"

"Say that word one more time," growled Desòchu, "and I will hit you far harder than I did last night. And I will break something more important than your ego."

Nifùni clamped his mouth shut, his eyes flashing with anger.

Chimípu sat on the corner of the bed Nifùni had claimed. "You disagree?"

"Of course I disagree. A hundred thousand is a lot of money."

Rutejìmo could feel the tension gathering around him. Mapábyo and Byochína both looked at him quizzically. He twisted his hand together and opened his mouth to rebuke the claim, but Desòchu shook his head, and Rutejìmo remained silent.

Chimípu shifted so she was sitting cross-legged on the bed. "Then, tell me about the job."

Nifùni looked at Desòchu and Rutejìmo with a scowl etched on his face.

"Fùni, please?"

Nifùni glared at Rutejìmo for a long time, then he sighed. "I was drinking by myself when she showed up and asked if I was a courier. Since that is what I was," his gaze drifted to the bed, "muttering about, I agreed. She said she wanted a message delivered and she was willing to pay twenty thousand."

"You said a hundred," said Chimípu.

Nifùni gestured to Rutejìmo who flinched. "It was twenty to start, but when Rutejìmo showed up, he started to say no, and she kept raising the price. Eventually, she just offered an entire roll of pyābi if we would take it."

Desòchu spoke up. "Take it where?"

"To any large city and the clan that controls it. I asked if Wamifūko would work, since they are on the way home, and she said yes. It just had to be there in the next few days. I figured we were heading home anyways, so it wouldn't be such a struggle."

"What's her name?" asked Chimípu.

"I don't know."

"What clan was she?"

"I don't know."

Rutejìmo cleared his throat. "Kosòbyo, I think. She had a green and gold tattoo on her cheek, a snake. And another on her wrist."

"I doubt that." Nifùni puffed out his chest as he spoke. "Kosòbyo is in charge here, they wouldn't need us for something like that."

Rutejìmo wanted to point out that Nifùni never asked the woman for her clan, but said nothing.

Desòchu leaned against the small dresser next to the bed. He clutched the wallet tightly and there was concern on his face. "She was desperate?"

"I guess." Nifùni looked up at the ceiling, "Yeah, she was desperate."

No one said anything for a moment.

Nifùni looked around at the others. "Look, can't we vote or something? It's enough money to make up what we lost."

Desòchu looked at Chimípu who looked back. He nodded after a second. "We'll vote."

Everyone went to their bags to gather their voting stones. Rutejìmo had one for every year since he passed his right of passage except for the one year he was ostracized from his clan. For a moment, sadness draped over him as he remembered where he had left it: at the bottom of the urn with his unborn child.

Nifùni sat down on the end of the bed.

Desòchu gestured Rutejìmo to the other one.

Rutejìmo stepped over the sleeping bags on the floor to go where his brother indicated.

"Okay, on Nifùni's bed if we go looking for her. Jìmo's if we turn it down."

Taking a deep breath, Rutejìmo started to gather up all his stones, but then only pulled out one. Carefully, he set it down on the bed next to his thigh. It was a way of expressing that he agreed with his decision, but he wasn't willing to put the full weight of his age behind it. It was also a tradition that one of his friends had, before he died.

Desòchu's eyebrow rose, and Rutejìmo saw him adjust the number of rocks in his hand.

On the other side of the room, Nifùni poured out his entire measure of voting stones on the bed. Seven bright red rocks landed in a heap.

A moment later, one of Chimípu's landed next to Nifùni.

Nifùni looked at Rutejìmo with undisguised glee.

Desòchu shook his head and reached over to Rutejìmo before dropping five down.

Mapábyo joined him, adding all five of hers.

It came down to Byochína. She stood in the center, looking back and forth as she played with her stones.

Nifùni cleared his throat. "Come—"

"Silence!" snapped both Desòchu and Chimípu.

Then, with a tear in her eye, Byochína tossed a single stone to Nifùni. "I'm sorry, I believe you, but..."

Nifùni let out a long gasp of frustration. There was only nine on his side and eleven on Rutejìmo's.

Desòchu gathered up his stones. "We find a different job. Pair off and check the message boards. Look for something that can be done in a day, two at the maximum."

Byochína held out her hand, her voting stone still in it. "Come on, Nifùni." She looked back at Desòchu. "We'll take the east side, Great Shimusogo Desòchu."

Dragging his feet, Nifùni stood up and headed out the door after her.

Rutejìmo stared down at his stones.

Desòchu patted him on his back. "I trust your feelings, Jìmo. If you thought there was something wrong, then it was probably for the best we didn't get involved."

D. Moonfire

Chapter 14

Presents

All magic has resonance, which only responds violently when two incompatible forces are brought together.

—*Primer on Crystal Sphere Techniques*

The merchant's store was quiet and peaceful, lined with blank books and writing utensils ranging from simple charcoal to magical devices that never ran out of ink. The artifacts were in glass cases, marked with a thin yellow line to indicate their sensitivity to resonance. Those with little magic, such as Rutejìmo, could use them safely but the petabiryōchi, a word he didn't know, would spark or explode if Chimípu walked too close.

Mapábyo led the way around the store, gathering up a few inexpensive gifts for Piróma, a blank book and some paper-wrapped charcoal. The pages crinkled as she ran her fingers along the other papers. She stopped at a wooden case and pointed out a dizzying array of metal tips inside.

Rutejìmo wasn't sure what they were, but the ink-splotched paper with calligraphic writing suggested they were also writing devices. His gaze dropped to the price, two thousand. It wasn't the most expensive item in the store, that was a five thousand pyābi pen that somehow had no resonance but could write for hours.

He sighed, and memories of the morning's vote returned to his thoughts. The Shimusògo were not a rich clan and a hundred thousand pyābi would have gone a long way to letting him buy gifts like the fancy papers for his daughter and Pidòhu.

His son would still be happy with a new ball though, no matter how much money they spent on it.

Mapábyo glanced at him, a beam of sunlight dancing on her almost black skin. "You made the right choice."

Rutejìmo smiled and gestured to the case. "It doesn't feel like it now." He looked at it. "Before I came here, I never knew about these things. But, seeing them, I want to get them for my daughter because I think she would love them. I want to shower the clan in presents because they have done so much, but I turned it down just because it felt wrong." He sniffed. "Maybe I am a coward."

Mapábyo's eyes flashed in the sun as she stepped up to him. "Never," she hissed, "use that word to describe yourself."

He opened his mouth.

She held up two fingers, silencing him. "You were never a coward. You are not a failure. You are Great Shimusogo Rutejìmo, the man I married, the father of my children, and the blessed of both Shimusògo and," she hesitated before lowering her voice to a whisper, "Mifúno."

He shivered at her words.

"And realize that I," she tapped between her breasts with both fingers, "didn't marry a coward. I married you."

Rutejìmo bowed his head. "Yes, Great Shimusogo Mapábyo."

"Good, now let's buy these things." She held up the items she had selected "And then see if that meat merchant is ready for us to make her delivery."

Ten minutes later, they were walking out of the butcher shop. Mapábyo held her travel pack loosely in her hand, the bottom only inches from the ground.

"Damn the sands," she muttered.

Rutejìmo was also disappointed, but he tried to keep it from his voice. "She did say we would only get the job if they couldn't find their usual runner. Apparently, they found her."

"I know, but it would have been nice. This city is expensive."

"You mean, the gifts we're buying are expensive."

She looked down at her bag. Her lower lip peeked out slightly. "Do we have to sell them back?"

Rutejìmo shook his head. "What if we camp out of town for the rest of the trip?"

"Your brother said that we have to put on the appearance of being stable. Cowering in the sands wouldn't give the right impression."

He sighed. "Damn, why can't it be easy?"

Mapábyo leaned into him. She said nothing for a long moment, then kissed his shoulder.

He slipped his arm around her waist and tried not to think about the money.

"Shimusògo!" Byochína ran toward them waving a hand. Her speed wasn't driven by Shimusògo's speed, but she outpaced two horses trotting down the street before cutting in front of them and onto the wooden sidewalk. She stopped in front of the couple while looking around.

A prickle of fear ran down Rutejìmo's spine and he took a step away from Mapábyo.

"Have you seen Nifùni?" she asked steadily, the run not even breaking her voice.

Mapábyo shook her head. "No, why?"

"I went in to ask about a delivery, and when I came out, he was gone. That was about twenty minutes ago."

"Why did he leave?"

Byochína held up her hands. "I don't know! He wouldn't have just wandered off. What if something is wrong?"

Fear twisted Rutejìmo's gut. There was an obvious answer why Nifùni would have abandoned his clan. "Maybe he found that woman. The one we voted on this morning."

"No," Mapábyo said firmly, "he wouldn't go against a clan vote. Besides, how could he find her in a city this big?"

"Sorry," Rutejìmo groaned, "I shouldn't have said it. It was just my head getting stuck. Maybe he just found a bar serving free drinks?"

"Or a pretty girl?" said Mapábyo.

Byochína twisted her hands together. "Just in case, we need to find him. I don't want him getting drunk alone in this city. Faster is better, don't you think? Do you think we can speed?"

Mapábyo gestured to an intersection in front of them. "I read that the one-way streets allow some magic, but most don't. If we stick to the one-ways, then Rutejìmo could race along the others. His power is much weaker than ours and won't cause feedback."

For the briefest moment, guilt slammed into him, but it was quickly replaced with determination. Even though he was the slowest of the clan, Mapábyo was right. At his top speed, he produced almost no resonance with artifacts. He swallowed his pride and nodded. "I can do it."

Rutejìmo pointed at the front side of the butcher's shop. "There are two one-way streets that intersect about a block that way, back where the writing shop was. We could check in there, say every ten minutes? If you two take the one-ways, I'll circle around and look. A plan?"

Byochína bowed. "Shimusògo run."

"Shimusògo run," said Mapábyo and Rutejìmo.

Settling his pack over his shoulders, Rutejìmo cinched it down and then sprinted forward just as his dépa raced past. The world blurred for only a few chains before the dépa disappeared. He jammed his bare feet into the ground and skidded to a halt.

When he stopped, he ignored the cries of outrage and peered around. When he didn't see Nifùni, he accelerated for another chain and looked again.

In minutes, the constant starting and stopping left his muscles aching and his feet sore. It felt like walking across the desert without food or the long runs keeping up with the rest of the clan. He wanted to slow to a jog, but the fear that he would miss Nifùni continued to twist his guts.

He kept going, one chain and stop. One chain and stop. The world became a blur of nothing but people yelling at him and a constant appearance of stores and houses.

Rutejìmo was just crossing over one of the one-way streets when he caught a flash of green and gold. He glanced toward it and spotted Dimóryo leading two other Kosòbyo guards away from him. She walked with purpose as she shoved her way through the crowds.

The feeling of fear rose and burned the back of his throat. He didn't think her presence was a coincidence.

The moment passed, and then he was past the intersection. Swearing, he came to a halt, his bare feet scraping against the cobblestones. A few bricks pried free before he managed to come to a halt only a foot away from a metal light pole. Gasping, he turned and jogged back to the intersection to follow the three guards.

It only took him seconds to catch up to them and a second longer to determine their destination. There was a crowd of people five blocks ahead with more desert folk running toward it.

"Sands," he muttered and accelerated past the Kosòbyo guards. He knew he was violating a law in front of them, but if Nifùni was in trouble, he needed to get there first.

The dépa circled around the crowd and Rutejìmo followed it. On the far side, it had disappeared so Rutejìmo came to a sliding halt and looked at the crowd's focus.

A woman in Kosòbyo colors lay in a pool of blood that poured out of her ears, eyes, mouth, and between her legs. It stained her green dress and smelled both coppery and acidic. One hand clutched against her breast and the other had clawed into the paving stones until the whites of her bones were visible.

Bile rose in his throat. He had tended thousands of dying but something about how the woman died was unlike any other death. It looked closer to plague than a weapon, except she had died quickly and violently.

When he caught sight of a snake tattoo, he forced himself to look further. He had not seen the woman's face in the cloak, but he remembered the tattoo on her cheek. He frowned and took a step closer. From his vantage point, he couldn't see much with the blood coating her face.

He spotted just a hint of a tail in one of the few unmarred spots of her face. His gaze focused on her hand, also covered in blood, and he spotted another tattoo peeking out.

Rutejìmo didn't know if it was the same woman or not, but she looked similar enough for him to worry for Nifùni's life. Turning around, he looked for any sign of his clan member, but the crowds were gathering too quickly. He leaned to the side, looking past people covering their mouths and making faces as they approached.

Hissing through his clenched teeth, he shoved his way past the brightly-colored dresses and more somber suits. As soon as he could get clear, he sprinted a chain away and looked around.

The difference of almost seventy feet was stark. There were only a few people remaining and the street was almost empty.

Proprietors stared out the doors of their shops, but otherwise everyone had gathered around the murder scene behind him.

"Come on, Nifùni, where are you?" Rutejìmo muttered to himself.

He spun around and scanned his surroundings. He was about to accelerate to a new position when he spotted one of the street lights sparking. Beyond that, about a block away, someone was picking up papers that had been scattered almost a rod's distance in a straight line from the lamp.

Rutejìmo followed an imaginary line between the lamp and papers. He saw more signs of high-speed movement: torn up bricks, a cracked window in front of a store, and a smoking sign that he guessed used to glow.

Setting his jaw, he tightened his grip on his pack and accelerated into a sprint. Instead of following Nifùni's probable path, he turned at the next intersection and headed back to where he was going to meet the others. He had to tell them before running off on his own.

He stopped at the crossroads where Mapábyo and Byochína were waiting. "Nifùni's in trouble," he said and spun around.

Three dépa raced past them, and Rutejìmo sprinted after them, knowing his wife and clan would follow. He wished he could also summon Desòchu or Chimípu, but they were on the opposite side of the city, also looking for Nifùni.

As soon as they reached the same path as Nifùni, Mapábyo and Byochína accelerated past him in a blast of air, running faster than he could see and covering the distance at twice his speed. With their passing, streetlights exploded into flames and glow lights above doors flared. Previously invisible runes on doors and windows shone out as alarms responded violently. A glass window of a store cracked around the runes before the entire window exploded into the depths of the building.

Even with them out of sight, he could easily follow their wake. Now there were fires on both sides of the road and the screams of outrage and anger echoed shrilly against the stone walls.

He caught up to the three of them in less than a minute. The two women's paths ended by two gouges that tore up paving stones and cracked a gutter.

Nifùni stood at the entrance of an alley between two three-story buildings. He clutched the edge of the bricks until his knuckles matched his pale face.

Both women were yelling at him at the top of their lungs. Garbage and papers swirled around all of them from the dying remains of the wind of Mapábyo and Byochína's speed.

Byochína punched his shoulder with every sentence, the steady impact keeping up with the rapid-fire questions that gave Nifùni no chance to respond.

Around the three, there were city folk watching with furious expressions. Signs of resonance damage were everywhere, including magenta sparks that poured out of a sign across the street and burning bricks along one sidewalk.

Rutejìmo paled and then stopped next to them. "Further in the alley. Let's not attract any more attention."

"What did you do!?" Byochína was screaming, her eyes flashing and her hands balled into fists.

"In the alley!" snapped Rutejìmo before shoving his wife further in. "Now!"

Mapábyo glared at him but then pushed Nifùni before her as Rutejìmo forced her out of the open.

Nifùni stumbled back, clutching the Kosòbyo woman's bone case to his chest. His mouth was open to speak, but neither Byochína or Mapábyo were giving him a chance to say anything.

Rutejìmo focused on getting them further into the darkness, shoving more frantically with every passing second. He expected glares or resistance, but they were both focused on berating Nifùni.

He managed to get them to a junction where two alleys met in the center of the block. Piles of garbage obscured the four openings leading out, but he could see the street in each direction. The smell of urine and rot was overpowering, but at least the walls and trash would mute their voices.

"We voted!" screamed Byochína.

"It was a majority!" continued Mapábyo.

"You went against everything!"

"What was in your moon-damned—"

"Sun-dazed—"

"Blasted—"

Knowing that neither would stop, Rutejìmo tried to speak up. "Please, let's be quiet—"

But both women continued to scream at Nifùni who was pinned against a crumbling brick corner and shuddering with every shouted word.

Rutejìmo looked around, nervous that someone would be attracted to their yelling even with the alley to shield them. He tried to rest a hand on Mapábyo's shoulder, but she batted him away.

Taking a deep breath, he stepped in front of Nifùni and spun around to face the two women.

Mapábyo tried to shove him to the side, but Byochína's attempt to move him came from the other direction. The slap across his eye hurt as much as the punch impacting his ribs. He felt one crack, but it was hard to see which one caused the injury through the sparks that floated across his vision.

Both women froze, the outrage on their face turning to shock.

"P-Please," he groaned as his rib throbbed, "quiet down."

"J-Jìmo?" whispered Mapábyo. "I-I didn't mean—"

"Great Shimusogo Rutejìmo, please forgive—"

Rutejìmo held up his hands as the last of the sparks faded from his vision. "I don't yell as loudly as Desòchu, and I know I have no authority, but we need to stop attracting attention. And that means not yelling." He glared over his shoulder. "Even if he may deserve it."

Mapábyo and Byochína ducked their heads. "Sorry, Great Shimusogo Rutejìmo."

Rutejìmo turned around. "Nifùni, did you accept that job?"

Nifùni, his eyes wide and his body shaking, nodded. "I... I thought it was going to be a simple run. And then I could just surprise everyone."

"What happened?"

"I saw her w-when Chína was... was in the store." Tears ran down Nifùni's cheek. "And I thought I could just take her money and th-this..." He held out the bone case but Rutejìmo didn't take it.

"And the money?"

Nifùni dug into his pocket and pulled out a blood-stained roll of pyābi.

Behind Rutejìmo, Mapábyo let out a gasp. "You killed her?"

"No! No, I swear, I didn't. She said the message needed to be taken to someone who could defend themselves. Someone ran up and punched her chest. I saw a snake or something flash by, like Shi-Shimusògo does, and then she started bleeding from her eyes."

Rutejìmo's blood ran cold at the sobbing words.

"I-I ran," sobbed Nifùni. "I didn't know what to do."

Behind him, neither of the women said anything.

Taking a deep, shuddering breath, Rutejìmo forced the words out as calmly as he could. "We need to either go to the guards or run. That woman was a Kosòbyo."

"B-but," Nifùni sobbed through his tears, "the man who punched her was a Kosòbyo also. I saw the colors and the snake. There is only one snake spirit in town."

"He's right," said Dimóryo from behind Rutejìmo, "they were both Kosòbyo, but she was a traitor." Her voice was low and threatening.

Rutejìmo jumped and then turned to look at the guard. The easy smile he saw the night before had disappeared. Golden energy ran along her fists as she stepped into the alley. Sparks dripped from her knuckles, sizzling on the ground as she paced closer. He could also see spectral fangs peeking out from her lips.

His breath locked in his throat. Glancing to the side, he saw another of the guards approaching one of the other alley entrances. Like Dimóryo, his hands glowed with the same dripping energy, but no fangs were visible.

Mapábyo dropped her hand to the long dagger at her side.

Rutejìmo stopped her with a shake of his head. "This isn't a fight yet."

Behind him, he heard someone else trying to sneak up. He barely heard the scuff of boots over the heavy breathing from everyone's yelling. There were three in Dimóryo's group. Mentally he tried to plan his route down the fourth alley and spread his hands to start guiding the others toward it.

"We need you to surrender, Shimusogo Rutejìmo." Dimóryo continued to stalk forward. Her hands continued to drip acidic magic, and he knew why she had no weapons. She was a hand-to-hand fighter, a relatively rare talent in the western side of the desert. He guessed that Kosòbyo's talents granted poisonous touch from Nifùni's description and the woman's corpse.

His hand slapped against Byochína. She tensed when he touched her, but he smacked her hard without looking back. After a moment, she stepped into the alley he wanted them to go down and backed away faster.

"We have not opened the case, Great Kosobyo Dimóryo." Rutejìmo was surprised by his own calm voice though he was screaming inside. "We are couriers and nothing more."

Dimóryo stepped over a cracked bucket and through a puddle. Her dark hair fluttered around her back from the golden energy rising off her forearms. "You accepted the contract."

"It was a mistake."

"Yes, but the deal was made. You talked to Techyomása. You know that something is happening. That makes you a threat."

"We are no threats." Rutejìmo shoved his wife back into the alley but kept his eyes on the guards who pressed forward. He could smell the acidic energy wafting down the alleys, filling the air with a stench that overpowered the urine and foulness.

"You are westerners. You don't understand when to be silent. You don't know the real story."

Rutejìmo glanced around to make sure the others were close to him. Sweat dripped down his face, and his heart pounded in his chest. It felt like the moments just before some brigand tried to kill him. "What are you going to do?"

She clenched her hands into fists, and a large glob of energy fell to the ground. It struck the ground and began to smoke. A heartbeat later, there was nothing but a hole. "You are a threat to Kosòbyo."

Dimóryo charged forward and the tension snapped.

"Down the alley!" snapped Rutejìmo as he drew his tazágu. The fighting spike was a long weapon in a narrow alley, but it was his only defense. He managed to shove it into position before Dimóryo's fist came for him.

The impact shook him to the bone, and the tip of his weapon scraped against the side of the alley. A splash of acidic magic splattered around the weapon, searing his face and shoulders.

"Jìmo!" screamed Mapábyo.

"Back!" he yelled, unable to look to see if they listened.

Dimóryo swung with her other hand, an uppercut.

He managed to rotate his weapon to catch it. The impact drove him back again, and the hilt scraped against the opposite side of the alley. He jammed it into place to stop her, but then had to yank it from the wall to parry another attack.

She kicked at him, but he caught it with his shin. Over a decade of running left his leg as solid as stone and she bounced from the impact.

Behind Dimóryo, both the other guards were running toward the ends of their alleys.

Rutejìmo yelled without looking back. "Get clear of this alley, they are coming around!"

Dimóryo yelled her own orders, using unfamiliar words and numbers. Her attacks didn't slow. She pummeled at Rutejìmo, striking his weapon as he frantically twisted it to parry each blow.

One of her strikes missed him and slammed into the brick wall. It left her side open for an attack, but Rutejìmo used the respite to back away from her.

She frowned and twisted her wrist. Shards of brick flew everywhere as she yanked it free and charged forward.

Rutejìmo focused on defending himself, parrying as her attacks came fast and hard. His opponent didn't have the speed of Desòchu or Chimípu, but the slender warrior was far stronger than she looked. He could barely keep up with her relentless attacks.

And then he missed. Her fist came underneath his weapon and caught him right in the chest, a solid strike against his sternum. The energy of the attack threw him off his feet. He shot backwards out of the alley and across the street.

"Jìmo!" screamed Mapábyo as he flew past her.

He landed on the far side of the street and rolled backwards. The far gutter caught his shoulder and flipped him before he smacked into the glass front of a store. The window shattered around him and rained down. Glass sliced his skin leaving shallow cuts.

Mapábyo's scream didn't end. It continued to rise into the high pitch of a bird in agony. He managed to get to his feet as a flash of golden power burst out from her. It resonated inside him, and he felt the urge to scream just like her, to call for Shimusògo for help. He knew the warriors had the ability to call for the entire clan, but he had never heard of a non-warrior using the spirit to scream.

Dimóryo ran out of the alley. "It's a call! Silence her!"

Rutejìmo scrambled to his feet, desperate to defend his wife before the Kosòbyo warrior reached her. He cut his hand on the glass and tripped on a massive wheel of cheese to get out of the wreckage. He could see more large rinds around him, much of it with glass sticking out of the wax.

He stumbled out of the store with his weapon in one hand. When he saw Mapábyo frantically defending against Dimóryo, his heart almost stopped. There were already burns on her face and arms from the warrior's attack. She sobbed as she tried to block the attacks, but she couldn't keep up with the rapid-fire hammering.

She was also still screaming, the high-pitched scream echoing in his head as much as his ears.

Behind her, Nifùni and Byochína fought their own opponents. They were scorched by the acid magic, but their opponents were marked with bleeding cuts also.

Dimóryo jerked forward and kicked out, catching Mapábyo in the pubic bone. Before Mapábyo hit the ground, the warrior jumped up and clasped her hands together to bring it down on Mapábyo's head.

"Jìmo!" screamed Mapábyo.

"Pábyo!" Rutejìmo sprinted forward using a burst of Shimusògo's power to cover the distance. He caught the blow against his shoulder. The impact drove him down to his knee as the acidic magic splashed against his back. He felt something crack from the blow, but he used his fading strength to push back and swing his tazágu around.

The tip of the fighting spike swung around before he realized that Dimóryo was further back than he thought. The sharp tip was poised to slice through her neck. With a grunt, he yanked it back, spoiling the blow but leaving his side open.

Dimóryo's fist hammered into his ribs, and the world exploded into pain as his lungs were forcefully emptied. She struck again and again before he could yank back from her attack.

Rutejìmo gasped for air, his vision blurring. Acid burned at his chest and he could smell his clothes burning.

"Why did you pull that blow, Westerner?" hissed Dimóryo.

Rutejìmo shook his head.

Byochína let out a scream of pain.

Rutejìmo almost looked but he caught Dimóryo tensing. He held himself still and tried not to think about the searing agony in his side, his ragged breathing, or the sweat dripping down his face.

The warrior straightened. She wasn't even winded by her attacks. "Who ever heard of a kojinōmi who refused to kill?"

"The desert kills enough, she doesn't need me to add to her tally."

Any response she would have given was interrupted when two flaming disks sliced through the air between Rutejìmo and Dimóryo. A thump of an explosion slammed into him, followed by two muted screams.

Rutejìmo reflexively followed the shots with his gaze, too late to see the impact, but both Byochína's and Nifùni's opponents had been thrown chains away by the impact of the fighting bolas. He spotted Shimusògo's name on one of weights as it burned away.

He turned back just as Chimípu stopped in front of him, her body vibrating with the sudden stop. Her weapon, a long sword, glowed with golden flames as she faced Dimóryo.

Energy cracked around her and Desòchu. Multicolored energy arced along the ground, tracing the gaps between the paving stones as it reached to the nearest artifacts. Streetlights, windows, and doors exploded from the violent response to the foreign resonance of the Shimusògo warriors. Two buildings began to smolder and a flickering light flashed from the interior of one store as something inside began to short.

A blast of wind slammed into them. Expecting it, Rutejìmo braced himself but Dimóryo stumbled slightly.

Desòchu came to a stop on his knees next to Rutejìmo. Even before the blast of wind passed, he was ripping the burning shirt from Rutejìmo and tossing it aside. "What happened?"

Rutejìmo gasped and looked at the others. "We need to run. Now."

His brother looked at him hard, then nodded. He pulled Rutejìmo up to his feet. Stepping back, he looked around with the muscles of his body taut. "Chimípu, take the rear."

Chimípu's response came as the golden flames burst along her body, tracing every line of her form and igniting into a halo of power. A translucent dépa superimposed itself over her as she clenched her body.

Desòchu raced over to Nifùni and Byochína who were both staggering toward each other. He grabbed their shoulders and forcibly turned them so they were facing Rutejìmo.

Rutejìmo looked away to help his wife to her feet.

Mapábyo squeezed him tightly. "Are you okay?"

Rutejìmo started to answer, but then Desòchu raced past.

"Follow!" yelled his brother.

Dimóryo's fist crashed against Chimípu's sword. Flashes of golden power burst away from each impact of steel against bare hand, a concussive wave exploded out, tearing up paving stones as it expanded. The rapid blows buffeted Rutejìmo, like someone smacking him with an invisible hand. The stench of acid and burning hair filled the air.

Rutejìmo turned away from the fight and raced after his brother, trailing behind the others. Desòchu wasn't leading them out of the city but along a route cleared by Chimípu's and his passing. Compared to the damage that Mapábyo and Byochína left, the two warriors had created a wide swath of destruction. Entire buildings had caught on fire, the stones already melting from the feedback damage. There wasn't a single intact window or standing stall.

The crowds that had normally filled the roads were gone, leaving a straight path to the edge of the city. However, groups of guards in Kosòbyo colors rushed past the burning buildings and into the wreckage. At first there was only a few warriors but more streamed in from both sides of the road until there were hundreds. Most of them appeared to be unarmed but their hands glowed with flames. He had no doubt that they shared Dimóryo's acid magic.

At the furthest edges of the city, a pair of massive mechanical snakes burst through the roofs of two buildings. The brass shells of the snakes shone in the sunlight as they rose two stories above the buildings that housed them. Hunks of wood and chucks of rock bounced off the bodies.

To both sides, Rutejìmo saw more snakes rising out of the buildings.

Desòchu accelerated ahead of the others, far faster than anyone else could run.

Rutejìmo stumbled in shock and then tripped on a paving stone. He fell face first, but his speed flipped him over. The impact against the ground drove the air out of his lungs. He scrambled back to his feet and forced himself to take a deep breath while looking back at his brother.

Desòchu tore a large paving stone out of the ground. The surrounding stones cracked from the impact. He straightened into a spin, whirling the stone around until it ignited into a disk of flames.

He fired it toward the nearest group of Kosòbyo warriors. The burning shot left ripples in the air. Desòchu scooped up two more rocks and fired them before the first one hit.

One of the warriors stepped into the path of the flaming stone and planted her feet. Her hands increased in brilliance until golden waves spread out from her palms. The light was blinding.

Desòchu's three shots slammed into her and exploded against the waves.

More warriors continued to pour in from the side streets, including a group of five only a block away from Rutejìmo. He heard their calls as they started to run toward him.

Rutejìmo gasped and turned back just as one of the mechanical snakes slithered into the street and started to work toward them. Fire dripped from its mouth, and a cloud of steam poured out from vents along its spine.

Desòchu picked up another rock and spun it around to fire it. As the stone became a glowing disk of flames, a vortex of power rose above him. Papers and glass blew away from him, clearing the ground at his feet.

When he released it, it wasn't toward the Kosòbyo warriors or the mechanical snakes. Instead, he fired it back down the street, past Rutejìmo and toward Dimóryo. It ignited into golden flames and expanded into a sphere of pure power that sucked papers and small items in its wake.

Rutejìmo spun around before it passed and braced himself. The passing shot tore at his skin, ripping the remains of his shirt off. It arched over him almost too fast to be seen.

Chimípu, her body a blur as she fought three opponents, came to a sudden stop just as Desòchu's shot reached her. As if she plucked something from the ground, she grabbed it mid-flight and threw herself into a spin on one foot. The ground underneath her cracked as a tornado burst out of her movement, spinning high in the air with a spiral of golden feathers and flames.

The force of the blast knocked Dimóryo and the other Kosòbyo warriors back.

Magenta lightning bolts traced along the ground from Chimípu's body, shattering stone as her power rose. Any artifacts in the area had long since disintegrated, and the lightning raced for the nearby warriors, burning them as it arced between their bodies. The glow along their hands flared in response, adding to the lightning crackling between the four warriors.

The spinning disk continued to grow more intense until it was as blinding as the sun. Stones were ripped from the ground and spiraled around her, clipping Dimóryo as they blew past.

The Kosòbyo warrior staggered back, blood painted on her face.

Chimípu released the rock. It shot back down the street toward Desòchu and the gathering Kosòbyo warriors. It was low to the ground, but its speed tore up the street, pulling a cloud of broken glass, rocks, and debris into a spear.

Rutejìmo saw it coming but there was no way he could brace himself. He ducked his head and tensed.

The pressure wave crushed him against the rocks and yanked him off the ground. He was sucked after the sphere of brilliance as it rocketed down the street. It destroyed everything on both sides in a wave of power.

Rutejìmo screamed as he was tossed into the air, pummeled from all directions. He tried to find the ground, but he was spinning around too fast to orient himself. The impact could kill him, but he couldn't stop screaming.

Chimípu's hands caught him and yanked him down the road after the blast. There was nothing but a smooth trench where one of the main streets of Kosobyo City used to be.

Rutejìmo tried to catch the ground, but Chimípu's speed was too fast. The earth was a blur underneath him and he couldn't sprint fast enough. Instead, he flailed helplessly as she pulled him after her shot.

A blast of heat slammed into him as they raced through a wall of fire but it was gone before it could do more than suck the moisture from the back of his throat.

They passed Desòchu who had just gotten the others back to their feet. A heartbeat later, they were racing after him.

Humiliation flashed through Rutejìmo. He couldn't keep up, he was being dragged. He knew that he would slow them down, but it didn't help that he was being pulled along by Chimípu's tight grip.

They passed through the wreckage of the Kosobyo warriors. One of the mechanical snakes laid across three buildings, the brass edges melted from the impact of Chimípu's blast. The other snake was missing its head.

Then they were past the carnage and out of the city.

Chapter 15

Banyosiōu

The cast outs, or banyosiōu, is the highest punishment an elder of the clan can inflict. It declares the recipient dead to the clan and to society. Few survive the first week.

—Tinsil de Polis da Kandor, *Sands of the Dead*

Nifùni flew back from Desòchu's punch. He landed on his back against a sheet of rocks that hid the Shimusògo from anyone in the city. With a groan, he tried to get up but then fell back. His hand slipped and left a smear of blood across the white rocks.

"You could have killed us!" bellowed Desòchu as he stormed after Nifùni. His body burned with flames that seared the rocks. He grabbed Nifùni's shirt and yanked him from the ground. The following punch that caught Nifùni in the gut sent a shudder coursing through Rutejìmo's body.

Nifùni flew back again, landing on a scree of gravel. He groaned and tried to get up. Blood ran down his chin and throat. More of it was splattered on the rocks.

Rutejìmo looked at the others. They were all covered in burns, blood, and dust. None of them were making any effort to stop Desòchu's beating.

Chimípu's lips twisted in a snarl of anger. If Desòchu wasn't her senior, it would have been her beating Nifùni within an inch of his life for what he did.

Looking back, Rutejìmo caught Nifùni looking at him. There was a desperate pleading in the younger man's eyes, a sorrow that scraped along Rutejìmo's own memories. Five years ago, he had been in Nifùni's place, praying someone would stop the beating from Desòchu. Then, Rutejìmo had ruined the Shimu-sògo's reputation by spending a night with his first shikāfu, a warrior of the night clan named Mikáryo.

The memory sickened Rutejìmo, and he wanted to look away. He had suffered more than anyone else from Nifùni's betrayal. Burns covered his arms, chest, and face. At least two of his ribs were cracked, and the tight bandage over his chest made it difficult to breathe. But, even with his injuries, he silently prayed Desòchu would stop.

His older brother stormed over and grabbed Nifùni around the throat. The light flaring around his body grew brighter as he easily hauled the flailing man from the ground. Desòchu shook him hard and then threw him back toward Chimípu and the others.

Byochína and Mapábyo stepped away without saying anything.

Nifùni sobbed as he looked up at Chimípu.

At the sight, tears gathered in Rutejìmo's eyes.

Chimípu kicked him in the shoulder, a flash of power giving her the strength to flip him over.

The thud dislodged more rocks, and Rutejìmo bit back a sob of his own.

"P-Please?" Nifùni spat out a tooth. "I didn't mean for any of this."

Desòchu grabbed him with both hands and yanked him off the ground. "We can never come back to this city because of what you did! You have ruined the Shimusògo name for the entire Eastern Desert!"

Nifùni's legs flailed back and forth as Desòchu shook him.

"More importantly, you betrayed the clan! We made a decision! We voted! And you—" Desòchu shook harder "—are bound by that!"

Nifùni's sobs and whimpers were punctuated by the impact of his chin hitting his chest or his head being thrown back.

Desòchu released his right arm, pulled back, and punched Nifùni underneath the chin.

The younger man flew back.

A crack rumbled around them, disturbing the dust and sand.

Rutejìmo tensed before the impact.

Nifùni hit the ground a rod away with a meaty thud and a wail of agony.

Slamming his foot down, Desòchu took a deep breath. "I am Desòchu, and I speak for Shimusògo."

Rutejìmo's breath stopped in his throat. Years ago, Desòchu had cast him out of the clan for a year. He had been declared dead by the clans and became a banyosiōu, an outcast treated as one of the dead. In the year that followed, Rutejìmo had almost died in the desert, lost a child, watched one of his friends die.

Frantic, he looked at the others, but he only saw the same expressions as he had that day. Mapábyo was crying, but neither she nor Byochína moved. Chimípu stood behind them, anger naked on her face.

"No!"

The word left of Rutejìmo's mouth before he realized it.

Silence.

Desòchu looked at him. "What?" The flames grew brighter around his body.

Gathering his courage, Rutejìmo stepped forward. "No, do not finish that sentence. You cannot."

Mapábyo gasped. "Jìmo, no, don't do this—"

"You can't stop me." His brother turned away from Nifùni. "This is my right. I speak for Shimusògo."

"Great Shimusogo Desòchu, please." Rutejìmo held up his hands. "We need him."

"He could have killed us."

"And we can deal with that later. But right now, there are only six of us, and we have no—" Rutejìmo stepped forward with his hands still out. "—allies in this part of the desert."

"I will not accept what he did!" bellowed Desòchu.

"I cannot let you do this!" Tears ran down Rutejìmo's cheek. He balled his hands into fists knowing that he couldn't stop his brother.

Desòchu's face twisted in a snarl. "I am Desòchu, and I speak for Shimusògo, not you!" His voice echoed against the stone ridges around them.

Rutejìmo opened his mouth, he didn't have any authority a-gainst an elder. He couldn't stop his brother. He closed his mouth for a moment, the despair rising inside him much like the wind blowing around his feet. He let out a sob of his own and ducked his head.

There was a long pause.

He stared at the ground, watching the sand rolling over his feet. A shard of glass still stuck in his sole, caught in the thick callous that years of running barefooted had provided. He didn't feel it, but there was a smear of blood on the end.

Rutejìmo looked back up, fighting with the pressing need to stop his brother.

Desòchu's feet crunched as he turned back to Nifùni. "I am Desòchu, and I speak for—"

Rutejìmo had to speak; he could not let Nifùni die. Whispers in the back of his head grew louder, demanding that he speak. He relented, despite everything else that told him to remain silent. "I am Rutejìmo, and I speak for Mifúno."

A blast of wind tore through the shelter, kicking up rocks and sands. It pummeled against their bodies. The flames around Desòchu and Chimípu wavered with the air, something that Rutejìmo had never seen happen, and then snuffed out.

Chimípu gasped and looked up.

Words whispered in the back of his head, too quiet to hear clearly but he could feel the intent. He had to keep speaking, and when he did, the words formed on his lips "I will not allow you to do this, Great Shimusogo Desòchu. We need him now, but he will pay for what he did. No matter what, no matter how, the desert will take her price for his actions."

Desòchu turned back at him, but there was no anger on his face. Just a stunned shock. "Rutejìmo? What did you—"

The force that drove him to speak poured out of him and the wind died down. In the stunned silence that followed, he listened to the hiss of sand falling and the clinks of rocks striking the ground.

He tried to take a deep breath, but he felt like he was breathing through canvas. A tightness gripped his chest, squeezing down as the world spun around him. He opened his mouth to try breathing harder, but he couldn't force the air into his lungs fast enough.

Looking up, he stared at his brother. The flames had returned around Desòchu's body, but they were thin and translucent.

"I-I," he exhaled as white spots swam across his vision, "I... can't... breathe."

And then he was falling. He closed his eyes as the darkness swallowed him.

Chapter 16

A Second Wind

Very few can speak for Mifúno, the desert spirit. She does not tolerate her name used for anything and death usually follows as soon as the words pass a fool's lips.

—Kosobyo Fidokùki

Rutejìmo groaned as he crawled out of unconsciousness. Every breath and twitch became agony as he fought the dreams of oblivion. He tried to reach out for the ground, to dig his fingernail in to pull him out of the hole, but instead his palms slapped against someone's hand.

Fingers tightened around him and held him in place, comforting and strong.

"Jìmo," someone whispered. He knew the speaker but their name refused to come to his thoughts.

He gasped for air, thankful when the icy coolness sank into his lungs. It helped clear his thoughts and he remembered how to open his eyes. Cracking one and then the other, he stared into the incomprehensible world and tried to remember how to see.

Images came slowly into focus, first the stars in the sky and then a woman with black skin who bent over his body. There were others watching him, men and women. They were bloody and burned, but they were his.

Their names came to him and his thoughts settled back into place, but he felt raw and empty. "P-Pábyo… Chimípu." He groaned and they helped him sit up. Everything wavered for a moment. For the briefest moment, in the space between two blinks, he saw their bodies as thin and translucent. But, when he blinked again, they were once again the familiar people he grew up with.

He gulped and Byochína pressed a water skin into his hands. He brought it to his lips, each movement as raw as a child's. He gulped and the warmed liquid ran down his throat to ease the dryness.

When he finished, he pulled it away. "W-What happened?"

"You passed out," Chimípu said with a smile, "right after you managed to surprise us all."

"Did Desòchu hit me? I was disagreeing with him, right? W… Why was I?"

Desòchu knelt at Rutejìmo's feet, a strained smiled on his face, looking more like a teenager who had just been caught by one of the elders. "No. And after what you just did, I don't think I could ever hit you again."

Rutejìmo held Mapábyo's hand and wiped his face with his other. A smear of dried blood darkened his palm, and he stared at it. "Remind me not to do that again."

Raising an eyebrow, Desòchu said, "You mean, you should never disagree with me?"

Still staring at the blood on his hand, Rutejìmo shook his head. "No, letting my brother open his mouth." He glanced up, afraid that he had somehow said something wrong.

Desòchu chuckled and patted Rutejìmo's knee. "You did the right thing, little brother."

Rutejìmo looked around. "Where is Nifùni?"

"Safe," said Desòchu as he stood up. He walked away and Chimípu and Byochína joined him as they sat down around a small alchemical fire and a pair of blue glow lights.

The rocks crunched as Nifùni came up from the darkness. His head was bowed as he knelt next to Rutejìmo. "Great Mifuno Rutejìmo, I—"

"Shimusogo Rutejìmo."

Nifùni looked up. "What?"

"I am Shimusògo."

"You are also Mifúno, and you saved my life."

Rutejìmo felt a pang of sadness. "No, no, I didn't." He held out his hand and rested it on Nifùni's shoulder. "Your body is still moving, and you still breathe, but you have already been killed. Mifúno's attention has a price, and," he thought about the warrior who he cast out, "it isn't a pleasant one. We will make it home, but... it would be best if you come to peace with the fact that she will take what is hers."

Nifùni sniffed, and a tear splashed down. "I didn't mean it."

Rutejìmo pulled him into a hug. "Neither did I, but it still happened."

Nifùni held him tight as sobs tore through his frame.

The pressure on his cuts and burns hurt, but Rutejìmo remained silent as he comforted Nifùni. The young man had a dire future for his life and scratches seemed like the least of either of their problems.

Mapábyo got up and joined the others, leaving the two alone.

After a few short minutes, the tears stopped, and Nifùni pulled back. "I'm sorry, Great Shimusogo Rutejìmo."

Together, they got up and headed to the flames. Sitting heavily next to Mapábyo, Rutejìmo took an offered piece of cooked meat and chewed on it.

Desòchu let out a long sigh. "We need to know what to do."

"Run home?" asked Chimípu.

"Maybe, but from what?" he said. "Are we just fleeing the Kosòbyo? Or is this something bigger?"

Mapábyo spoke up. "The case?"

Desòchu nodded. "I think we should open it."

Sharply inhaled breaths answered him.

"I know we don't ever look at the message, but they almost killed us, and we just left a large, smoking hole in the center of town. So, if this is a trivial note, then we need to go back and offer our throats in forgiveness. If it isn't, we may be running faster than ever."

No one said anything for over a minute.

Rutejìmo cleared his throat. "We vote? I say open it."

"Open it."

"Open it."

The others chimed in. When silence draped across them once again, Desòchu nodded. "Then we open it." He pulled the bone case into his lap and broke the seal with his knife. He twisted it open, keeping the end aimed toward his lap.

Coils of paper slid out. They were different types and colors, some aged and some crisp with newness. All of them were covered in writing, correspondence, and diagrams.

Desòchu frowned as he looked at the papers.

"Good thing," Rutejìmo said, "that Pidòhu taught all of us to read."

It was a poor joke, and only Mapábyo gave a nervous chuckle.

Desòchu passed around the papers. "Start reading, just scan over things. We need to figure out what this is about."

Rutejìmo's papers were old, and the edges crumbled when he touched them. He carefully puzzled through them, struggling with the unfamiliar way the eastern clans wrote their words. The first was a letter written in a rough hand of someone barely able to write, a Kosobyo Mioráshi. It talked about the birth of her daughter, Kanéko.

A few pages later, there was another letter from Mioráshi. Her daughter had shown no signs of Kosòbyo's power. The response was copied in a letter, ordering that Mioráshi let her northern husband take the daughter and train her. Rutejìmo felt sick to his stomach, the idea of a desert woman mating with a northerner disgusted him. It spat on the face of the spirits.

"What is a gyotochizōmi?" asked Byochína, "I don't know that word."

Rutejìmo frowned and peered at her. "Is it like a chyotechizōmi, a dragon spirit?"

"Here," Mapábyo held out a page to Rutejìmo. "This is Piko-mìro's legend, isn't it? When he trapped the zōmi in the Wind's Teeth and then threatened the entire desert with it?"

"Yeah, that's the legend." Rutejìmo frowned and took the page. "But they call it a gyotochizōmi here. They are probably the same thing."

"But there are no more chyotechizōmi left in the world." Nifùni looked pale as he held his pages in a shaking hand.

Desòchu cleared his throat and held up a page filled with dense, neat writing. "Not according to this. Some Kosobyo Kanéko is allied with a chyotechizōmi and they are luring it to Kosobyo City to capture it."

"But," Nifùni said, "Tachìra forbids the zōmi souls. After the Wind Teeth, he and Mifúno," he glanced at Rutejìmo, "declared that no sand would ever bind one again."

Chimípu held out a page. "But Chobìre didn't. These are letters to the southern smiths of the night, asking for help."

"That can't be." Desòchu shook his head firmly. "The Kosòbyo are the bastions of light. They are one of the greatest clans of Tachìra. They would never ally themselves with the night, never. That's why they have a month named after them!"

"Hizogōma turned to the night," added Rutejìmo. It was one of the legends that all of them had grown up listening over the fires. When one of Tachìra's staunchest allies turned to their e-nemies and betrayed everything, it had started a war that killed millions. He sighed and set down his papers. "If this is true, then this would be a greater blow against the sun. If they can tap into the power of zōmi, then they would become great allies of the night."

"It would be a war," whispered Mapábyo.

"No," Chimípu said, "it would be a slaughter. When Hizo-gōma became the night, it set off a war that burned this desert for a decade. But, if Kosòbyo could do it before anyone could stop them, and they had the chyotechizōmi's power, then there would be no one stopping them. They are already the most powerful clan in the desert."

No one said anything.

The tension grew until Rutejìmo had to break it. "What if we're wrong? What if we tell everyone this and these are all lies?"

Desòchu looked at him. "Then Kosòbyo will wipe Shimu-sògo from existence. If we are lucky, it will be only a slow death. But the Feathered Snake has not been known for forgive-ness or mercy. You've seen how they responded to us and to this." He held up the case.

Rutejìmo swallowed and nodded. "What do we do? Do we vote?"

"No," Desòchu said. "This would risk all of Shimusògo. We six can't make this choice. Not for our families, our children, and our home."

The others nodded, and there was the glistening of tears in the blue light from the glow spheres.

He cleared his throat. "We have to bring it home. Let every-one decide, let everyone vote. And then we follow that deci-sion."

Rutejìmo spoke up. "Whether this is a lie or the truth, Ko-sòbyo is going to do everything they can to stop us."

"Then we run fast."

"I can't run that fast, Desòchu." Rutejìmo felt the tears filling his eyes.

Mapábyo grabbed his hand.

"No, I won't leave you behind." Desòchu shook his head and then again. "What if we give everything to Chimípu and she runs. She is—"

"No," snapped Chimípu, "I won't abandon our clan."

Desòchu looked at her with a pleading look. "You are the fastest runner the Shimusògo have ever had. If anyone deserved his power, it is you, and he gave it to you for a reason. I can't think of anything more serious than making this delivery, Great Shimusogo Chimípu."

Tears ran down Chimípu's face. "But, if I leave you, you may die."

Desòchu looked down. "I will die for my clan, and I will fight for them to the end. Even if it means the five us will perish, this is something that must be done."

"I-I'm," said Nifùni, "already dead..."

There was an uncomfortable silence as Nifùni struggled with his words.

"... but I agree. Send Chimípu, and we will chase after her. We are slower, but we won't abandon Rutejìmo. She can come back for us as soon as the vote is made."

Chimípu sniffed and shook her head.

A dark realization came to Rutejìmo. He dug in his pack, looking for a pair of bags. He found both. One was orange and the other red, Shimusògo's colors. He also pulled out his voting stones and poured them into the red bag.

"Jìmo," started Chimípu, "What are you—"

He held up the red bag. "My vote for telling the world." He held up the other. "A vote for keeping it a secret. We vote now, and you deliver it. Even if we can't make it, you will speak for us."

"No," her voice came as a soft wail.

"Chimípu, I will not pay you to make this delivery, but I will ask you to carry these for me and return them when you get back." It was almost the same thing Pidòhu had told both of them when he, Rutejìmo, and Chimípu were trekking across the desert during their rite of passage.

"Damn you, Rutejìmo. Damn you to the sands." She got up and came around the flame.

He sniffed and handed the bags to Mapábyo.

Chimípu knelt next to Rutejìmo and hugged him tightly. She pressed her lips to his ear. "Damn you, little brother. I won't let you die."

He smiled and hugged her back. "Then run fast. When the sun rises, run fast."

"Shimusògo run," came the broken whisper.

Chapter 17

Splitting Up

No plan survives untouched.

—Tarsan proverb

Rising bile woke Rutejìmo with a start. He clawed at the ground to pull himself up. Fingers dug into sharp rocks before he hauled himself into a sitting position. Sweat dripped from his face as he swallowed hard, desperate to avoid vomiting before he had even opened his eyes.

As he gasped for breath, he felt the cold night air prickle his skin. A warmth radiated along his hips. He cracked open one eye and peered down. At his side, Mapábyo shivered underneath their shared bedroll. His end of the roll hung on his arm and left her exposed.

He crawled out and carefully tucked it back around her. Mapábyo smiled in her sleep and curled up in the blankets.

Trembling, Rutejìmo stood up and knuckled the sleep from his eyes. It was light, but not quite sunrise. Most of the clan slept in a circle around the fire but Nifùni's roll had been moved about a rod away from the others. Two other rolls, Desòchu's and Chimípu's, had been set up, but the fabric was still smooth and they looked untouched.

At the thought of his brother, Rutejìmo inhaled sharply, and the bile rose again. He had claimed to be one of the Mifúno, spoken as an elder of a clan he had no right to speak for. For all he knew, there was no one who ever considered the desert to have a clan. And, to his surprise, he wasn't struck dead instantly for doing so. He didn't know what it meant or why he was still alive. He only hoped the whispered voices in the back of his head were not his imagination, and he didn't just commit suicide by saving Nifùni's life.

He glanced over at the younger man. Nifùni had betrayed them, putting all their lives at risk. Even though Rutejìmo stopped Desòchu from ostracizing him from the clan, Rutejìmo knew he had only stalled the inevitable. Was he driven to speak so the clan knew the full extent of the damage inflicted by accepting the contract?

"Jìmo?" whispered Chimípu.

Rutejìmo saw her and Desòchu sitting a rod away along the ridge of the rocky scree. They were facing the desert. He got up and padded over. Coming up to the ridge, he saw movement in the false dawn and came to a halt. His eyes scanned the horizon, picking out black dots swarming along the other dunes and rocks. It took him only a heartbeat to realize the flickering didn't come from the rising heat but from auras and magic. There were warriors across the desert.

"H-How many are there?" he asked.

"At least a thousand." Desòchu muttered. "Five different clans, maybe more. They've been moving since light, probably settled in at night after it was dark."

Rutejìmo could see horse riders and clans on mechanical spiders. Three of the massive snakes with Kosòbyo colors were slithering a few miles away. Outside of the city, they appeared to be hundreds of feet long.

Above him, he could see flocks of birds flying straight across the desert. Instead of a cloud or "V" pattern, the birds were arranged in an unnatural line that looked more like a search pattern than anything a flock would do on their own.

"Hawk clan of some sort," Chimípu said quietly.

"At least two of them. But I'm worried about that," he pointed to Kosobyo City, barely visible along the horizon. Above it a single black dot sailed around in lazy circles. "Anything that we can see from this far away has to be large."

"A clan spirit?"

"Or one of Chobìre's raptors."

Rutejìmo shivered at the thought. Tachìra had eight divine horses that ran the desert to influence his will. Chobìre, the moon spirit, had giant birds that did the same. They were all mounts for the champions of the two spirits in their endless battle over Mifúno.

He gulped and tore his gaze away from the distant bird. "Shouldn't we be panicking now?"

Both warriors shook their heads. "We were about to get everyone up, but we have a half hour before the sun rises. Those are all day clans, except maybe the raptor. None of them will attack until Tachìra wakes."

"And then Chimípu will be running."

Chimípu ducked her head.

Desòchu shook his. "We've been talking for a while now. Neither one of us thinks that plan will work anymore."

"Why not?"

"There are at least three speed clans out there and two jumpers. If Chimípu leaves us, then we either have to scatter to avoid being attacked or bunch up to be slaughtered."

Rutejìmo sat down heavily. "Sands." The rock underneath him dug into his buttocks, but the despair and frustration made it hard to do anything but look at the two warriors.

"Yes," Chimípu grunted, "I believe we've both said that. Repeatedly."

Rutejìmo looked at her. "Can't you do that shooting thing? You could...." He almost said "kill" but the word stuck in his throat.

She shook her head and gestured to the desert. "That only works if they are bunched up. I have one, maybe two of those until I rest. Everyone is spread out looking for us. There isn't any group large enough to hit. Maybe one of the Kosòbyo snakes, but I don't really know what they can do."

"And if we get down there," continued Desòchu, "we can pick them off one-by-one, but with that many, it's just a matter of how many we kill before we're killed ourselves. No one can stand against an army."

"But you can break one if you do enough damage." Chimípu said.

Desòchu looked at his brother. "So, we're trying to figure out how to save everyone. Or at least give us a chance to save some of us."

Rutejìmo's stomach twisted. He knew that someone was going to die, but it was hard to say it. For years he had served the clan by treating the dead, and he imagined he would be there for the deaths of everyone he knew, but if they scattered, he couldn't be there when they needed him the most.

He forced his thoughts away from the sudden despair by clearing his throat. "With you and Chimípu protecting us, we could make it."

Desòchu nodded and then shrugged. "Yes, but it would also make it obvious where we are going, which means they could set up a trap that even we couldn't survive."

"You want us to split up," Rutejìmo said.

Desòchu sighed. "It's an ugly answer. Shimusògo run together for a reason, except when it's safe. But, we all travel at different speeds and if our paths aren't obvious, maybe one of us can slip through the net they are spreading out. Easier to catch a rock than a sandstorm."

Rutejìmo ran his hands along the rocks as he struggled with his emotions. He could feel their hesitation and fear. Knowing that one would die was one thing, but there was more. After a few minutes, he realized what it was. "I'm the most at risk, a-ren't I?"

Both the warriors nodded, neither of them looking at him.

"I'm the slowest and not always that bright."

Chimípu shook her head. "Jìmo—"

"No, it's true, Mípu. The only way to give me a chance to get home in time is to send me in the straightest line, which would make me the easiest to ambush."

With a sigh, he returned his gaze down to the rocks. He picked one up and rolled it in his palm, struggling with the swelling of emotions. He was going to die. Probably alone in the middle of the desert where no one would lead him to Mifúno's embrace.

Rutejìmo almost threw up, but he managed to keep it down. The answer was obvious the moment they mentioned it. But, it took him a few minutes to quell his fear to let the words out. When he managed to look back up, he could feel the tears burning his eyes. "Let's tell the others we're splitting up."

He caught only a look of relief and sorrow in their eyes before he looked away.

Ten minutes later, all six of them were standing on the ridge looking over the gathered clans. There were thousands of them and even from the distance, their powers were evident. Rutejìmo spotted speed clans racing with clouds of dust and rocks, groups that appeared and disappeared among the sands, and even archers that seemed to be content to remain along the highest ridges despite nothing for miles around them.

"W-We can't do this," said Mapábyo with tears in her eyes. "We can't survive this."

"We can if we spread out," said Desòchu in a low voice, "I'll have routes for all of you. Just make sure you never tell anyone the names and places. Not even each other. There may be clans that can hear from a distance."

"Then how will we know where to go?" asked Nifùni. He stood a few feet from the others and a step behind.

Desòchu smiled weakly. "I've grown up with all of you. We've had so much time together that I can reference a location by what happened there, something that only we know. That way, we don't leave a trail for someone to catch. Never talk about it, never say where you are going. Assume someone is always listening."

Rutejìmo felt a prickle along his side. He looked behind them and around, but saw nothing. Embarrassed, he turned back around.

"We'll split up the documents among all six of us."

Rutejìmo spoke up. "And one stone each."

"What? Why?" snapped Nifùni.

"Because if one of us makes it, then there will be a vote. Make your answer clear." Rutejìmo didn't want to dwell on the reasons they wouldn't make it back to vote themselves.

Nifùni shook his head and stepped up. "No, I refuse to..."

Rutejìmo felt the prickle again. Ignoring Nifùni's words, he turned around and peered across the campsite. They had already packed their belongings in silence and eaten quickly. Their packs were lined up near the dead fire, ready to snatch at a moment's notice.

He silenced his thoughts and felt his attention drawn to the far side of the camp. Slowly, he turned around and walked across it, his bare feet crunching on the sand.

He felt Chimípu's presence more than saw it. She walked next to him in silence, but her body burned with pale golden flames. Unlike the couriers, the warriors could retain their powers at night for a short time. "Jìmo."

"Something is here." He spotted a straight, sparkling line a few feet away. Inhaling sharply, he rested his hand on Chimípu's shoulder. "Mípu, I think we have company—"

The flames around her grew brighter, and the muscles underneath his palm tensed. The heat rippled along his body, not burning but clearly present.

"—but it may not be an enemy."

The line twisted, revealing the two-dimensional shape of Fidochìma, the old man Rutejìmo had met a few days before. The body blossomed into three dimensions as the man dropped to his knees and bared his throat. His outfit was dusty and blood-stained. Some of the arrows in his quiver were notched, and one looked stained with blood. "Great Shimusogo Rutejìmo, please forgive this old fool."

Chimípu stepped back and drew her weapon with a hiss.

Desòchu appeared on Rutejìmo's other side, weapon drawn and body burning. A moment later, a blast of air buffeted Rutejìmo's back. "Jìmo, who is this?"

"I am Fidochìma, and I speak... for no one right now."

The words brought up a memory for Rutejìmo. He had said the same thing right after he was cast out of his clan. He lost the right to speak for a clan because he had none. Fidochìma had lost his own clan recently.

Rutejìmo stepped forward, but both Chimípu and Desòchu stopped him by slapping their hands against his chest.

"It could be a trap," said Desòchu in a low voice.

Rutejìmo shook his head. He could feel the breeze buffeting his back and the sand rolling along his feet. "No, it isn't. He's looking for me. He's a banyosiōu now."

Both Desòchu's and Chimípu's hands dropped from his chest.

"H-How can you tell?" hissed Desòchu.

Rutejìmo stared at Fidochìma for a long moment, and the whispers arose in his head. "Because he killed a man that was already dead."

Fidochìma shuddered but said nothing. A tear sparkled in his eye.

"Jìmo," whispered Desòchu, "we are about to run for our lives. If this is one of the... kojinōmi things, we don't have time for this."

Rutejìmo nodded and stepped forward, lowering himself in front of Fidochìma.

The old man, face covered in sand, looked up. "Forgive me."

"I cannot, I'm sorry." Rutejìmo sniffed.

"I hunted him down, I found him. He was sobbing in the corner of a cliff, terrified. He told me what you had done, and I knew I should have walked away. But, I didn't have the faith." Fidochìma clutched Rutejìmo. "I didn't trust her to take care of it. I killed him because he killed my granddaughter of a daughter. I killed him because I was so angry."

Rutejìmo rested his hand on Fidochìma's shoulder. He knew the need to talk.

"And then, I felt it. Something inside me died and withdrew. I felt... alone...separate from the world, and even my own family turned their back. I said nothing, and they turned their back on me. They knew before I stepped sideways."

Rutejìmo nodded. "I know. It hurts in a way you can't describe, not to anyone who hasn't died already."

"Y-You?"

"By my own brother's command. A year and then I could live again, but Tsupòbi had far more than a year. She," he didn't name the desert, "is far crueler than my brother could be. I don't think the man you killed would have ever been forgiven."

"And I think now I'm given his curse. The sands dug into my skin at the moment he died."

"She is very vengeful. Someone must suffer the full measure of what she bestows."

"Wisdom I should have listened to," whispered Fidochìma, his voice cracked.

Rutejìmo chuckled dryly. "I'm not sure if I'm wise, but I can say this. She has a purpose in her actions. She is cruel and beautiful, but also loving. You can get back into her graces, but not by simple bribes or empty actions."

He pulled Fidochìma in a hug, tensing only slightly at the thought of being stabbed. Embracing the older man, he whispered, "I can only give you the same advice I gave the man whose curse was given to you. Find a city or a place to live and stay safe. There are others who have also died, and they will help, but only if you remain silent and listen. The others see you, but they can't acknowledge you. Just be willing to see the way they can talk to the dead; it won't be with words."

Fidochìma rested his head on Rutejìmo before pulling back. "Half my age and filled with wisdom. I guess I was wrong, there is greatness in the desert."

Rutejìmo blushed.

"Thank you, Great Shimusogo Rutejìmo."

Rutejìmo nodded and then pressed his finger to Fidochìma's lips. "Silence. The dead are silent." He sniffed as the tears burned his eyes. He wished someone had told him that when he was cast out, it would have saved him weeks of agony. But it would have set him on a path to lose Mapábyo.

Fidochìma, an old man of a night clan, bowed and then turned sideways, disappearing in a sparkle of light.

Rutejìmo stared at him, jealous that Fidochìma had a way of escaping in stealth when he had none. Then he pushed himself up, swaying before he regained his balance. The two warriors had left when Rutejìmo and Fidochìma were speaking, but Rutejìmo didn't remember their withdrawal.

He looked out over the desert, away from the city. There were fewer clans out there looking for him, just a wide expanse of rolling sands. The plumes from their run would be visible to anyone looking.

"Jìmo," Desòchu said as he walked back up, his bare feet crunching on the rocks.

Rutejìmo turned to his brother.

"You're the last." Desòchu handed Jìmo a heavy bone case, the original one. "I've already given routes to the others."

"And mine?"

Desòchu's lips pressed into a thin line. "Start with the bed that Byochína kicked you out of." It was a campsite from a week ago. Rutejìmo had accidentally crawled into the wrong bedroll in the middle of the night, much to the amusement of the others and his embarrassment.

"And then to the place you died the first time." Wamifuko City. "I would not normally send you anywhere like that, but you have more allies there than anywhere else."

Rutejìmo nodded, the world spinning around him as he focused on his brother.

"And then to where your friend broke his leg." A set of Wind's Teeth where Pidòhu, Chimípu, and his rite of passage started.

"Finally, to where I learned the true Shimusogo Way." Home, right inside the entrance where most of the clan stopped Desòchu from killing Rutejìmo.

Rutejìmo fought back the tears, but he bowed his head in acknowledgment. "Will I see you along the way?"

Desòchu jerked and then nodded. "Yes, but I won't tell you where."

"Race you home?" It was a thin joke, and he couldn't force himself to smile.

"I'll give you a head start," came the dead-panned reply.

"When do we leave?" asked Rutejìmo just as the sun rose above the horizon. A ripple of power coursed through his veins and all six let out sighs of pleasure and despair.

"Now."

Everyone ran for their packs and scooped them up. Rutejìmo looked across at the others of his clan and felt a blackness fill his heart. The faces looking back at him were drawn and nervous, no doubt feeling the same thing.

They were going to die.

Desòchu cleared his throat. "Pábyo and Jìmo with me. Chína and Fùni run with Mípu. Mípu and I will create cover by kicking up a cloud, and you four run inside it, peeling away when we hit the first curve—" He pointed to Mapábyo and Byochína

"—and then the second—" His shaking finger gestured to Rutejìmo and Nifùni.

"—and we—" He finished pointed to Chimípu who took a deep breath.

"—will sprint from there. We have the longest routes since we are the fastest. Any questions?"

No one answered.

Desòchu wiped the sweat from his brow. "Shimusògo run."

"Shimusògo run."

And then they were.

Chapter 18

Brothers

"I see you" has become an intimate way of greeting and leaving a loved one, but the origins of the phrase have been lost in history.

—Kakasaba Mioshigàma

Rutejìmo ran in a cloud of dust and rocks, half-blinded and terrified some enemy would jump him even in his brother's plume. The dust and sand scraped against his face and tickled the back of his throat. His eyes locked on the translucent dépa that guided him as much as the translucent bird that his brother chased. Shimusògo would lead Rutejìmo out of the cloud when the time was right, but the long seconds of running blindly planted grains of doubt deep in his thoughts.

Next to him, Mapábyo paced Rutejìmo easily. He could see her own dépa a few feet to the side of his, flickering in and out of his vision. While he could always see his no matter how much he struggled, the other dépas were harder to spot during moments of stress. He was thankful that the two remained together, it meant that Mapábyo would stay next to him as long as she could.

They shared unhappy glances at each other every few seconds. They were approaching the point where she would leave him, and in a matter of minutes, he would be alone.

He wished he could talk to her. Talking while running was difficult for Rutejìmo. At his highest speed, he had to concentrate on moving without tripping. Every step carried the threat of falling, or hitting something, or being attacked.

Normally, Mapábyo ran slower to pace him, but their run wasn't for comfort or happiness. His brother knew exactly how fast Rutejìmo could run, and he kept the three running at the point Rutejìmo found it hard to breathe and concentrate.

He thought about the words he wanted to tell her. He wished he could slow down long enough to hear "I see you" one last time, or to just touch hands. But, he couldn't. Stealing the occasional glance was the most he could do while they ran for their lives.

Desòchu's initial sprint would take them in a wide circle around the gathered clans. His speed kicked up a miles-long plume of dust and rock to obscure the couriers when they peeled off for their own paths.

At least, that is what they hoped would happen. How could they plan around those who could jump from the shadows or run as fast as the Shimusògo? Even with their speed, the hawks would see them long before their plumes settled to the ground. He couldn't see how any of them would survive, despite his brother's and Chimípu's faith they could make it.

Rutejìmo concentrated on following Desòchu. The despair grew harder to fight, sapping his strength and will. He wanted to stop, to slide to a halt and let the Kosòbyo come for him. In his mind, he could pretend he would somehow slow them down to let the others survive. His heart, however, knew he wasn't capable of doing anything that would even give the other warriors a moment to hesitate.

Mapábyo's dépa pulled away from Rutejìmo's. It was time for her to leave. She ran closer, the wind of her body creating eddies of sand around their feet. Her dark skin flashed in the sun as she leaned over and yelled past the rush of air between them. "I see you!"

He bit back a sob.

She accelerated into her full speed and easily outpaced Rutejìmo. Her body blurred through Desòchu's sand storm and Rutejìmo lost track of her dépa. A heartbeat later, she veered away in one of the sharpest turns Rutejìmo had seen and rocketed out of sight in an explosion of sand.

He watched as long as he could, but it was only seconds before he passed the point where she turned away. Pressure squeezed his heart as he fought the urge to stop. Only the dépa and his brother kept him running forward as his wife ran away.

Rutejìmo lifted his head into the wind to let the sand scour the tears from his face. He had to have faith, though despair chased after him dangerously close. He caught flashes of his brother's glowing body and threw everything he could into following. He would never reach Desòchu, much like he would never catch his dépa, but it was better than letting fear slow him down.

A few minutes later, they approached the point where Rutejìmo would turn away. His planned path would take him in almost a straight line along a map, the most direct route, taking him over inhospitable terrain until he reached Wamifuko City. He could see it in his head, and it left him depressingly vulnerable. Entering the city would be risky if Kosòbyo's allies were informed, but he had friends among the Wamifūko.

He gulped, preparing himself for days of traveling alone. The fear reached up to claw at his thoughts, ripping deep furrows in his shaky confidence.

His dépa abruptly disappeared.

Shocked, Rutejìmo continued for a few more rods before he realized his brother had jammed his foot into the sands and come to a rapid halt. Gasping, Rutejìmo did the same, his body shaking as he blasted a deep groove in the heated sand.

He stopped and closed his eyes as the wind scoured him from behind. It peppered his back, scratching his exposed skin with sand, before settling down around him a familiar hiss.

Desòchu walked back to him, his bare feet scrunching in the sand. It was a stark sound compared to the deafening quiet after running.

"Sòchu? What's wrong?" Rutejìmo took a deep breath and glanced around.

Desòchu's hair fluttered in the wind, and he wiped the sand from his face. "I have to say something."

"Aren't we running?" Even as Rutejìmo said it, he knew that his brother wasn't going to run. He cringed at the words before Desòchu could say them.

"You are."

His stomach twisted into a knot, and he groaned at the discomfort. "You are staying." It wasn't a question.

Desòchu nodded slowly and turned to look at the clans searching for them.

The various clans raced toward the tip of Chimípu's plume and toward where Desòchu would have been if he hadn't stopped. Rutejìmo could tell they were trying to head him off when the nearest ones turned sharply toward Desòchu and himself.

On the far side, Rutejìmo could only see Chimípu's plume, but knew that Byochína and Nifùni had already veered off on their own routes. The massive cloud rolling behind Chimípu looked like a storm, wider and taller than anything he had seen before. Flashes of golden feathers rolled in the cloud, highlighting twisting lines of power that kept it from settling.

Rutejìmo closed his eyes for a long time, struggling with his gasping breath. When he could speak, he did without looking at his brother. "Why?"

"Because I can slow them. And if I can do enough damage, it will give us a few minutes or even a half hour."

"Can you really stop a thousand warriors?" Rutejìmo opened his eyes and looked across the sands. He could see plumes of racers, both on horse and foot, along with the flicker of jumpers as they shrunk the distance rapidly.

Desòchu turned back, the sun glistening on his face. "If it means saving my clan, yes."

Rutejìmo sniffed. "Chimípu knows, doesn't she?"

"Yes." He waved his hand toward Chimípu.

Rutejìmo looked up just as three streaks of flames burst out of the tip of Chimípu's plume. The shots were accurate but spread out. One struck a group of horse riders who exploded in a shower of flesh and flame. Another hit two people standing on a ridge with no obvious weapons. The last struck one of the mechanical snakes that slithered toward her.

The snake shuddered and tilted to the side, smoke pouring out of the side. Before it hit the ground, though, it twisted and caught itself. Polished bronze shimmered in the sun as it rose back up and opened its mouth. Launching its head forward, a ball of green fire exploded from its maw and shot toward Chimípu, but she was already past where it slammed into the ground.

Three more bursts of light shot out before Chimípu accelerated away, disappearing with the speed of her movement.

"No," whispered Rutejìmo. He stepped toward his brother and held out his hand. "Please, then just run with me. We need you if we are going to survive. I need you too."

Desòchu covered the distance between them and rested his hand on Rutejìmo's shoulder, his body hot with the energy rolling off him. "Jìmo. You are a good man and my greatest mistake."

"You're a warrior of the clan!" Rutejìmo shoved the hand off. "You can survive. I'm the one—"

"No!"

Rutejìmo stepped back with surprise.

"There are many warriors of Shimusògo, but there is only one kojinōmi." He sniffed and shook his head. "Damn the sands, Jìmo. There are dozens who can tell us of the Shimusogo Way. But there is only one who followed the Shimusogo Rutejìmo Way. You are—" he tapped Rutejìmo's shoulder with two fingers "—the reason I was given these powers."

Rutejìmo ducked his head. His body hurt, but his heart felt like Desòchu had crushed it. He knew Desòchu would die just as he knew his brother would fight with the last breath of his body to make sure they survived.

"Brother, please. Let me do this. Great Shimusogo Rutejìmo, let me protect you."

A tear rolled off Rutejìmo's cheek and splashed on the sands.

"This is who I am."

Rutejìmo nodded. "Shimusògo run." He looked up, choking on the words. "S-Shimusògo run."

Desòchu held out a courier case, his own. "It's empty. I never gave anything to myself. You have everything in yours. Because you will run."

Rutejìmo stumbled forward and hugged Desòchu tightly. "May Tachìra shine on your death."

Pulling back, Desòchu nodded. "Shimusògo run."

He turned on his heels and exploded into movement.

Wind sucked past Rutejìmo. It kicked up the surrounding sands in a cloud that plumed after his brother. He ignored the scrapes of rocks against his skin as he watched his brother ignite into flame racing toward an army he had no chance of stopping. A translucent dépa, brighter than Rutejìmo had ever seen before, appeared over Desòchu's form, and he accelerated.

Desòchu passed by a rock outcropping. Rutejìmo didn't see him pick up a stone, but with a flash of light, a shot streaked ahead of the warrior to punch into the chest of the closest runner less than a quarter mile away.

The shot exploded into blood and flame as it continued into the ground kicking up a large cloud of darkness.

Firing more rocks as he ran, Desòchu charged straight for the nearest opponents. Most of his shots struck flesh and bone. The resulting clouds of crimson settled to the sand as he blasted past them, kicking up the corpses of his enemies.

Rutejìmo sobbed as he watched his brother burst through a crowd and out the other side. Bodies were ripped off the ground by his passing. Splashes of blood painted the sand, but he was long past them before it settled.

A wave of light arose from the archers a few miles away, a hundred arrows burst into flames as they sailed toward Desòchu in a bright cloud. It would have been majestic, if they weren't aimed at Rutejìmo's brother. Rutejìmo could do nothing but hold his breath, unsure of how his brother could survive an attack from above.

Ragged black and blue streaks cut across the sky toward the wave, not traveling in a straight line but sharp angled turns jerking their way into the arrow cloud. The energy, a startling contrast to the gold and white on the battlefield, was dark and violent. It looked like lightning until Rutejìmo peered closer and saw the streaks were also arrows that flew like nothing he had ever witnessed.

His breath quickened as he followed them to the source. Fidochìma stood at the Shimusògo's camp, black bow out in the brightness of the morning light. His body glowed with a pale white light. He drew back and more of the pale light gathered at his fingers. When he fired, it became an arrow that split into two and then four then over a hundred. Each one angled itself across the battlefield and into the cloud of arrows, decimating it with each strike.

Above Fidochìma's head was the barely visible disk of Chobìre, the moon, already reaching down toward the horizon. The night clan warrior had chosen to spend the last of the moon's light fighting for a man he had never known.

Rutejìmo bowed his head as the tears ran. Two people were going to die to save him, and he could do nothing. He had to turn around, but he couldn't. He couldn't move from the spot as he watched his brother's light weaving in and out of the gathered warriors.

Rutejìmo's vision blurred, and the wind kicked up around him. It peppered his face. "R-Run, Jìmo," he whispered, trying to shove himself away. But the words weren't enough to force him to move. Instead, he stared at the battle and fought the bile rising in his throat. He knew how it would end, but he had to see it.

Fidochìma's arrows continued to shoot across the battle, knocking away the other arrows and punching into the sides of the hawks. Bodies and shafts plummeted to the ground. But, each time he fired, there were fewer of the angular lines bursting from his bow. Each shot weakened as the moon dipped further toward the horizon.

Rutejìmo lifted a foot and then put it down. He couldn't run away.

Desòchu's sprint caught another warrior, and with a flash a body hit the ground. The golden streak of the Shimusògo warrior continued along, burning a path through the ground as he circled toward the next group of opponents.

Just as he reached his opponents, one of the mechanical snakes reared up and belched out a green fireball. It caught Desòchu and the warriors before exploding.

Rutejìmo's heart stopped beating for a second.

Desòchu wasn't burning gold as he flew out of the explosion. Instead, streamers of green flames clung to his body as he rolled against the ground, bouncing hard before landing. The impact left clouds of sand rising in the air.

The flames from the snake's shot dissipated to reveal bodies of Kosòbyo's allies on the ground. They were burning brightly, bones already visible from Rutejìmo's distance.

Desòchu scrambled to his feet, his body once again igniting into flames. He shot forward in a cloud just as a second fireball landed in his place. He fired back twice, the two golden shots pathetically small against the giant snake. The first bounced off the shell, but the second punched into the machine's left eye.

The ground underneath Desòchu rose into a sharp wall, and Desòchu jerked to the side to avoid it. Two arrows punched into his chest, and he stumbled again, his blood splattering the ground.

Gasping, Rutejìmo stared at the distant fight as his brother stumbled forward. He could see more warriors streaming toward Desòchu, the slower clans had reached his brother.

"Desòchu!" screamed Rutejìmo. He shook his head and stepped back. He tried to tear his eyes away, but he couldn't. His brother was about to die.

And there was nothing he could do about it.

A translucent dépa blasted past him, going in the opposite direction. Shimusògo commanded him to run, but he couldn't move. His vision blurred with tears.

Wind buffeted his face, and the dépa circled around, racing past him again and again.

In the battle, the warriors gathered around Desòchu, blocking him from accelerating. Weapons flashed as the fight grew brilliant from the glowing bodies and searing attacks. Rutejìmo could see bodies falling and he watched each one, terrified to see his brother hitting the ground.

The battle broke apart briefly, peeling back to reveal Desòchu. He stood in the middle of his opponents, his chest covered in blood and his body shaking. Two arrows still stuck out of his chest, piercing his bottom ribs. Cuts crossed his body and blood spurted out from his injuries. Weak flames coursed along his body, wavering as he stood defiantly.

Seeing his brother's inevitable demise brought a sharp wave of terror coursing through Rutejìmo's veins. It shoved him away from the battle harder than the wind or Shimusògo could ever manage. He couldn't watch the end. He couldn't see his brother die.

Choking, Rutejìmo spun around and stumbled away. His bare feet tripped in the sand, but he managed to keep his balance. A few steps later, he found his purchase and dug his toes in to sprint forward.

The dépa raced past him again, and he chased after it, blindly running because he couldn't see through the tears in his eyes or the despair in his heart. It took only a second to reach his limit, but then he was fleeing Desòchu's final fight.

Chapter 19

Nightmares

Sleeping alone in the desert is dangerous. Even in a time when no one has magic, there are always creatures hunting for a quick meal.

—Janithin Vans, *Fear of the Dark*

Rutejìmo sat alone, surrounded by nothing but the icy blanket of his nightmares. His eyes ached as he stared into the black that surrounded him. The moon wouldn't rise for a few more hours, and only a few stars sparkled in the sky.

It was the safest time to sleep in the desert, when no clan had powers, but Rutejìmo couldn't close his eyes. Every time he took too long to blink, or his thoughts sank toward unconsciousness, the nightmares blew across his mind. It was the same thing, Desòchu's final fight. Nothing could tear his mind away from those last few seconds of his brother's life.

He sniffed and fought a sob rising in his throat. He clamped both hands over his mouth and nose, shielding them as he shuddered with the effort. He couldn't make noise; someone might find him. Something might kill him. It didn't matter if it was a creature, nature, or human. He was vulnerable and alone, a weak man with a weaker heart.

Tears rolled down his knuckles. He gripped his face tighter and forced his eyes to remain open. He couldn't save Desòchu. He watched his own brother charge into battle, and he just stood there. He did nothing. In his mind and fantasies, he tried to play out a world where he ran after Desòchu and they both survived. But, even as he clutched to the hazy fantasies, reality crushed his hopes.

Rutejìmo was not a warrior. After so many years, there was no doubt about it. He was weak and slow. He hadn't killed anyone, at least not with a physical weapon, and he couldn't—even in his dreams. He tried to change his fantasies, to be the brave warrior with glowing feathers. It only lasted a few seconds before Desòchu became the hero in his dreams and then died, his blood splattered across the sand and the light fading from his eyes.

The tears ran faster, dribbling down his arms, soaking into the sand. He trembled as he dug his hands into his jaw, preventing it from opening. Only the wheeze of his breath rushing through slick fingers filled the night around him.

His stomach gurgled around the cold pit of food he managed to shove into his mouth a few minutes ago. It sat in his gut, a cold weight that refused to ease the discomfort. He couldn't risk an alchemical flame to cook it or even a glow light to push back the night. In a moonless night, even a spark could be seen for miles.

Rutejìmo drew in air through his fingers, choking on it as he tried to force himself to breath. He managed to draw in one breath, and then another. Each gasping shudder took all his will just to bring air into his lungs. He concentrated on it, trying to push away the waking nightmares that bubbled underneath his thoughts.

After a few minutes, his mind drifted away from the endless loop. He remembered another time he was alone in the night, sitting helpless. Someone came for him, a Pabinkúe rider named Mikáryo. She had threatened to kill him in exchange for her sister's death and always called him "pathetic," but she saved him that night. It wasn't until morning that he knew how much she had done, when he saw the giant snake she had killed.

He wished she would come back, stepping out of the darkness with the single word that defined everything about him: "pathetic." Mikáryo didn't appear to his silent wish. No pitch-black horse stepped across the sands. There wasn't even the hiss of someone walking. There was nothing around him but the impenetrable black marred by a few stars.

Fear bubbled up, a thousand images flashing through his mind. After a few minutes, he had to risk even a flash of light to push away the darkness. With one hand over his mouth, Rutejìmo reached for one of his glow lights. Three of them rested in his lap. He fought the key at the bottom, picturing the effort to twist it around until the mechanism inside began to produce light. His mind continued forward knowing that someone would see it.

His breath grew faster as he played out the horror in his mind, of a warrior attacking in the middle of the night. His thoughts rewound and went down a different path, of being killed in his sleep. And then another, each one more horrifying than the others as he experienced a hundred deaths just because he needed light.

The globe slipped from his finger and clinked loudly against the other two. He flinched, and the unbidden horrors arose again. It wasn't the light, but the sound that drew his death. Scene after scene burned in his mind until he sobbed into his palm.

He knew how it would end. In five years, he had seen the worst ways people could die. He had seen disease, old age, and injuries from fights, falls, and crushing. He saw the pain painted across naked faces and shared them in his heart. A thousand deaths hung in his memories, unwritten on paper but still willing to remind him that he would not die in a bed or with comfort. It would hurt, and he would scream. And there would be no one to guide him to Mifúno's breast.

Rutejìmo inhaled sharply and lifted his head to feel the wind, but there was nothing. The air had grown still and suffocating over the last few hours. Not even the hiss of a breeze interrupted the silence that he filled with his weak cries.

His hand stroked along the glow lights and over his hip. He stopped when his palm rested against the hilt of his knife. He knew how to die, that much being a kojinōmi gave him. He could picture killing himself and his body tensed with the anticipation of the one strike he needed.

But then he would be abandoning his clan and family. Two children waited for him in Shimusogo Valley. In a few years, Kitòpi would grow into a fine young courier, maybe even a warrior. He had the right attitude, the drive to push forward even when he got hurt. Chimípu was the same way, a spark that pushed her beyond the limits of just running. She had become Shimusògo's greatest warrior because of the spark.

Piróma, on the other hand, was as different from her brother as Rutejìmo was from his. She was quiet but observant, following a path different from the others. In many ways, she resembled Tateshyuso Pidòhu. Pidòhu had been weaker than the others but more intelligent than Rutejìmo could ever hope for. He and Piróma already shared a common interest in reading, writing, and drawing.

The tears started to dry on his knuckles, but he still felt the ache in his eyes. He couldn't kill himself, not when there was even a slight chance he could see his two children again.

Trembling, he pulled his hand off his knife and reached over to dig into his pack. He found the *Book of Ash* and his pen, but he couldn't see the pages. He set the glow lights aside and fumbled with the book to set it in his lap. Blindly, he oriented it correctly using the rough binding as a guide and then flipped to the back where he knew there was a blank page.

His body aching and exhaustion plucking at his senses, he took a deep breath and let the nightmares flow. As they did, the images still sharp in his mind, he began to write. Not a single line to document Desòchu's death but everything he remembered, every grain of sand and horror he felt. He switched to poetry when he couldn't write straight, and then back to detailing the scene. He poured his despair and helplessness onto the page, trusting that years of writing in the dim light would keep the words legible in the morning.

He wrote down his nightmares on a page he couldn't see, because it was the only thing he could do.

Chapter 20

An Unexpected Companion

Only a warrior knows the true measure of cowardice.

—Klistan dea Xerces

Writing all night, Rutejìmo had not slept, but he couldn't stop to find shelter. Instead, he lost himself in fleeing the enemies that chased him. He ran steadily, but only because of his years of practice. His body moved, even though his heart wanted to stop.

He continued to chase the translucent dépa racing ahead of him. No matter how fast he ran, he would never catch it, but the effort gave the Shimusògo their abilities to run. As he concentrated on the clan's spirit, the sharpness of his grief faded away beneath the euphoria of the power rippling through his veins.

A small measure of him was thankful that Desòchu's planned route took him along rippling lines of dunes instead of through rocks or against the wind's grain. He traced his path along the bottom of the ridges, hidden from sight except for the occasional need to crest a ridge to find a new valley. It was steady and monotonous, both a curse and a blessing.

Rutejìmo had run since sunrise. He only stopped long e-
nough to duck into an oasis to refill his water skin. Normally,
he would stop and interact with the clan protecting the waters,
but he couldn't afford to remain in public long. The reputation
of Shimusògo would suffer with his rudeness, but they were
on the opposite side of the desert and Rutejìmo thought they
would understand if they knew his reasons.

Upon reaching the end of one valley, he started to race up
the side. The dépa crested before he did and he followed it,
casting a mile-long plume of sand behind him. It marked his
path, and he wished that the power didn't create an obvious
sign of his passing, but he couldn't change how Shimusògo granted his gifts. He hoped no one was looking before he ducked
back into the next valley.

But the dépa remained along the ridge.

Rutejìmo tried to go down the other edge, but he felt the
spirit drawing him out into the open. After a few seconds of trying, he relented and ran after it.

It was a bright blue day, with not a single cloud in the sky.
The searing light of Tachìra cast across the reddish-orange
sands around him. It heated his skin, but Shimusògo's power
kept the worst of the burn away from him. However, the burns
Rutejìmo had earned from his recent purification ritual didn't
have the same protection. The aching pain pulsed with his
footfalls.

A second translucent dépa raced by, slowing down to match
speeds with his.

Rutejìmo jumped at the sight of it, but then sighed in relief.
He looked over his shoulder as Nifùni raced up.

They nodded to each other and then ran together.

Almost immediately, some of the tension twisting Rutejìmo's stomach relaxed. He was with someone he trusted. The
effort to run grew easier with Nifùni pacing him.

They ran until a half hour before sunset, coming up to the isolated campsite where Rutejìmo had embarrassed himself by crawling into the wrong roll. Together, they came to a hard stop that left deep gouges in the sands right up to the rocky scree that framed one side of the site.

Rutejìmo's body jerked as the ground grew harder, but his callused feet barely felt the difference before he came to a neat stop and walked out of the groove he had just created.

Nifùni bowed to him. "Great Shimusogo Rutejìmo."

"Great Shimusogo Nifùni. I wasn't expecting to see you."

"Neither was I. Great Shimusogo Desòchu planned well. I came along... Jìmo?"

Rutejìmo wiped the sudden tears from his face and turned away.

"What happened?"

"Great Shimusogo Desòchu stayed b-behind." Rutejìmo tried to keep his voice steady but it cracked in the end.

"What!?" Nifùni rushed forward. Rutejìmo tried to look away, but Nifùni stepped around and grabbed his shoulders. When Rutejìmo looked up, Nifùni's face was pale and stricken. "What do you mean!?"

Fighting the sobs rising in his throat, he shook his head. "He died defending the clan and to give us more time to escape. I-I saw him fighting them off, but he was about to fall and... and I was a coward." He looked up and peered at Nifùni through tear-blurred vision. "I ran."

Nifùni paled even more and looked back the way they came. "That isn't being a coward."

"You said it yourself, I couldn't fight."

The muscle in Nifùni's jaw tightened. "I was wrong."

"How can you say that? I ran from a battle—"

"A fight you would never survive."

"But, I ran!" Rutejìmo's voice drifted across the hissing sands.

"At least," Nifùni said in a whisper, "you didn't kill everyone."

Rutejìmo stopped at the sound of Nifùni's voice.

Nifùni gestured back across the sands. He sighed and his hand dropped to his side. "The problem with running alone is that the only person left to talk to is yourself." He spoke in a low voice. Rutejìmo knew exactly what Nifùni was feeling. "And the memories that keep playing over and over. Reminding you of your failures, weaknesses, and everything you've done wrong," he added. "When you try to sleep, it refuses to let go."

Nifùni looked back, his eyes haunted. He nodded after a time.

Rutejìmo lowered his gaze. "It never goes away. Every run, I'm reminded of my life. It just runs in circles in my head, never slowing, never stopping."

"But, you never stop."

With a snort, Rutejìmo slipped his pack off his shoulder. "How can I? There is always going to be someone better than me, faster than me, stronger than me. I'll never be a hero." He headed into the camp, his eyes narrowed as he peered around for an attacker.

The site was plain, only a niche in the rocks where someone mounted a metal ring for a fire pit. A six-foot brick wall had been built around the campsite to shelter it from the winds with two entrances on the east and west; it was a day clan camp from the openings.

There were few places for someone to hide, but Rutejìmo still circled around the shelter looking for signs of recent use. He spotted none and he returned inside.

Nifùni had already set up his tent, a lightweight fabric that clipped to metal loops mounted in the brick. He was working on Rutejìmo's, pitching it opposite to his.

Normally, the last person to stop at camp prepared it, but with only two of them, it was quicker to work together.

Rutejìmo knelt by the ring and held up the metal container with the alchemical gel they used for cooking. "Can we risk a fire?"

Nifùni sat back on his heels. A droplet of sweat traced the side of his face as he looked up in thought. "I hope so. Last night was cold." He pointed to the surrounding wall. "That should keep others from seeing any flames, but let's put our packs around the entrances just in case. I'd like hot food tonight."

Rutejìmo's stomach grumbled in agreement. He gathered up the packs and remaining supplies and piled them high against both openings of the shelter. A few minutes later, he was cooking dinner for both of them.

While they ate, Nifùni made no effort to speak. It wasn't until they were sitting in the darkness, staring at the pale blue glow of a single globe that he interrupted the uncomfortable silence.

"I'm sorry, Jìmo. I didn't think it would end up this way."

Rutejìmo stirred his thoughts from his own dark spiral of replaying Desòchu's death. Writing the night before had faded the agony of his memories, and it didn't choke him as much, but he still couldn't stop grieving. He lifted his head and looked up at the stars above him, wondering if he would ever live long enough for the ache to fade.

"Why did you stop Great Shimusogo Desòchu from c-casting," Nifùni choked on the word, "me out? Was it really because you needed me?"

Rutejìmo struggled with his thoughts, trying to pull them together to speak.

"Great Shimusogo Rutejìmo?" Nifùni's voice was pleading.

With a deep breath, Rutejìmo spoke softly. "Five years ago, Desòchu declared me dead to Shimusògo. It took me a long time to figure out what that meant, and I almost died because there was no one to help me. If Desòchu declared you dead back there, you wouldn't have survived the night."

"But we don't acknowledge the dead."

Rutejìmo shook his head. "No, we don't talk about the banyosiōu. The warriors still watch us, waiting for us to draw a weapon or be a threat. Otherwise, it would be easy to pretend to be one of the dead, sneak in somewhere, and then draw a weapon. They don't look at us, they don't speak to us, but only when we are not a threat."

Nifùni inhaled sharply. "Us?"

"Yes, us. Because even though I may have saved you from Desòchu's wrath, I promise that, sooner or later, you will be cast out of the clan. One person has already died because you went against us." Rutejìmo's voice grew sharper. "You may have risked the entire Shimusògo clan because of your greed."

"We are poor!" Nifùni's voice echoed against the shelter walls.

"It would have been hard, but we could—"

Nifùni stood up, his head rising out of the light of the globe. "No! I lost that money. I was in the group that got robbed. Not even Great Shimusogo Chimípu could get it back."

Rutejìmo fought the urge to stand up. He looked up into the darkness, the world spinning. "No, the clan lost that money."

"I was there! I wasn't—"

"—strong enough." Rutejìmo interrupted him. He had heard the same things in his own head many times. "You wanted to save Bakóki and be the hero. You wanted to be the one staggering home, covered in blood after saving the day."

Nifùni's mouth closed with a snap.

Rutejìmo continued, his voice low as he struggled with his tears. "You don't like living in the shadow of Great Shimusogo Desòchu or Chimípu any more than I do. But, when you go to bed at night—" He shook his head "—you tell yourself that at least you're better than me. It's how you sleep, isn't it?

Visible in the blue light, Nifùni's hands balled into fists. He turned and stormed away. "What do you know? You're a coward."

Rutejìmo listened to the footsteps as Nifùni left the shelter and walked around. A faint thump filled the air and Rutejìmo could imagine him leaning against the outer wall.

He bowed his head again, fighting with his own fears and doubts. "You say I'm a coward, Great Shimusogo Nifùni. And I am because I don't fight. I have never killed anyone, and I never will. The idea sickens me, and I can't do it."

Nifùni snorted.

"I do what I can. I kneel next to the dead as they die." Rutejìmo sniffed as the tears came and a faint breeze picked up. "When your mother was hit by that arrow, I was the one holding her when her last breath left her lips. I had to be the one who listened to your father's tears, pretending I couldn't hear them as she whispered how much she loved you into my ears."

Silence.

"When your sister died from the plague, I was the one who knelt in the shit and blood to reach her. No one else would do that. I had to pick her up," Rutejìmo's voice cracked, "a-and carry her to the flames. It didn't matter if I would get sick just for touching her, I'm the one who tends the dying—no matter what. There is no one else."

He took a long, deep breath.

"I may be a coward, so I do the only thing I can do. And that is what we are doing now. The only thing we can do."

Chapter 21

The Dying

The hard choices never come on easy days.
—Tisolan Misas, *Queen of the River Knives*

For the first time, Nifùni struggled to slow to Rutejìmo's pace instead of Rutejìmo striving to match his. They were racing along the ridge of a cliff, following a well-worn path that wound along the edge of rocky cliffs. Every few minutes, the dépa that Nifùni chased would accelerate, and he would follow, easily passing Rutejìmo. Then, Nifùni would look back with frustration before slowing down to match Rutejìmo's pace.

Every time Nifùni pulled away, a slash of guilt tore through Rutejìmo. He knew that Nifùni chaffed under the slower speed, but there was no way for Rutejìmo to force any more speed out of his body. He knew his limits and he ran at them, gasping for breath as he tried to avoid disappointing his clan.

Even though they were heading along the same route, they would be going separate ways in the morning. Nifùni said something about heading out early but made no effort to leave before Rutejìmo or to outpace him.

Fear kept Nifùni running with him. And Rutejìmo's slowness only frustrated the other courier with every passing mile.

To distract himself, Rutejìmo imagined catching his translucent dépa. It was impossible, but he managed to lose himself in hopeless daydreams until they came near the end of the cliff route. The final segment of the road swept around the western edge and gave Rutejìmo a view of the desert before him. Seeing nothing but leagues of sand gave him hope. No one could jump them when every movement kicked up sand and there were no shadows to hide in.

Night would be harder, though, since they would have to avoid any obvious shelters. Like the previous night, Nifùni and Rutejìmo would each take half the time on watch while the other slept. Exhausting, but four hours of sleep was better than none.

He spotted a small oasis at the intersection of rock and sand. A small shrine house, not large enough for more than a single room, stood less than a rod from the water's edge. The painted stone walls of the shrine were cracked and faded, exposure to the sun and wind had scuffed the walls.

A prickle of fear crawled down Rutejìmo's spine as they approached it. Both men slowed down to a stop and held still while the dust from their running blew past them.

From the edge of the water, a lone guard looked up from her book. It was an older woman, maybe in her fifties, clutching a tall spear with one gnarled hand and the crinkled spine of her book with the other. Her face wrinkled into a scowl, and her deep-set eyes seemed to disappear in the folds.

Rutejìmo held his breath as he bowed. He spotted the name of her clan on her clothes and the walls of the shrine, Nyochikōmu, but he wasn't familiar with the clan. There was nothing to indicate her clan's powers, but he guessed a long spear meant that she was a warrior despite her advanced age.

The old woman scoffed. "Twenty to refill your skin, two hundred for one of mine. I have other supplies, but they aren't cheap."

He let out his breath in a rush of relief. In his experience, the guards that made no effort at friendliness were also ones who didn't ask questions. "Thank you, Great Nyochikōmu. We have four skins to refill."

She held out a wrinkled hand. "Eighty and on your way."

Nifùni and Rutejìmo each put forty pyābi in her palm and held out their skins. When she nodded, they circled around her and knelt at the waters to refill them.

Rutejìmo ducked the leather skins under the water's surface and watched the bubbles rise. He sighed and glanced at Nifùni.

His clan member's eyes were fixed on his own skins. He held his jaw clamped shut, the muscles trembling. Rutejìmo's heart sank as he watched Nifùni move with sharp, angry movements.

After a few seconds of hoping Nifùni would look back, Rutejìmo turned away. He had said too much the night before and Nifùni obviously held it against him. Telling Nifùni that he was doomed to be a banyosiōu did little to help either of their moods. Silently berating himself, he focused on refilling his flasks.

As soon as the two skins were full, Rutejìmo set about checking supplies in his pack. He counted the number of rations and checked the level left in the jar with the alchemical gel.

"Jìmo, let's go."

Rutejìmo looked up at Nifùni and then back. "Give me a second."

"No, now."

Frowning, Rutejìmo shoved his supplies back in his pack. He stood up and bowed to the old woman. "Forgive us, Great —"

"Jìmo!" snapped Nifùni, "let's go!"

The sharp tone raised a prickle of fear. He turned around. "Is someone coming?" He scanned up along the trail and then across the sands. He stopped when he saw two wisps of smoke rising further along the cliffs as the trail curled to the south, away from both home and Kosobyo territories. The wind buffeted the wisps into oblivion, but the twin curls of white and yellow were unmistakable.

"Don't go there," growled Nifùni.

Rutejìmo sighed but didn't take his eyes away from the smoke. Someone was dying or had just died. He didn't need to look down at his feet to feel the sand wafting around his feet. The sudden tickle of grains told him that the desert called to him. "I have to. Someone needs me."

"No, we need you more. We run for our lives, Jìmo. And spending two days doing... whatever you do... is just going to put both of our lives in danger."

"But, Great Shimusogo Nifùni, I have to—"

"No!"

The old woman jumped at Nifùni's outburst. She twisted the haft of her spear, and her blade ignited into golden flames. Letters flickered along the surface, the name of the weapon.

Rutejìmo glanced at her and then back.

"Listen, Jìmo. You better make a choice now. Because either you are a Shimusògo or you are... that!"

"A kojinōmi?" whispered Rutejìmo.

Nifùni paled, and it was his turn to look at the woman. When he looked back, his lips were tight but his voice lowered into a harsh growl. "Yes, one of those. So, which one are you, Shimusògo or sand-damned kojinōmi?"

In his head, Rutejìmo heard the question differently. Shimusògo or Mifúno. Was he a courier or a kojinōmi? He knew he could strip off his clothes and take on the mantel of white, maybe forever. Not even the Kosòbyo would attack him then, but he could never return to his clan.

"Choose, Jìmo. Because in a minute, I'm going to run to save this clan and I will—" Nifùni shoved two fingers against Rutejìmo's sternum. "—leave your cowardly feet behind!"

Rutejìmo turned back to the smoke. It continued to rise in the air, fading in the wind. It was a stark reminder that someone was dying out there, maybe terrified, alone.

A tear ran down his cheek as he struggled. If he answered the call, he could be risking not only his life but Nifùni's and the others. At the same time, someone could be suffering, and only he could tend to them.

"Rutejìmo, someone is going to answer that. We have to go, now. We have to run before they catch us." Nifùni grabbed Rutejìmo by both shoulders and turned Rutejìmo to face him. "Jìmo, someone else will get it."

Rutejìmo started to look back, but Nifùni's grip tightened. "Jìmo."

Lowering his head, Rutejìmo sniffed. "We need to run."

"Good. Finally, you are making the right choice." Nifùni released him and gathered up his bag and water skins. "We'll have to run all day to make the...." His voice trailed off, and he glanced at the woman.

Tearing his gaze away, Rutejìmo nodded. "I know." He hefted his pack on his shoulder. Turning around, he bowed to the old woman. He wasn't surprised when he felt more tears drip off his cheeks and strike the ground at his feet. He stammered for a moment. "I-I'm sorry."

Her dark gaze, barely visible in the deep wrinkles never shifted.

He bowed again. "I'm sorry, Great Nyochikōmu. I-I have to leave." He wiped the tears from his eyes, wishing he didn't feel sick from abandoning his duties.

Strapping his pack into place, he bowed again.

She didn't move.

"Jìmo, come on!"

Rutejìmo turned and jogged over to Nifùni.

"About time," snapped Nifùni. He stepped forward as the translucent dépa passed him.

Rutejìmo started after him, jogging until Shimusògo appeared, but the dépa never came. He slowed after a few rods and stopped. Frowning, he turned around looking for his clan spirit.

In the back of his mind, he knew why he couldn't use it. He wasn't going to run after Nifùni. Even knowing that the others may need him, the pull of Mifúno was stronger. He sighed and looked back over the sands.

Nifùni had stopped a half-mile away, a dark figure standing in a swirl of settling sand. From the distance, Rutejìmo could still pick out the angry look on his face.

Rutejìmo shook his head. "I'm sorry, Great Shimusogo Nifùni. I can't ignore this." He spoke even though Nifùni couldn't hear him.

In the distance, Nifùni turned and sprinted away, disappearing in a plume of sand that rapidly streaked across the sands. Rutejìmo could feel the man's anger as he raced away.

Shaking his head, Rutejìmo turned.

The old woman stood less than a foot away from him, glaring up at him from her shorter height.

He jumped back. "Sands!"

Her wrinkled face somehow screwed up tighter, and she stepped toward him. Despite her age, there was no suggestion she couldn't keep up with him no matter how quickly he ran. She moved fast, not as much stepping through the intervening distance but simply appearing at the end of her movements.

She tapped her spear against the ground lightly. "If you don't run," she said in a wavering voice, "then you will die."

Rutejìmo nodded and gestured toward the smoke. "Y-Yes, Great Nyochikōmu, but they need me too. How do I choose one over the other?" He shook his head. "I can't. I may be a coward, but—"

She held up her hand, stopping him. "There is no cowardice in running toward death."

Memories resurfaced, of watching Desòchu charging into battle. "I-I don't run toward death all the time."

"Running to a death filled with blood and violence and running to one filled with sickness and injury are the same. The only difference is what we call those who rush toward death. The glorious deaths are for us warriors, the noble deaths are the ones we don't talk about. The kojinōmi."

Rutejìmo shivered at her words.

She stepped back. "I am Atefómu, and I speak for Nyochi-kōmu."

He bowed. "I am—"

"—and I do not see the dead." She turned around. "Even if they leave their possessions here for safe guarding. On the shelf of the shelter."

She appeared next to the shrine, leaving no hint of her passing. She tossed forty pyābi on the shelf. And then she appeared on the stone next to the spring, holding her book as if she had never moved.

Chapter 22

Old Ways

The kojinōmi cannot ask because they cannot speak, but they are given shelter and food for their presence.

—The Ways of the Dead

Rutejìmo groaned as he opened his eyes, his head fuzzy with sleep and his body aching from his day-long walk across the desert. He could feel sharp pains along his ankles and sides from sand fly bites. Along his shoulders and head, the familiar sear of sunburn rippled along his senses. The wound in his side ached, and he rested his hand on it, tracing the scab. Touching it added to the multitude of other discomforts and pressures that woke him from his sleep.

Knuckling his eyes, he sat up. A fur blanket slipped off his shoulder and slumped into his lap.

Rutejìmo froze. He didn't have a fur blanket. It was too heavy to carry across the desert. Shaking, he lowered his hands and peered around at his surroundings, a room just large enough for a single bed, a wardrobe, and a door. Light came in through the skylight of what appeared to be real glass. The sun shone on the walls revealing murals of children and adults. Unlike the outside of the shrine, the inside was obviously maintained and recently painted.

His eyes scanned his surroundings, trying to identify the owner. He saw clothes neatly folded on the dresser. He could see letters embroidered along the hems. Leaning over the edge of the bed, he read the name of the clan. Nyochikōmu. He must be in the shelter at the spring, though he didn't remember how he got there or even setting down his supplies.

Struggling with weak muscles, he crawled out of bed and stood up. He was naked and still raw from his purification ritual. He looked around for his own clothes, but couldn't find them. For a moment, he considered grabbing some of Atefómu's clothes, but he left them alone.

Instead, he staggered to the door and opened it. It was right before dawn, and the pale blue light suffused everything with halos in his blurry vision.

Atefómu sat where he first saw her, holding the same book and spear. Her wrinkled face hid the movement of her eyes and gave no hint of her moving or reading. It was as if she was a statue.

Rutejìmo used his hands for balance against the shelter wall as he limped around the corner and retrieved his belongings. And then he headed to the pond where it drained out into a thin stream. A sign that said "Bathing" hung from a rock outcropping. Below it was a shelf with soap and rags with "10 pyābi" carved into the front of the sign.

He dug into his clothes for the forty pyābi she had returned.

"The kojinōmi do not pay."

Rutejìmo jumped at her close voice. He turned around, steeling himself for her presence. But even knowing she would be less than a foot away, it still startled him to see her wrinkled face so close.

Gulping, he bowed his head because there was no room for a formal bow. "Thank you, Great Nyochikomu Atefómu."

"There is no thanks," she said in her wavering voice, "because this is the way it is. Go on, I will help you break fast." She turned, and then she was gone. He didn't see how she moved, only that one moment she was standing in front of him and the other she was a rod away, kneeling at an old fire pit.

Shivering, Rutejìmo set down his belongings and went about cleaning himself from head to toe.

Half an hour later, he felt cleaner than he had since Kosobyo City. His stomach gurgled happily from a rich breakfast of eggs, strips of meat, and vegetables. He didn't recognize the taste of the meat but that didn't make it any less fulfilling.

Atefómu sat across the fire, her smaller plate still laden with her half-eaten breakfast. She was looking at him, he thought, but it was hard to tell with her deep wrinkles.

He gulped. "Excuse me, Great Nyochikomu Atefómu."

"Atefómu. No need for formalities right now."

Rutejìmo felt uncomfortable with the familiar way of speaking that the eastern desert seemed to have. He hesitated for a moment, then asked a question that hung over him since he left her the day before. "You said that if I went toward... the smoke, I would die. I was thinking about it as I ran there, wondering if you mean I needed to run or if answering that... call would kill me." He felt uncomfortable talking about being a kojinōmi out loud. It was something he wasn't allowed to do back home, but the eastern ways seemed to be more... lax concerning the dead.

She didn't move for a moment, then she set down her plate. "Shimusògo..."

"Oh, I'm sorry. I am Rutejìmo, and I speak for Shimusògo."

Atefómu bowed her head to him in acknowledgment. "Who did you find at the smoke?"

"I... I'm not supposed to talk about it."

"An old man surrounded by family, a scar on his face and missing fingers on his left hand?"

Rutejìmo inhaled sharply. "H-How did you know?"

"He was my sister's husband. Her third husband because the first two died. She was a kojinōmi also, and I protected her against the desert as she struggled to follow the old ways, just as you do."

Rutejìmo set down his plate as she continued.

"And, just like her, I found you unconscious on the sands in the middle of the night. Helpless against the night. I guard you because of what and who you are."

"I'm sorry."

"For what? Not telling you what I was about to do? Or for you killing yourself trying to follow ways that don't make sense anymore?"

"I," he tugged on his damp shirt, "I don't know any other way. It was the way... I was taught and what felt right."

To his surprise, she smiled. It was a strange transformation with her wrinkled-filled face, but it was also the first expression that she had shown. "She said the same thing when we talked about it. She had the same book as you. In fact, it was hers a long time ago, before she passed it on to another kojinōmi."

"I didn't know."

"Of course not, why would you? But, I remember the smear of soot when she had a seizure and the burnt corner when I threatened to destroy it because being a kojinōmi was killing her."

"Yet, it wasn't burned." He flushed. "You didn't destroy it."

Atefómu shook her head and looked down at the fire. She shook her head twice before she spoke. "No, because I realized that being a kojinōmi was the same as being a warrior. What I told you before is true, and also that we don't talk about how they are both champions. Warriors get glory and fame, kojinōmi die alone in the dark. They die in the dark, holding their sister's hand, as some disease eats their insides."

A tear welled up from one of the deep wrinkle and dripped along her face, tracing the lines that years had dug into her.

"No one talks about the dead," said Rutejìmo.

"No, but they should. What you do should put your sacred ashes right at the front of the other vases of your clan. It is easy to face a sword or hammer. It's hard to face plague, age, and the thousand other ways we die. A warrior ends life that is suffering, you ease it. It is far harder to be at peace than it is to kill."

Unable to say anything, Rutejìmo nodded.

"You are Mifúno's warrior, Rutejìmo. You will die like us, serving Mifúno just as I will die serving Nyochikōmu."

He nodded again.

She took a deep breath. "And that is why I didn't tell the people looking for you that there were two travelers."

Rutejìmo looked up sharply. "W-What?"

"They came for you yesterday, while you were burning my sister's husband's body. Eight men from three clans, looking for runners of Shimusògo." Her voice grew harder. "They threatened me before even asking a question, filled with their own pride and righteousness."

"What did you tell them?"

"You will not like the answer."

A feeling of dread trickled down his spine, a suspicion that gathered in his mind. Rutejìmo clutched the rock he sat on. "Please, Great Nyochikomu Atefómu, I need to know."

"I told them that one runner had passed by and entered the desert." She pointed in the direction Nifùni ran. "I told them he was alone and that he had no allies." She spoke with a dead-panned voice, as if she was describing a meal or a sparring session.

"Nifùni? The courier I was with? What happened to him."

"Dead. They came back this way, still proud of themselves for serving Kosòbyo." She pointed back up the path. "They went home like cowards. With his head in a bag and cheering for their success." A glob of spittle appeared at her feet but he didn't see her spit.

Rutejìmo stared at her in shock, his mouth opened. Only two days ago, Nifùni was alive and yelling at him; he was trying to outrace him, and being frustrated that he couldn't. And then, in a flash, he was dead.

He shook his head, trying to deny it. "No, no, you couldn't have done that."

His fingers dug into the rock as he looked up at her. Seeing her deeply furrowed face and knowing that she wasn't devastated by her actions, he wanted to lash out at her. But, at the same time, he knew he couldn't. He wouldn't survive against a warrior. Even if he could, Rutejìmo had never killed anyone in his life. He couldn't change that, even for his clan.

He choked, trying to force words out. His vision blurred before he could work his mouth to make a sound. "W-Why?" It came out weak and quiet.

Atefómu groaned as she stood up. "Because I didn't see the dead." Her voice never rose in tone, only creaked more with her emotions. "But I also served you for helping me."

"Helping... how?"

"I have no love for anyone who threatens me, nor do I have respect for Kosòbyo and their allies. They are bullies who use their position as Tachìra's greatest allies to further their own goals. Whatever reason they want you dead, they were willing to start fights that no one would ever win."

She pointed back across the sands, in the direction Nifùni ran. "They think they have killed the only Shimusògo nearby. They have closed the trails on the other end of the mountain, which means you have clear running along a path that is not guarded."

"You killed my clan!" Tears ran down his cheek. "You killed Nifùni!" He let out his breath, it came in shuddering gasps.

"Yes, I did." Her voice didn't falter. "And if you wish to strike me, feel free." She dropped her spear on the ground and came around to him. Standing before him, she put her hands behind her back and lifted her chin.

Rutejìmo stared at her bared throat; she was willing to give her life for her choice. He couldn't even raise his hand. He stood up, stepped back while shaking his head. Tears threatened to spill out and he wiped at them, hating that he wasn't strong enough to save his brother or Nifùni.

The spear appeared in her hand. "I'm a warrior, Rutejìmo. I will be until the day I die." She was in front of him again, moving faster than he could see. "I killed him, and if you wish to take my life in exchange, I will give it freely for making that choice."

"Why? It can't be for helping a stranger."

She reached out and pressed one wizened hand against his elbow. "Yes, because you were a stranger. You didn't know what was at the smoke. You didn't know you were running to my sister's husband. But, when you had a choice, you chose to help a stranger instead of yourself. And your clan would not."

Rutejìmo sank to his knees and sobbed.

"You are not a coward. You may think you are, but you aren't." He blinked, and then she was gone. Another blink, and she was back.

A heavy thump landed next to him, and he peered over. It was a large bundle of wood, wrapped in paper and string. A prayer had been written on the paper, and he could smell the incense nestled inside. They were supplies for burning the dead, blessed wood and sacred scents. He never had to gather them on his own because others would leave them near the dying for his use.

"Burn your clan, and give his spirit some peace, but forget some of the old ways. You serve Mifúno even if you don't purify yourself. Even if you skip the ritual in this time of need, Mifúno knows you are her champion. Don't ever forget it. And don't be afraid to speak about who you are. Everyone needs to know. My sister did not, and I wish not to see anyone suffer in silence like her again."

Rutejìmo looked up at her. "What if I can't?"

"Ways are changing. If you remain who you are, they will know." She smiled broadly at him. A heartbeat later, she was sitting back at her rock, holding her spear and her book as if she had never moved.

Rutejìmo wiped away the tears and stood up. He didn't know if she was right. The young kojinōmi who served Mifúno near Kosobyo City had refused to help one of the night clans, something that Rutejìmo would never consider doing. Their ways were changing, some for the good and some for the bad.

He straightened his back and took a deep breath. Gathering his pack and the wood, he gave one final bow to the old woman who didn't move.

The translucent dépa raced by, shooting out into the desert. Shimusògo would find Nifùni's body despite the wide expanses of sand and the ravages of the wind. He would burn the young man's body and then keep running, even if he had to skip the purification.

He didn't know what would happen, but he still had a message to deliver, and he couldn't abandon Shimusògo for Mifúno any more than the reverse. He would serve both.

And then he ran.

Chapter 23

Asylum

The Wamifūko are forbidden from traveling beyond a chain of their town, on the pain of destruction.

—Kosobyo Buhíchyo, Lord of the Second Kosobyo Army

The arrow slammed into the sand a rod ahead of Rutejìmo.

He tensed at the sight of the bright red feathers blossoming into flames.

The gravel around the arrow began to vibrate.

Knowing that it was about to explode, he closed his eyes, shielded his face with his arm, and raced past. A sharp crack shot out behind him, and the concussion wave shoved him roughly forward. He stumbled and continued along, chasing the dépa as he reached the long shadows cast by Wamifuko City.

The city had been carved out of the mountain by the Wamifūko. Massive stone claws, each one a mile in height, rose from the base. The clan had shaped them with their magic and used the outcroppings to form sixty-four gates that lead into the city. It was the promise of the Wamifūko that they would protect anyone within their boundaries.

Rutejìmo hoped he would survive long enough to find out.

He blamed himself for not expecting an ambush, but days of travel without incident had tempered his fear. If it wasn't for a chance wind that blew sand in his face, he would never have noticed the ambush.

That was six miles ago.

Another arrow slammed into the ground before him. The point of the head slipped from the gravel, and it fell to the side. The shaft rolled for less than a second before it ignited into flames. Another two arrows pierced the ground in a line. They were too close to outrace the explosions.

He threw himself against the ground, digging his feet hard against the sharp rocks. As his speed and Shimusògo's magic carved a deep furrow, he leaned back as far down as he could, using his momentum to keep him from falling but also building up a mound of rocks between him and the arrows.

Just as he reached the point where Shimusògo would disappear, the arrows exploded. Three rapid punches slammed into the gravel at his feet, kicking up stones and dust that smashed into him. Sharp edges of rocks tore at his legs, hip, and shoulder. He could feel more shards punching into his skin and scraping against bone.

The heat seared his face, but he closed his eyes and threw himself to the side, running before he even hit the ground. He accelerated in a flash, despite the agony of moving. His other wounds, an arrow in his right shoulder and gashes from near misses along his side, reported with sharp agony, but he couldn't stop.

Rutejìmo slapped his hand against the ground and shoved himself up. His feet caught the ground, the dépa already ahead of him. He shot forward and scanned the quarter mile remaining between him and the city.

Besides the four archers riding behind him, there were three other clans moving to block him. He didn't know them by their colors, but he couldn't imagine any other reason they would be racing to block the gates nearest to him.

He heard the twang of bows. Air rushed past him, and four more arrows hit the ground before his feet.

Rutejìmo raced around the first two, then turned sharply back toward the city before they both exploded. More rocks whizzed past him as others punched through his pack and grazed his arm. He winced from the impact and prayed he could make it before another one of the arrows struck him. He was already leaving a bloody trail behind him and didn't think he could take much more before falling.

The next set of arrows missed their mark, and he passed them long before they exploded. He panted for breath as he straightened his path and sprinted for the gate.

The other clans had reached their positions in front of each of the nearest gates. The gate that Rutejìmo had aimed for was blocked by a clan using spears. All their weapons were set to receive him, their red and white banners hung from short crossbars near the blades. Behind them, a rank of fighters waited with swords in both hands. Their blades burned with golden flames and sparkling letters.

Rutejìmo focused past his opponents, on the gate. The Wamifūko wore heavy armor and had highly stylized helms. In the desert, it would be dangerous to wear such armor, but they never left the confines of their city. He hoped to see a horse-headed one, his friend Gichyòbi, but the impassive guard standing at the entrance holding a massive spear in both hands wore a cat-shaped helm.

The Wamifūko were bound to not travel more than a chain from their city. It was common knowledge in the Eastern Desert, and his opponents knew of the clan's limitation. They remained a chain's distance from the walls and well outside of the city's protection.

Rutejìmo stared at the gate, trying to find a path through the warriors blocking him. He could barely breathe after the last few minutes of running, with all the evasive maneuvers. He knew that his injuries slowed him down, and he was just one man against a dozen. If he shifted direction, they would block him again. To outrace them, he would have to move closer to the walls, but then he would be more at risk from whatever killing magic they had.

He looked to the further gates, the ones that weren't blocked. Each one had a crowd in front of them, mostly merchants entering the city as the markets opened, and he had no doubt that Kosòbyo's allies were among them. He could try to find a less protected entrance, but he wasn't sure if he could survive the archers behind him long enough to find it.

Drawing out his tazágu, Rutejìmo bore forward. He had no intent of killing anyone, but it would be useful in parrying attacks. Taking a deep breath, he prepared himself for more injuries and charged forward.

A ripple of movement along the gravel warned him of another ambush. He jerked to the side as a stone-colored snake burst out of the ground and shot forward, missing him by inches. More ripples appeared, and he had to concentrate to wind his way through them as the snakes shot forward. He felt one fang catch his trousers. He kept running, but the snake had somehow latched onto his clothes and thumped on the ground before him. He could feel its body snapping with the wind and the weight slowing him down.

Rutejìmo slashed his weapon down, striking the snake and dislodging it. When he looked up, he was far closer to the spears than he realized. With a cry, he dug his foot into the ground and turned sharply.

One of the blades caught him across the cheek, cutting a line clear to his ear before he managed to accelerate away. The pain exploded across his face, and his right eye blurred with the agony.

Rutejìmo stumbled but managed to keep moving. He ran parallel to the city walls. Spears slashed at him, each strike leading a wave of force that extended past the end of the weapon. One hit him along the thigh, slicing deep into the muscle.

His leg gave out. With a scream, he threw himself beneath the readied spears and onto the ground. He pitched forward, twisted until he could dig his feet into the hard-packed earth. He slid along it until he jammed his feet harder, forcing them under the crust until the surface shattered from his speed. Ragged plates of stone burst out from both sides as he rapidly slowed.

Another spear swung over him, and he ducked back, narrowly avoiding it.

When he saw the other fighters racing toward him, he realized that if he stopped, they would kill him. He thought furiously and then realized he had a way to get past the line, but it would hurt more than he could imagine.

He winced but then rolled out from underneath the spears and shot away from the city. He couldn't regain his full speed; his leg injury resisted his efforts to run faster. After only a chain of distance, he circled back and charged the wall. His breath came faster and his heart slammed against his chest as he stared at the spears being set for him. Blood dripped down his side and his leg shook with the effort to keep running.

Just as he approached the spears, he jammed his feet into the ground to stop.

The blades lowered to pierce his body.

Rutejìmo held his breath and let his momentum pull him up. For the briefest of moments, he stood at the head of his own furrow, but then the inertia of his movement yanked him up off the ground and flung him up and over the spears.

Waving his hands, he could do nothing as the side of the city rushed at him. The sheer height of stone reached far past his vision, but then it filled his view until there was nothing else but wall.

He only had time to scream "Sands" before he hit it face-first. His nose cracked from the impact and stars exploded across his vision. The solid stone stopped his movement instantly, and he was crushed against it.

Rutejìmo let out a long, tortured groan. And then his body peeled off the rock and he fell. He was surprised that he didn't hear more cracked bones, but it was hard to sense anything past the pain of his fractured nose and the blood sheeting down his face.

He hit the ground, bouncing once before slumping against the rock. Blood poured down his face, smearing across his eyes and casting everything into a crimson haze. Agony seared across his body, reporting everything from his shattered nose to the wounds from the arrows. He could breathe, but each time he inhaled, a sharp pain radiated from a cracked rib. His leg burned with his injuries and he didn't know if he would ever run again.

Rutejìmo couldn't move. He stared up at the sky and the single stone claw that rose above him. He had made the city, but he was going to die in its shadow. There was no way any of the Wamifūko could reach him between the gates.

Footsteps rushed toward him. He tensed for the blow.

The first opponent jumped up, his body silhouetted against the sky. He raised a spear over his head and began to thrust the weapon downwards, aiming for Rutejìmo's chest.

Rutejìmo's held his breath as he waited for the end.

A second spear swung across his vision, the blade almost a yard long. It appeared to come from between Rutejìmo's feet, but they were pressed against the rock wall. The weapon caught Rutejìmo's attacker right below the ribs, slicing through cloth and flesh in a single slash.

Instead of a spear blade striking him, it was a rain of guts and blood that poured down. Striking his body in wet thuds, pounding into him before sliding off. The stench of offal and gore choked Rutejìmo.

A heavily armored figured stepped over Rutejìmo, walking out of the stone wall itself. Steel boots landed on both sides of Rutejìmo's head. A moment later, something heavy slammed into the ground and a wave of power radiated from the impact. It shifted Rutejìmo's body to the side, and his head thumped against one of the boots.

"I am Gichyòbi, and I defend Wamifūko!"

Rutejìmo sobbed at his friend's familiar voice.

Someone spoke up. "Give us the runner, Wamifūko, and we won't enter your city."

Gichyòbi's voice boomed loudly over Rutejìmo. "You will have him when Chobìre shits in Tachìra's skull and not a moment sooner."

Someone grabbed Rutejìmo and pulled him toward the wall. Rutejìmo let out a gasp trying to call out for Gichyòbi. He flailed around for his weapon but his tazágu slipped from his hand.

"Jìmo, Jìmo! It's Kidóri! Calm down, I have you." It was Gichyòbi's wife.

Rutejìmo let out a sob of agony as she pulled him to her chest. She was a curvy woman with no armor, a stone tender of Wamifūko instead of a warrior like her husband. Rutejìmo didn't know how she reached him anymore than how Gichyòbi came to rescue him. Blinking past the stars and blood, he peered over her shoulder just as two more warriors stepped out of the stone.

One of them walked through the bloody smear that Rutejìmo's nose had left on the wall. The mark transferred to his chest as he stepped away from the stone and around Rutejìmo and Kidóri.

Someone away from the walls cleared his throat. "I am Chitàre and… I speak for Kosòbyo."

Rutejìmo turned his head to see the speaker, pausing only as Kidóri held him tighter and pushed him down. He frowned, but the need to see the man responsible for this attack pushed Kidóri's behavior aside. He peered over his shoulder and tried to ignore the blood sheeting down his face and soaking Kidóri's arm.

The Kosòbyo man panted as he came to a stop in front of Gichyòbi. He wore the gold and green of the clan, but his button-down suit looked out of place so far from Kosobyo City. Sweat soaked the fabric around his neck and armpits. He held up his hand and gulped for air.

Warriors from at three others clans gathered behind him. There were at least thirty of them, all of them with drawn weapons or glowing hands. Rutejìmo spotted the archers that had chased him and the spear fighters that tried to block him.

Gichyòbi grunted and twisted his spear, digging the butt into the ground.

Chitàre took a deep breath and straightened. His pale brown skin shone with sweat. "Y-You don't want this fight, Wamifūko. Only a fool would take on Kosòbyo over the life of a single man."

"Why do you want him?"

"The Kosòbyo don't have to answer that."

Chitàre's allies finished gathering behind him. None of them were smiling, and more than a few were scratching at their joints. A haze of their resonance grew more obvious, bringing the sharp scent of contrary magic that cut even through the blood coating Rutejìmo's face. Sparks of energy hovered between the warriors. It wouldn't take much more before the sparks became arcs of power much like when Chimípu had used her power in Kosobyo City.

Next to Gichyòbi, there were only two other heavily-armored warriors. Three against thirty. Rutejìmo had seen Gichyòbi fight before but never against such extreme odds.

"Stay down," whispered Kidóri. She tightened her arm around Rutejìmo, holding him close to her breast. She didn't seem to mind the blood soaking into her dress.

Gichyòbi grunted, his voice hollow in his metal helm. "In that case, Wamifūko will answer with the deepest respect to the greatest clan of the desert." He bowed deeply before he continued. "The Kosòbyo can kiss each and every ass of the Wamifūko for their decision to bind us to the confines of our city because of our actions during Hizogōma's betrayal."

Chitàre's lips tightened for a moment. "That was three hundred years ago."

"Stones have a long memory."

"Would you really fight us then? The Wamifūko lost the last time they went up against us."

Behind Chitàre, his allies braced themselves.

Gichyòbi slammed the butt of his spear into the ground again. It shook underneath Rutejìmo, the stone rumbling from the impact. The other two Wamifūko warriors did the same, and power crackled in the air around him.

Rutejìmo frowned. He had never felt resonance from Gichyòbi before, but the rumble set off itching inside his joints. He ducked his head and winced at the pain from his movement. The blood seemed to have stopped, though he didn't know why. He reached up and touched his cheek. It came back covered in bloody sand.

His breath came out in a shudder. More sand blew across his skin, kicked up by a breeze he hadn't noticed before. It clung to his finger and stuck to his face. He could feel it gathering along his cuts and injuries.

Shifting, he peered down at his leg. Sand had gathered along the cut in his muscle, filling it and staunching the blood. More rolled over his thigh. At first, he looked for the pattern that said Mifúno needed him but it wasn't anything that he had seen before. It repeated itself, tracing rippling lines across his skin. It was something, but he didn't know what the desert was trying to tell him.

Rutejìmo stared in stunned shock as the desert tried to communicate, but it was hard to concentrate with the two warriors still speaking.

"—and you don't really have a mountain left to destroy, Wamifūko."

Rutejìmo glanced up to see Chitàre pointing to the top of the city.

Gichyòbi grunted. "We can rebuild. We did it once before."

Chitàre cocked his head. "You would risk destroying your city and your clan for a single man? Someone not of your clan?"

Kidóri tightened her grip on Rutejìmo.

"When it comes to the life of this man, I will send my entire clan to war against Tachìra himself."

"And what makes this man so important?"

Gichyòbi paused. "Because Wamifūko tells me he is my clan. Because all clan spirits tell their warriors to protect him. Day or night—"

Chitàre paled slightly at the reference to the night clans, but Rutejìmo doubted anyone else saw it, not knowing the Kosòbyo's secret.

"—he is one of ours. Every clan, every warrior. He may wear the name of Shimusògo, but he is everyone's. You should be protecting him, not trying to kill him."

Rutejìmo shivered. Gichyòbi once mentioned the need to protect Rutejìmo just as one of his own clan. He suspected that other warriors felt the same because many had come to his defense when they would have otherwise ignored a courier.

Chitàre snorted. He waved his hand casually, twisting his fingers around as he did. "No need for drama. I'm sure we can negotiate."

"I've made my terms," Gichyòbi snapped.

The ground rippled near Rutejìmo. He gasped as he saw a snake rising out from the rocks, slithering forward. With a whimper, he tried to crawl away, but Kidóri held him still.

"D-Dóri!" he cried.

Gichyòbi raised his spear, reached back, and slammed it down without looking. The butt crushed the snake's head into a smear of blood. Venom burst out from the creature's fangs and painted a smoking line across the rocks. The warrior twisted the spear in the remains of the twitching snake before returning it to his side.

An uncomfortable silence stretched out across the gathered men.

Chitàre's face twisted in a scowl. "Hand over Shimusogo Rutejìmo, or we will kill you."

Gichyòbi chuckled. "In that case..." He took a deep breath and spoke in a booming voice. "I am Gichyòbi, and I speak for Wamifūko! I forbid the clans of Kosòbyo, Pochyogìma, Modashìa, and Kokikóru from entering this city." He slammed his spear down, and a wave of power rumbled from the impact. "Ever!"

Chitàre's lip peeled back in a snarl. "Kill the runner."

The two Kosòbyo warriors charged forward, followed by the thirty others. Their yells echoed against the stone wall behind Rutejìmo. Energy crackled around them, a haze of sparks and arcs coursing around their bodies.

Chitàre raised his hands, and a giant, translucent snake burst out of the ground before him. It rose high above the fighters as it reared back. Fangs the length of swords shone with green flames. Venom dripped to the ground, leaving blackened holes in the solid stone beneath. Two frills of green feathers fanned out from the back of its skull.

Behind Chitàre, the snake continued to roll out of the ground, stretching easily two chains along the hard-packed earth. When the tail came out, it was tipped with a series of rattles and a long needle-like tip.

It rattled loudly and the feathers matched the rapid beat of the spectral snake. Golden eyes burned with flames, and Rutejìmo felt his attention being drawn toward it.

"Don't look," snapped Kidóri. She shoved him down. "Never look in the eyes of the snake."

Rutejìmo turned away just as the other two Wamifuko stepped toward the charging warriors. They both swung their spears out in a long, wide arc. The heavy weapons whistled through the air before they impacted the first of the warriors. The steel edges burst into flames and sliced into bodies. There wasn't even a jerk as they cut through bone.

The blades cut through the first two ranks, including the Kosòbyo warriors. An explosion of boiling blood burst out in a cloud, splattering Rutejìmo in a heated mist of gore.

He flinched away from it. When he looked back, he caught sight of the spectral snake's eyes. Something gripped his heart, and he felt pressure pinning him in place. He tried to whimper, but he couldn't do anything but lose himself in the golden eyes that stole his attention.

Gichyòbi jumped in front of Rutejìmo and broke the line of sight. His leap had carried him over the charging warriors. He hit hard, swinging his weapon down toward the ground.

Instead of bouncing off the earth, the blade easily slid into the stone as if it wasn't there. Gichyòbi's gauntlet dipped into the ground as he swung forward. Rutejìmo followed the movement through Gichyòbi's shoulders before the weapon came up in front of him.

Gichyòbi jumped again. His spear cut into the spectral snake, affecting the translucent creature as if it was physical. The blade sliced it open, cutting upwards through it, but instead of blood, only golden energy poured out of the gaping wound.

The spear came out of the head of the spectral snake. His blade left a glowing curved line that sailed high above the snake, almost a chain from the ground.

Gichyòbi spun the spear around and brought the tip down in Chitàre's head. There was a meaty thunk, but Rutejìmo couldn't see it impact the man's head. He did see the blade as it punched into the ground between Chitàre's feet. Seconds later, a shower of blood rained down around the haft.

The power that pinned Rutejìmo crumbled instantly. He inhaled sharply, a sob of humiliation and fear.

Kidóri pushed him down, holding him tight to her body and close to the ground.

Gichyòbi bellowed over the fight. "I will defend Great Shimusogo Rutejìmo as if he was Wamifūko! Anyone who dares touch him declares a fight against the mountain, and will die!"

The fight sputtered for a moment. Among the sea of blood and guts, only half of the Kosòbyo allies remained. Most of them were looking nervously at their fallen comrades. They separated away from each other, giving Rutejìmo a clear view of Gichyòbi.

The Wamifūko warrior stood with his spear impaling Chitàre from skull to groin. He stepped away from the corpse and twisted his spear hard. The entire haft flashed gold and Chitàre's body exploded in a shower of blood. The wet splatter of body parts rained down on the battle.

Gichyòbi stepped forward, his steel boots splashing in the remains of Chitàre's brains. "Enemies of Wamifūko. You have one chance. Either you all drop your weapons and cease your spells or every single one of you will die. You bound your blood to Kosòbyo, and you are all dangerously close to painting the stones with your lives." His bellow echoed against the wall.

A sword dropped to the ground. And then another.

Rutejìmo held his breath, watching as the warriors started to surrender.

One of the archers snapped up his bow and fired at Rutejìmo. The exploding arrow sailed the short distance, the feathers already glowing.

Kidóri yanked Rutejìmo to the side and threw her hand up. The ground boiled out from underneath Rutejìmo, rising into a shell that curved toward and above them. There was a loud crack and then a muffled explosion. The shell cracked and crumbled, falling apart amidst smoke and flames.

Rutejìmo gasped and clutched Kidóri's arm tightly to his chest. He could feel her shaking.

The three Wamifūko warriors responded as one. Their spears swung wide as they stepped toward the Kosòbyo allies. Three blades sliced through flesh and bone. They cut through glowing swords and spears as if they were nothing but paper.

Their attacks continued past the bodies, the speed and force of the blow too much for anyone to stop as they swung back into the path of the Wamifūko themselves. The blades swung toward the other warriors and Rutejìmo could see there was no way to dodge.

Rutejìmo cringed in anticipation of his friend's unavoidable injury.

The blades passed through the armored figures harmlessly. They stepped away from each other, again powering their swings to catch the warriors that were outside of the initial attack.

Bodies hit the ground in a wet shower of gore. A sea of red pooled out from the remains, soaking into the cracks and gouges of the ground.

"And that," whispered Kidóri, "is why you stay down. The blades of Wamifūko cannot harm stone."

Gichyòbi stepped over to Rutejìmo, his boots squelching in the gore. As he did, he spoke sharply to the other two warriors. "Seal the city, we are at war."

Both men bowed their heads, brought their spears up above their heads, and then slammed the butts against the ground. Power burst from the impact, and a boom rumbled through the ground. They raised them up and slammed them down again. A beat of one, two, one, and then four. There was a long pause and then they repeated it.

More booms echoed from the gates. Rutejìmo turned to look at the nearest gate. The two guards were moving. One slammed his spear down in the same pattern as the others. The other guard blocked the entrance and pushed back the line of merchants entering the city. Further down the line, the other guards did the same.

At all but the nearest gate, stone doors closed behind the guards. Amid the enraged cries, the guards stepped back into the stone and disappeared.

Gichyòbi bent down in front of Rutejìmo. "Can you walk?"

Rutejìmo shook his head. "I-I don't think so."

"Here, Great Shimusogo Rutejìmo, let me help you."

Without letting go of his spear, Gichyòbi shoved his gauntlet into the ground underneath Rutejìmo and pulled up. At the same time, Kidóri did the same and they balanced him between the two of them.

Rutejìmo cringed as his ruined leg thumped against the ground. He reflectively pulled at it, and to his surprise, it lifted off the ground. The wound burned but the muscles still worked.

He gasped and tried again, lifting his foot up and setting it down. It hurt, but then again—everything hurt. He pushed through the pain and set his foot down. His toe dragged against the ground where Gichyòbi and Kidóri were carrying him toward the gate. "S-Stop, please."

Both of the Wamifūko stopped. Gichyòbi turned to him, the horse helm hiding his face. "Jìmo?"

Rutejìmo slipped his hand down and pressed it against his wound. He could feel the burn of the cut shooting up his leg, but it was no longer a deep slash. Instead, the sand had packed tightly into the wound.

He tried to look down at it, but a pressure rose in his head. It felt like the spectral snake which had drawn his attention, but instead of pulling his eyes toward it, he felt his gaze slipping away from the cut. Concentrating, he looked harder at the wound, tracing his hand down to the bloody cut.

For the briefest of moments, he saw sparkling yellow-green eyes in his leg but then the mental pressure tore his gaze away.

Gulping, Rutejìmo set his foot down again. His bare feet splashed against someone's intestines. He ignored the gore and put more pressure on it, using Gichyòbi for balance as he did.

When his leg held, he pulled away from the two Wamifūko.

"You can stand?" Kidóri sounded surprise.

"Y-Yes."

Gichyòbi looked around, the metal of his armor scraping together with his movement. "We are exposed out here. Wamifūko will protect you for as long as you are within the walls."

Curious and terrified, he made a hesitant step, and his leg held. He took another. Pain radiated from the wound, but the muscles weren't ruined.

He took a deep breath. He didn't know what Mifúno had done or how she did it, but he could keep moving. Gulping, he forced himself through the pain toward the open gate. He was thankful that he had allies in the city but dreaded the knowledge that Mifúno had taken a personal interest in the remainder of his short life.

Chapter 24

Declaration of War

When one claims to speak for a spirit, they take responsibility for the entire clan.

—Cultural Differences in Practice

Rutejìmo cringed as Kidóri grabbed his chin with one hand and jammed an ice-covered cloth against his face. She ground it against his broken nose, sending bursts of pain along his cheeks and forehead, before shoving it flat against his face.

He let out a cry and tried to escape, bucking violently to dislodge her, and clawing at the ground and her thighs. His touch left bloody smears along her dress and skin. He didn't have the strength to buck off the woman straddling his chest and pinning him to the hard mattress. The cold of the cloth suffocated him but quickly numbed his skin.

"I'm almost done," she said as she leaned forward. Her hand slipped from his chin, but he had no chance to pull away as she gripped both sides of his face tightly and jammed her thumbs against the ragged ridge of his nose.

"No, no, don't do—" he started.

She forced the cartilage back in place, and his cry became a high-pitched wail that echoed painfully against the walls.

Unable to see past the lights exploding across his vision, Rutejìmo tensed and waited for the agony to pass. For long moments he wondered if he was going to die, but when she pulled back her hands, the sharp pain quickly became a dull throb. She pulled the cloth away, the fabric stained bright with his blood.

A few rivers of melting ice mixed with tears rolled down his cheeks as he blinked and tried to focus. It took more effort to release his hand away from her thigh; he didn't remember when he stopped flailing and grabbed her.

Kidóri leaned back until her buttocks rested against his hips. "That's the best I can do. You are probably going to have a crook for the rest of your life, though."

She leaned over and grabbed a roll of bandages.

He focused on her movements, watching her through the haze of tears in his eyes. He didn't think he was going to have long to live, but it wasn't because of the broken nose. The fight demonstrated that he wasn't able to defend himself. The only thing he could do was run, and even then they almost killed him.

Kidóri smiled sadly as she unrolled a few feet of the bandage. "This will ache for a little bit, but it will feel better soon. Just a few more seconds, do you think you can take it? Gichyòbi has a nice beer waiting for you."

Even with the agony radiating across his face, Rutejìmo nodded. "N-No promises that I won't cry more."

An emotion flashed across her face, regret and sadness he guessed, but she nodded instead of saying anything. With the same lack of grace, she lifted his head and began to wrap his nose and face with gauze. Her touch seared his nerves, but the pain was nothing compared to the setting of the cartilage or the initial impact with the wall. A whimper escaped his lips, but he clamped down on it for the long seconds before she finished.

When she finished, she rested the back of her hand against his cheek. There was sadness and something else in her eyes, and he felt an uncomfortable twisting in his stomach. He looked away sharply to avoid the chance she might try to explain her emotions.

In the door to the room, he saw Gichyòbi's and Kidóri's two youngest children, a boy and a girl, watching curiously. Both were almost old enough to leave the home, but Rutejìmo still remembered when they were babies.

Kidóri crawled off him and wiped her hands on a towel. "Don't worry, I'm sure Pábyo will think it is handsome."

He turned away from the children and shoved himself into a sitting position. The guest bed, covered with an old blanket, creaked under his weight. His injuries twinged in response to his movement, stifled by the drugs in his veins and the bandages around his limbs. He looked down at his wrapped hand. The burns along his palms and the cuts from the arrows ached, but he was still alive. Looking up, he forced a smile across his face. "Thank you, Great Wamifuko Kidóri."

Kidóri patted him lightly on the head. "Don't give me that 'great' shit, Jìmo. I'm thankful you are alive."

When she sat on the bed, it tilted alarmingly to the side. At the door, the two children crept further inside. She turned her head and held up her hand. "Tèji, bring up some of the stew and your father's bread. Wait, bring up yesterday's bread. Today's experiment was horrible." All three made a face. "And Ópi, draw a couple mugs of the good lager."

"Hey!" rumbled Gichyòbi as he came up behind his children. He still wore his heavy armor but carried his horse-shaped helm underneath his arm. The metal creaked with each movement. "Who has the right to give away my good stuff?"

Kidóri looked up at him. "Do you want to sleep in the basement?" Her tone was serious, but Rutejìmo knew they teased each other heavily. He couldn't help but smile a little.

"At least the lager doesn't snore." Gichyòbi entered the room shoulder first, then straightened inside. "But I'm afraid I need Jìmo for two very serious tasks first."

Rutejìmo tensed at his low voice.

"I'm sorry," Kidóri said to him before she stood up. "I'll have some cold mugs waiting for you when you get back."

She slipped around her husband and pulled the two children out of the room. The wooden door closed behind her.

Gichyòbi looked around the room for a moment, then gestured to the bed. "May I sit, Great Shimusogo Rutejìmo?"

The tension in Rutejìmo's stomach intensified. Gichyòbi never used formal names inside his house, not with Rutejìmo. He nodded and then clutched the bed, knowing that the heavy weight would threaten to dislodge him.

Gichyòbi sat slowly down, but it caused the entire bed to shift under the heavy weight. The nearest leg to the armored man cracked but held. "The council is listening right now."

"C-Council?" Rutejìmo's voice cracked and he winced at the sound of it. Then whimpered again as his muscles protested his movement.

"After the events in our... past, the Wamifūko decided to be led by a council of five elders. Obviously, I'm Master of the Gates, but there is also the Mistress of the Streets, Master of the Hearth, and the Mistress of the Maps. The last one is the eldest of the elders and coordinates between the four of us." Gichyòbi scratched his face before he reached out and pressed his palm against the stone wall near the bed. "I'd give you more of our history, but we are pressed for time. We need answers and you're the only one who can give them."

Rutejìmo nodded and pressed his bandaged hands into his lap. He looked at Gichyòbi's hand. The gesture was too deliberate. He remembered how the warriors came out of the stone, something he didn't know the Wamifūko were capable of.

"Why was Kosòbyo chasing you, Rutejìmo?"

Rutejìmo glanced at Gichyòbi's face and then at his hand. He struggled for his words for a moment, then gestured to the wall. "Do I have to touch the wall to answer?"

Gichyòbi smiled broadly. "No. They can feel the vibrations of your voice."

"I notice—" Rutejìmo stopped. In all the years that he had known Gichyòbi, he had never heard of the Wamifūko's ability to hear through stone. It was obviously a secret and not something to talk about. He cleared his throat and said, "When we were in Kosobyo City, we... accidentally took on a job to deliver a message. The woman who hired us was killed, and the Kosòbyo attacked us."

"Do you know why?" Gichyòbi's smile had disappeared.

Rutejìmo nodded, the memories of Desòchu's last hours rushing into the front of his mind.

"Can you tell us?"

Rutejìmo shook his head.

"What happened?" asked Gichyòbi.

"Great Shimusogo Desòchu died to give us a chance to escape. He took on the clans and... told me... he told me to run. I was a..." Rutejìmo almost said "coward" but then he remembered Atefómu's words.

Tears burned in his eyes. "I couldn't stop him. He had to do... what he had to do."

Gichyòbi spoke in a low voice, "And you did what you were supposed to do. I know it won't give comfort, but Desòchu wouldn't have wanted you to wait for him."

Rutejìmo wiped the tears from his face and looked where they soaked into his blood-flecked bandages. "I know. But it doesn't make it hurt any less."

"It never does," Gichyòbi said in a haunted voice.

"W-We know what the message says. I have part of it in my case." Rutejìmo looked around sharply until he saw his bag on a shelf. "It's in there," he pointed, "but we don't know if we can tell anyone. It may be a lie, but whether truth or not, it is dangerous to anyone who knows. That's why I shouldn't tell anyone."

He paused for a moment before he continued speaking. "We can't tell if Kosòbyo is trying to kill us because they think it's true or because it is false. Either way, they are willing to do anything to prevent it from being known. We were trying to deliver it back to the clan to make a decision on how to proceed and whether to warn others."

Rutejìmo's throat tightened. He wasn't sure what else he could say without revealing everything. "I-I hope the others made it. I can't be the only one."

"Rutejìmo."

Rutejìmo closed his eyes.

"Please tell us the message." Gichyòbi's tone was insistent.

Rutejìmo froze. There was something in the warrior's eyes. He was holding something back from Rutejìmo.

Clearing his throat, Rutejìmo stared into his friend's eyes. "You said two things."

Gichyòbi bowed his head. "Forgive me, Great Shimusogo Rutejìmo, but I have to pick the one that threatens my clan verses the one that keeps our friendship."

Ice ran down Rutejìmo's spine, pooling in his stomach. He held his breath and shook his head. "W-What happened?"

Gichyòbi glanced at the wall, then slowly pulled his hand away from it. "We disagree," he said softly.

"Please, Great Wamifuko Gichyòbi. What happened?"

The warrior looked at the stone and then back. "Last night, Great Shimusogo Hyonèku entered the city with the body of—"

Rutejìmo inhaled sharply. "No..." The world spun violently around him and he couldn't focus through the sudden tears.

"—Great Shimusogo Kiríshi. They were ambushed outside of a Tifukòmi oasis last night."

"She was killed?"

"Yes, by the Modashìa who were also trying to kill you. I suspect that the reasons are the same."

Rutejìmo shook his head, swaying as he lost his balance. He started to fall but Gichyòbi caught him. "T-they weren't even part of our group."

"Which means that Kosòbyo may be going after all of the Shimusògo."

Pushing away from Gichyòbi, Rutejìmo tried to crawl out of bed. "I-I need to see them."

"Great Shimusogo Hyonèku is—"

"He's my wife's father!" Rutejìmo grabbed the armored arm. "He's the man who cares for my children! If they died because of me, I... I..." He sobbed and bowed his head. "I can't fail them too."

Gichyòbi stood up and held out his hand. "Come, I will deal with the council later." He glared at the wall. "Or sooner, but it wasn't our right to hold knowledge of your clan."

Rutejìmo could barely stand, but knowing that Hyonèku was in the city pushed him forward. He grabbed the bone case and slung it over his shoulder. Leaving the rest of his belongings, he staggered out of Gichyòbi's house while leaning on the warrior.

The older man led him down empty streets normally packed in the middle of the day. Seeing the deserted street left Rutejìmo uncomfortable. He had spent months in the city, and it was never quiet before. The silence ground down on him, and he shivered from the pressure.

As they crossed a thoroughfare, Rutejìmo peered down the street to see a Wamifūko warrior standing in the center of an intersection. The warrior held his weapon ready and burned with glowing flames. The stone underneath the armored feet was scorched in a wide circle.

Beyond the warrior, he saw the normal crowds of the city.

"We've already had two attempts to break into the city," explained the warrior. "Whatever message you have has raised the ire of many clans. I've ordered a three-block length from you cleared of everyone."

"I-I didn't mean for this to happen."

"No, but the Wamifūko respond seriously when clans we previously respected decide to break our rules. The Kokikóru and Kosòbyo have both tried to force their way into the city while the Pochyogìma is simply threatening to."

Rutejìmo felt very small.

Gichyòbi stopped in front of a building with bricked-over windows. A guard stood in the entrance to the building. "We're here."

The guard stepped aside and saluted by slamming the butt of his spear into the ground. Rutejìmo expected a rumbling boom but heard only the crack of wood on stone.

Following Gichyòbi, Rutejìmo entered. Dust and spiderwebs indicated the building had been abandoned for some time. Recent traffic marked a blood-flecked path toward the bedroom while a path of something being dragged led toward the kitchen area.

He felt drawn to the kitchen, knowing there was a body there. His duties as a kojinōmi pressed against his thoughts, though no breeze could reach him inside the city to remind him of his duties.

In the living room, two gray dogs sat near the entrance, stained with blood. They had been panting, but they stopped as soon as Rutejìmo entered the room. Two sets of brown eyes regarded him in eerie silence.

Rutejìmo bowed to the dogs. The Tifukòmi clan could see through their animal's eyes.

Gichyòbi grunted. "Great Tifukomi Kamanìo refused to leave your wife's father's side."

"Because the Tifukòmi failed the Shimusògo," said an old man as he stepped out of one bedroom. "And we will not continue that failure by abandoning our charge."

The years had worn on Kamanìo. The short man's eyes were hazy, one more than the other, but they were just as sad as the day he saved Rutejìmo from dying in the desert. He walked with a cane, one leg trailing behind. He had fresh scars layered over old ones, the red lines tracing his nose and cheek. His outfit, a simple tunic of red and white, had been recently stained with blood.

Rutejìmo bowed. "Great Tifukomi Kamanìo."

Kamanìo and both dogs bowed in return. "Great Shimusogo Rutejìmo, I cannot ask for forgiveness from you. I know what the one we lost means to you." He staggered forward. "Please, accept my shame." He knelt in front of Rutejìmo.

Rutejìmo held up his hand. "No, don't do this."

Kamanìo raised his head, baring his throat. In his hand, he held a knife.

"No, I will not."

"Tifukòmi's honor demands you take this."

Kamanìo's hand was steady as the tip of the blade caught the light.

Power bubbled up inside Rutejìmo. He shook his head as it rushed up to fill him. It wasn't the euphoria of Shimusògo but the raw power of Mifúno, impersonal and terrible. The whispers demanded Rutejìmo take the throat presented, to accept the honorable death of a clan that had broken a promise to the desert.

Energy crackled along Gichyòbi's spear and armor. Golden lines spread out between Kamanìo and his two dogs, forming a webbing of emotion and thoughts shared between human and animal. Motes of energy rose from the warriors and drifted toward Rutejìmo, swirling as they brushed against the power welling out of Rutejìmo.

Rutejìmo whimpered as he fought the urge to grab the knife out of the old man's hand. He bit down on his lip, drawing blood. With another shake, he slapped the knife from Kamanìo's hand. "No!"

As rapidly as it appeared, the power faded. It left Rutejìmo swaying. He clutched blindly for balance, his hands scraped against Gichyòbi's armored side.

Gichyòbi grabbed him by the elbow and held him steady.

Kamanìo's and Gichyòbi's eyes were wide when Rutejìmo finally looked up.

Rutejìmo turned back to the man kneeling in front of him. "I can't take a life after seeing so much death." He held out his shaking hand. "You had to say what you must say, but I honor Tifukòmi by not accepting the life of one of their own. Death has surrounded me on this run and, I have no doubt, there will be more before it is done."

Kamanìo bowed his head. "I accept your decision, Great... Shimusogo Rutejìmo."

Unable to concentrate on Kamanìo's hesitation, Rutejìmo pushed himself off Gichyòbi and staggered toward the bedroom. No one stopped him as he inched into the room, afraid of what he would see.

Hyonèku had been laid out across a bed. His body was wrapped in bandages secured with leather thongs, including one set across his right eye. He could see where the edge of the slash came down across Hyonèku's face, ending at his cheek. There were more on his chest, arms, and sides. Blood seeped through the fabric everywhere, mapping out half a dozen cuts that would have killed a lesser man.

Cloth had been wrapped around his throat, and there was a large blot of crimson dangerously close to his jugular. The cloth glistened with fresh blood, but it wasn't pouring out.

Sadness punched Rutejìmo in the gut. He staggered further in and dropped to his knees against the side of the bed.

Hyonèku turned his head toward him, but the older man's one good eye didn't focus. There was blood surrounding his green iris and his pupil was large.

Rutejìmo lowered his gaze to trace a sweeping line from Hyonèku's ruined eye, to his throat, to his shoulder where only a bandaged stump remained. Bits of charred flesh stuck out of the coils of cloth. The sight of an injured Hyonèku reminded Rutejìmo of when another friend had died. Gemènyo had fallen from the cliff saving a little girl but he had died in the process.

Fighting the emotions welling up within him, Rutejìmo forced himself to continue inspecting Hyonèku.

The older man's leg was wrapped in two strips of wood and bandages. There was no blood, but Rutejìmo was familiar enough with broken bones to know what the two lumps meant: both bones were broken.

Tears ran down Rutejìmo's cheek as he pressed a hand against Hyonèku's chest. He didn't feel the pressure from Mifúno to do anything, though he searched his heart for any hint that the desert desired Hyonèku. When he felt nothing, he let out a soft gasp of relief.

Hyonèku jerked. "J-Jìmo?"

"Yes, I'm here."

Hyonèku smiled, though it faded almost instantly. "I thought I recong... knew that whimpering."

Rutejìmo flushed. "I wasn't whimpering."

Hyonèku chuckled and then groaned. "No, you weren't, were you? Don't worry, I'm not dead." He paused. "Not... are you?"

Rutejìmo shook his head. "I'm not here for you, old man."

"Ríshi?" The muscles of Hyonèku's face tightened.

"She's dead, I've heard."

"I tried to save her, but there were too many. They ambushed us," Hyonèku coughed and clutched his stomach with his good hand, "right at the end of the day. Snakes, scorpions, and so much magic. I-I lost her when they pulled me down..."

"Her body is in the other room."

Hyonèku looked at Rutejìmo, his eyes bloodshot and tears welling. "W-Will you be the one?"

Rutejìmo caught Hyonèku's only hand. "Yes, I will guide her. I promise."

Mapábyo's father gripped him tightly.

"I promise," Rutejìmo repeated.

"Could you also... promise to tell Desòchu and Chimípu to slaughter the bastards? Every single one of them?"

A sob rose in Rutejìmo's throat. He shook his head and held the hand tightly.

"Jìmo?"

It took all Rutejìmo's strength to speak. "Great Shimusogo Desòchu is dead, killed by the Kosòbyo."

Hyonèku's hand gripped Rutejìmo's tightly. "Sòchu? Sòchu is dead? How? Why?"

Rutejìmo fought his own tears. "Ni... one of us accepted a job that the others didn't want to take. We were attacked and had to flee the city. We were planning on running out as soon as Tachìra rose, but they were on us. My... my brother slowed them down so we could run."

He lost control of his emotions and the tears poured down his cheeks. "I had... I had... I had to leave him behind before they killed him."

In the silence that filled the room, Rutejìmo glanced at the door where both Gichyòbi and one of the dogs stood. He considered what would happen if he explained the message. After a long moment, he knew he owed Hyonèku more details of what lead to his wife's death. "One moment. Great Wamifuko Gichyòbi?"

"Yes, Great Shimusogo Rutejìmo?" Gichyòbi's voice was tense.

"If I tell only you, can you decide if you want the rest of your clan to know?"

Gichyòbi glanced at the walls and then nodded. "The council has withdrawn, Great Shimusogo Rutejìmo."

Rutejìmo turned his attention to the dog next to the armored warrior. "Whoever knows this will make an enemy of Kosòbyo. Are you willing to remain?"

The dog slipped past Rutejìmo to enter the room and sat down near the bed. A moment later, Kamanìo stepped up to the door. All of them entered before Gichyòbi closed the door behind him.

Rutejìmo turned back to Hyonèku. "It started when we first arrived at the city..." He told the story the best he could, bursting into tears when he reached Desòchu's death but continuing on to describe Nifùni's body when he finally found him and the final rites he gave the desecrated corpse of the man who was responsible for Desòchu's death.

When he finished, he was weak. He slumped against the bed and slid down to the ground. The effort to tell the story left him with no energy to remain upright. In the silence that followed, he could only hear his own panting and felt the shaking of his body from his rapidly beating heart.

"I-I had no right to go against our decision to keep it a secret. Nifùni did the same and people died. Telling you... people will die."

Gichyòbi shook his head. He was paler than Rutejìmo had ever seen him before. He leaned against the wall with his arms crossed. "Kosòbyo is turning against the sun? No wonder they are willing to kill to keep that a secret. Only one great clan has ever betrayed Tachìra and... hundreds of thousands died in the war that followed. Old wounds, rivalries, and hatreds opened up as the line between day and night blurred. As Tachìra and Chobìre fought, so did all of us."

Kamanìo sat on the floor between his two dogs. "When Hizo-gōma betrayed Tachìra, the stars in the night withered and died. Our nights are dark because of the people who were slaughtered in those wars."

Rutejìmo shivered at the forbidden clan's name, and his many memories of staring up at the night sky. There were less than a hundred stars at night, but that had been the case for centuries. The idea that a clan changing allegiances could impact the world so much terrified him.

Kamanìo continued. "If Kosòbyo does the same, we don't know what horrors will happen. We can't allow the snake to do this."

Rutejìmo squeezed Hyonèku's hand, he had not let go of it the entire time he spoke. "I... we don't know if it's a lie."

"It's the truth," said Kamanìo sharply, "and I'm willing to put my clan behind it to say that."

Rutejìmo shook his head. "How can you know?"

"If this woman had written a lie, they would be discrediting you. We would see runners going out to the cities and oases, not fighters and warriors setting ambushes to kill you. Kosòbyo has always been a manipulative snake, but he's going for the throat. And doing so quietly. That means there are not many sunrises before the snake bites Tachìra."

Gichyòbi grunted and glanced at the wall. He shook his head and then looked back to Rutejìmo. "Do we do nothing and let Shimusògo stand on their own?"

"Tifukòmi will stand by Shimusògo," announced Kamanìo, "I will not let the snake bathe my desert in blood."

Both dogs stood up sharply in response.

Gichyòbi tilted his head in acknowledgment. He held up his hand for a moment and stared at the wall. When he turned back, Rutejìmo could see a hardness in his eyes. "Making that choice is to declare war on Kosòbyo, Great Tifukomi Kamanìo. Are you willing to risk your clan against the most powerful of Tachìra's allies?"

"Former allies of the sun. And that snake will have a lot less once the desert knows his plans."

Hyonèku stirred. "Couriers die delivering messages like this." He slumped back to the bed, speaking to the ceiling to finish. "Ríshi died because of this message. Kosòbyo has already declared war on my family and my clan. I can't speak for Shimusògo but you can guess my vote."

Gichyòbi looked at Rutejìmo.

"I..." Rutejìmo sniffed. "I don't know what to say."

"Jìmo," croaked Hyonèku. "You speak for Shimusògo here."

Rutejìmo fought back the tears. He squeezed Hyonèku's hand one last time before staggering to his feet. He took a moment to steady himself. When he did, he took a deep breath. "I-I am Rutejìmo, and I speak for Shimusògo."

He had never before spoken for the Shimusògo clan with an elder present, but Hyonèku said nothing. Gulping, he forced himself to keep speaking even as he shook violently from the effort. "Kosòbyo has declared war on my clan, and I need help. Will you?"

Gichyòbi stood up. "I am Gichyòbi, and I speak for the Wamifūko. We will defend the Shimusògo with our lives, and if that means I have to shit on Kosòbyo's corpse to do so, then we will go to war. The Shimusògo and his allies will find shelter in our mountain for as long as the sun rises."

Both dogs barked as Kamanìo stood forward. "I am Kamanìo, and I speak for Tifukòmi. The oases will offer no shelter to Kosòbyo for as long as the sun rises."

Rutejìmo glanced at Hyonèku.

Hyonèku nodded, his eyes glistening. "You always surprised me, boy. I never thought it would come to this."

With a smile, Rutejìmo shook his head. He looked back at the others. He had just formally declared war on Kosòbyo. The realization of what he had done was immense, crushing down on him. He never wanted the responsibility for this, but it was the only thing he could do.

Silence filled the room. It wasn't a moment of celebration, but a moment of hesitation.

To break it, Rutejìmo cleared his throat. "I need to burn Kiríshi tonight."

The silence shifted instantly as everyone stared at him.

"Are you insane!?" roared Gichyòbi. "You just declared war on the Kosòbyo and want to go out of the city limits where I can't protect you!?"

"Yes!" snapped Rutejìmo, "because she is my wife's mother and I promised Hyonèku. Her soul deserves to be tended."

"No," Hyonèku groaned as he sat up, "you can't honor that promise. Not after what—"

"Other kojinōmi live in this city," added Gichyòbi. "They will do it."

Kamanìo and the dogs joined in, yelling and barking.

Rutejìmo knew he should let another kojinōmi burn Kiríshi's body, but it was something more than just caring for the woman who helped him and raised his wife. He needed to do it for Mapábyo, his clan, and himself.

The others continued to yell at him, filling the tiny room with overwhelming noise. It beat against him, slamming against his chest, and crushing him with the pressure. Even Hyonèku joined in the yelling, though his weak voice was drowned out by Gichyòbi, Kamanìo, and the dogs.

He waited a few seconds and then drew in his breath. "I am Rutejìmo, and I speak for Mifúno!" His voice slammed against the walls of the room and the power crackled around him. It sparked along Gichyòbi's weapon and the connection with the pack. Arcs of lightning speared through the air and scorched the stone as a field of brilliant, magenta light surrounded him.

The sound of his voice didn't echo back. Instead, a suffocating silence draped over the tiny room. A whisper of wind slipped through the cracks of the door, sending streamers of sand cascading across the floor.

Everyone stepped back from Rutejìmo, their faces pale. Rutejìmo stood in the silence. The fear he felt declaring war was completely gone, replaced with a determination to perform his duty.

Hyonèku whispered, "What happened to you, Rutejìmo? How can you speak for her? You'll... she'll kill you."

The whispers rising in the back of his head made it easier to speak for Mifúno than Shimusògo. Rutejìmo jumped forward. "I lost my brother, and I lost my clan. People are dying around me, but I have obligations to two spirits, not one. I am a kojinōmi—"

Everyone else ducked their head at the forbidden name.

"—and Kiríshi is still my friend and my family. She is the mother of my wife. She deserves my hand on her final path. So, I ask you as a friend, will you protect me while I honor her?"

"Not even Kosòbyo would interrupt a kojinōmi," said Gichyòbi, "they aren't that stupid. That would be like declaring war on the sand itself."

Rutejìmo looked at him, a silent question.

Gichyòbi shook his head. "But I would say the same for turning away from the sun. No, Kosòbyo would attack you, if it meant keeping you silent. I will protect you though the rest of Wamifūko will not."

Kamanìo bowed. "The Tifukòmi will die to shield you."

Rutejìmo turned to Hyonèku and knelt again. "I know you disagree, but—"

"No," interrupted Hyonèku, "I don't. I just... never thought the boy who almost failed his rites would ever be willing to risk his own life for this." He reached out and pulled Rutejìmo into his chest; the gesture was weak, but Rutejìmo sank into the embrace.

Hyonèku whispered into Rutejìmo's ear. "I'm proud of you, more than I have the words to tell you. Thank you for... everything."

Rutejìmo hugged him back. If Rutejìmo's brother could die in the flames of glory, then he could do the same.

Chapter 25

Sneaking Out

Wamifūko have many secrets hidden in their stones.

—Wamifuko Efeshīri

"**W**hat about your purification ritual?" asked Gichyòbi as they stood in front of his house. "Walking naked in the desert with a dozen clans looking for you is a good way to die. Not to mention, you still have to come back for your messenger case and clothes."

Rutejìmo looked up. It was almost sunset and he could feel Tachìra approaching the horizon. Pink suffused the sky except for a few dark clouds spreading above the city. He thought about Atefómu's words and the young kojinōmi he met near Kosobyo City. "Mifúno will forgive me. I'll perform the ritual until sunrise and then run."

Gichyòbi looked at him with an unreadable expression.

"I will be okay, Chyòbi," said Rutejìmo in a voice that was more confident than he felt.

The warrior cleared his throat. "The bone field is a quarter mile out of the city, well beyond the limits that Wamifūko were bound to their city. The spotters say that no one is near there.

The Tifukòmi are bringing Kir—her—the body there now after taking the long way around."

Rutejìmo had been there more than once as he performed the duties of the kojinōmi in the city. He glanced around before he responded. "Unless they know to look for it, they won't see the fires. And the Wamifūko pay to keep it well stocked for any of the kojinōmi who serve the city."

"You mean they think you'd be a fool to do this. They know what you are."

Rutejìmo sighed. "I have to, Chyòbi. She's… family, and I couldn't face Pábyo knowing that I didn't do what I had to do."

"You could, and you would have."

"But, this is…" Rutejìmo bowed his head. "I just have to."

"I know, but that doesn't mean I can't try to drive some sense into you. This is suicide, both the ritual and running on your own."

"No one else in the city can outrun the Shimusògo."

"That isn't true either."

"My family is in that valley." Rutejìmo turned to him. "My grandmother, my boy and girl. The others that I grew up with. Those are the people who bled for me and stood by me. I can't let them be surprised by Kosòbyo attacking any more than you could abandon your family and the city. I can't lose anyone else just because of this message."

Gichyòbi worked his jaw for a moment. His gauntlet creaked as he tightened his fist.

"I'm not the strongest or the fastest, but I have to try."

A nod. "Then, come into my house. We'll leave by the other exit."

Stunned, Rutejìmo followed the warrior into the house. "Here? We can leave from here? There is—"

When he saw a massive snake in the living room, he stopped. It took him a second to realize a frying pan had crushed its head. Judging from the wounds in the snake's body, it had been hit repeatedly until its skull was nothing more than red paste. The smell of cooking brain filled the room, not to mention the fried eggs that were splattered across the stone.

Kidóri stood next to another Wamifūko warrior. They were both looking at the twitching remains of the snake. She was shaking as she reached for the ground. Below her hand, the stone bubbled like soup.

"I take it we had visitors?" rumbled Gichyòbi.

Kidóri jumped before she turned on him. "Chyòbi, move your ass. This is the second snake I've killed in the last hour."

"The children?"

"We moved them to the council hall. Ópi is currently drawing on the sacred scrolls, but I'd rather they were protected then draw them into this. Snakes can't crawl through stone, but we can't leave them there for long. They aren't ready for it."

Gichyòbi grunted. "We're leaving through the cellar. Now."

Her eyes widened. Turning to the warrior, she smacked him lightly. "Guard the house," she snapped before heading into the kitchen.

Gichyòbi led Rutejìmo into the basement filled with large barrels of lager.

The large man shoved barrels and shelves out of the way until he revealed a large expanse of stone wall.

"That's a wall." Rutejìmo said, unhelpfully.

"Actually, a solid vein of chisogamāri that goes from here clear past the bone field. We can step out there safely."

"It's solid rock."

Gichyòbi turned to him. "Rutejìmo, I'm not going to lie. This is going to be one of the most painful experiences in your life. Men have died going through this. You will feel rock tearing you apart, shredding you down into less than paste. The pain is probably more than anyone else could imagine, but I know you can survive this. This is what the Wamifūko can do, but that doesn't mean you have to."

Rutejìmo looked at the stone wall. He felt sick to his stomach, but determined. "Are you trying to scare me off?"

"Yes," came the reply a second later.

Footsteps echoed against the stairs, and then Kidóri rushed in with two packs. One was Rutejìmo's old pack, now swelling at the seams with supplies. The other was a new bag, also filled to the brim. She stopped in front of Rutejìmo. "I took out most of your unneeded belongings, including your..." she looked away, "stones. I'll send them home with Hyonèku."

Rutejìmo pulled her into a hug. "Thank you, Great Wamifuko Kidóri."

She kissed him on the cheek. "We'll take care of your wife's father. I promise you, no snake will reach him so long as this family draws a breath. And he will have a full escort going home if he likes it or not."

"Thank you."

"Be safe, Jìmo. We all love you."

He hugged her tightly. "And I love all of you."

She pulled away with tears in her eyes. Turning around, she headed up the stairs without another word.

Gichyòbi held out his hand. "She said what I can't. Ready, fool?"

Rutejìmo took his hand. "Ready—"

His word ended when he was yanked into the stone. One moment later, his entire body ignited into icy flames. The stone dragged through his insides, tugging at his organs and scraping along his thoughts. The burn continued to spread through him until he felt like he had been dragged miles through gravel.

And then he was throwing up in the middle of a black field. The agony passed over him, but he couldn't do anything besides empty his stomach.

Gichyòbi strode away to where a pack of dogs and four human Tifukòmi stood. There was a wagon with a white-cloth shrouded body on top of it. Piles of garbage were heaped on the side; a few shreds of rotted food still clung to Kiríshi's pale form.

He knew his role in the ritual. He stripped down before pulling out his white clothes. As he did, his thoughts quieted, and he felt a peace surround him. This was his duty as a koji-nōmi, one he knew well.

He thought he would hesitate when he approached Kiríshi, but he didn't. Instead, he scooped her body from the wagon and carried it to the bonfire. Even with the cloth, he could see where an arrow had impaled her left eye. More wounds marked her chest, stomach, and pelvis. Most went clear through, including the one that pierced her skull. Blood stained her wounds and coated her body. It cracked from where it had dried, lined the wrinkles on her face and outlined the grimace she wore when she died.

He felt a pang of sadness as he remembered her smiling and laughing. The hours spent arguing over dinner, or the way she helped him when he was dead to his clan. He grew up with her, and he didn't want a single memory forgotten.

Already knowing what he was going to write in his book, he scooped up her body and held her tight. Tears dripped down his face as he pressed his cheek against her.

"I see you, Great Shimusogo Kiríshi."

────────── Chapter 26 ──────────

A Long Night

Even the greatest warrior can be defeated by hunger, thirst, and exhaustion.
—Kosobyo Takòji

When Rutejìmo started the rituals of the kojinōmi, he still had a measure of energy racing through his veins. The determination to serve Kirîshi and the declaration of war had kept him going strong for the first few hours. But as the night grew long, his strength fled, and he was left shaking with exhaustion.

He sat on the ground in front of the dying flames, his thoughts dipping into the abyss of unconsciousness, before he forced himself back to wakefulness with nothing more than his will and the desire to serve Kirîshi until the end.

In the long night, his thoughts drifted from one moment to another moment that occurred over the last few days. He had not had a chance to rest since he started off on the previous morning. Since then, he had been ambushed repeatedly on the route to the city, attacked at the gates, spoke for Mifúno, was pulled through solid rock, and then performed the ritual for Kirîshi. Each one would have left him exhausted, but all these events on top of two days without sleep tore at him.

One incident flashed through his mind, a half-remembered second that would have been forgotten if not for the long night. Just as he was trying to see if he could walk after being injured by one of his ambusher's spears, certain he had suffered a fatal wound, or at the very least a crippling one, he had momentarily seen sparkling yellow-green before his eyes were pushed away.

There was no such thing as magical healing in the desert. No clan had the ability to do anything other than mask pain, set bones, or stop bleeding. There was no true magic for healing.

He tried resting his hand on his thigh, right where the spear had cut into his flesh, but his hand struck against his knee. He frowned and tried again, lifting his hand pointedly and slapping it down. His body remembered exactly how to strike his leg, but his hand came down against the bony ridge of his hip this time. Twice more, he tried to touch his injury before the first whispers of the desert arose in the back of his head.

Hearing Mifúno at night seemed strange. The powers of Shimusògo came from the sun and ceased when it set. But Mifúno was always present, day or night. Her whispers recognizable through the chorus of a thousand voices he had sent to her. He heard Gemènyo's, the little girl who died near Kosobyo City, and even Kiríshi's. They spoke to him in maddeningly quiet whispers, the individual words only a hiss of sand but somehow the desert's intent slowly drifting through his mind.

Rutejìmo listened to them, wishing he could understand the desert's desire but letting his mind drift right on the edge of wakefulness and unconsciousness, in that moment when the whispers were at their clearest.

He tried to slide his hand up from his knee to his hip, to touch his wound, but the whispers rose sharply in a chiding tone. He stopped, hand trembling.

The voices of Mifúno pushed him back, like a parent correcting a child.

He obeyed, closing his eyes and sliding his grip back to his knee. If the desert wanted to keep secrets, he would listen.

She spoke to him again, in comforting voices and half-remembered memories. Images flashed through his mind, of a thousand times he had been stabbed, cut, thrown across the rocks, and even the time he fell off a cliff. Each time, he recalled grievous injuries, but each memory ended with the same pressure to look away and forget. Each time he obeyed and then forgot the severity of his wounds.

It was Mifúno's gift, the cruel touch of the desert spirit which killed with one hand and refused to let him see her comfort from the other.

If any doubt had remained of being Mifúno's champion, it was extinguished. She'd had her eye on him for many years, probably more than he knew. But, like the other warriors of the desert, there was only one fate for him.

Rutejìmo sighed. He was going to die at the end of this run, he knew it. The only thing he could do was run as fast as he could until Mifúno called him. It was going to hurt, he couldn't imagine it any other way, and it would be terrifying, but he would obey her will.

The acceptance of his fate pushed away the exhaustion. He finished his prayer and picked up the vase with Kiríshi's ashes. With a reverent bow, he closed it and felt the familiar scrape of rough pottery rubbing against itself. Using long strips of white cloth, he sealed it shut and then used wax to prevent water and insects from getting inside.

The world swayed around him. He clutched the vase tightly as he stood and blinked his bleary eyes. He lifted one foot, wincing at the sharp pain from a cut that had reopened, and then turned around.

It was almost morning. He could feel Tachìra rising in his heart. All he wanted to do was crawl into a bed and sleep until oblivion took him. Instead, he forced his feet to move forward away from the heated circle of ash that used to be a stack of seasoned wood, sacred incenses, and the body of Mapábyo's mother.

He made it less than a few feet before his leg gave out underneath him. With a groan, he sank down to his knees. The vase started to topple, and he clutched at it, holding it tight until his body stopped moving.

Ahead of him, he could see the silhouette of Gichyòbi and four members of the Tifukòmi clan with their backs to him. Even the dogs were positioned in a wide circle to avoid watching a ritual the living could not observe.

Rutejìmo heard sadness echoed in the whispers in his mind. His friends chose not to see what he did because death was a forbidden part of the living world. Ever since Atefómu pointed it out, he realized he wanted to share it with the others instead of bearing the weight of the dead in silence.

Crawling over to his pack, he stripped off his white clothes and folded them. He focused on pulling a fresh set of clothes out of his bag. They were all Shimusògo colors. Kidóri could have tried to hide him in Wamifūko fabric, but Rutejìmo would have refused to wear them. Even in times of crisis, one never lied about their clan. It was an unspoken law of the desert, to do otherwise would be to turn his back on his own clan's spirit. He never thought he would consider doing anything else, but that was before the Kosòbyo hunted the Shimusògo.

His ash-streaked hands shook as he dressed. Even pulling the tunic over his head was almost too much for him. Fresh blood patterned against the fabric as he settled it into place.

It felt wrong not to strip and start walking. For five years, Rutejìmo had performed the purification ritual even though it almost killed him every time. He dreaded it, but he still followed the ritual as it was written in *Book of Ash*. He could still feel the burns on his shoulder from the purification ritual he performed less than a week ago. It was a minor injury compared to the scrapes, bruises, arrow slashes, and cuts that had occurred since.

He stood up, panting with the effort. The rocks under his feet scraped together, and his joints felt the same. Swaying, he regained his balance and looked around again.

The others remained with their backs to him. They had their weapons drawn but Rutejìmo spotted no sign of violence or bloodshed. He sighed in relief. The allies of Kosòbyo didn't attack at night.

A moment later, he felt guilty for even thinking that the clan would violate one of Mifúno's laws. He did not exist when he wore white. He thought about keeping the clothes on for the run home, but he already knew that he couldn't do it. Unlike the young kojinōmi, Rutejìmo clung to the old ways. He would only run if he was running as one of the Shimusògo; he couldn't dishonor the desert by pretending.

Wind rose around him. It peppered his body with dust and sand from along the ridge of the valley. He looked down, to see if there were any patterns. Seeing none, he turned to the fire and bowed.

The ash and his clothes were gone, but he already knew they would be.

He turned back around and staggered to the circle of his protectors. His leg carried his weight, and he wondered if the desert continued to heal him. As he passed into the light, he rested a hand on Gichyòbi's shoulder while setting the vase into the armored man's palm with his other. "Thank you," he whispered.

Gichyòbi stirred and looked down at the vase, his face hidden in the horse helm. For a moment, he didn't move. When he stirred, it was to take the vase from Rutejìmo and set it down. Slowly, he raised his gaze up to Rutejìmo.

On the other side, one of Kamanìo's gray dogs started to pant as it sat down.

"You are very quiet," said Gichyòbi in a low voice. "I've never... heard you do this before."

Rutejìmo winced at the voice and the fact Gichyòbi was talking about the ritual. But then he remembered the old woman's words. Maybe the kojinōmi needed to be talked about. He smiled. "Silence is a prayer."

"Yet you moved constantly. Not even warriors fight the entire night and then charge into battle again."

"I wasn't exactly fighting. It's just...." Rutejìmo held up his hand, unable to explain it.

Gichyòbi twisted his helm off. When he looked at Rutejìmo, there was a strange expression in the warrior's eyes, as if he encountered something new and terrifying. He was haunted. "You ran all day and then... that all night."

"I... I can talk about it if... if you want."

Gichyòbi looked startled before he turned away. His armor creaked.

Realizing he had gone too far, Rutejìmo looked down but caught one of the dogs looking at him. He smiled weakly to the hound. "Right now, the only thing I want to do is crawl into a bed and sleep."

"You look exhausted." Gichyòbi said without turning back.

"I feel like there is gravel in my joints and in my head."

"You are still running, though?"

Rutejìmo didn't want to run. The euphoria of chasing Shimusògo would push away some of the exhaustion, but his body ached and burned. He wanted to scratch his nose, but it would only bloody his fingers.

He focused on the eastern sky, where the light was just beginning to brighten. One day. He could rest for one day and then run. But, he might be coming home to a slaughtered clan.

The idea of finding his children's bodies made his decision. He loved them with all his life. Weeks ago, he left knowing they were safe. And now, he may be the last chance of warning them before Kosòbyo attacked.

Gichyòbi cleared his throat. "Four clans, including Modashìa and Kokikóru, left for the southwest last night. In the cover of darkness. One of the clans was of the night."

The words shook Rutejìmo. Fear prickled his skin, leaving behind a sensation of crawling insects underneath his bandages.

"They left right after sunset as we were starting the ritual. There was a Kosòbyo in the group, according to... the person who told us."

Rutejìmo sniffed, his hope of crawling into a bed dashed. They were ahead of him, he had to run now. "Who told you?"

"A banyosiōu of the night, another runner with a dépa spirit."

Five years ago, ostracized from his clan, Rutejìmo had become one of the banyosiōu. He was treated as one of the dead, someone who could not talk or attract attention without the fear of being killed. His time ended after a year, and he rejoined the living. For most, becoming a banyosiōu was a punishment for the rest of their short, brutal life.

Rutejìmo knew the courier. They both worked for the same person back when Rutejìmo had been kicked out of the Shimusògo for a year. They were as close as day and night could be, the common bond of chasing a dépa giving them solace. But, Rutejìmo was allowed to return to the living and the other man was not.

Rutejìmo bowed his head. "Can you... give him something? Anything? In thanks?"

Gichyòbi grunted. "I will arrange it."

"Thank you. I have to run. Now."

Kamanìo looked up, his eyes were bloodshot from staying up all night. "Are you sure? You are exhausted and injured."

Rutejìmo looked around and saw his packs near some rocks. Padding over to it, rocks crunching underneath his bare feet, he scooped up the bags and slung them into place. His body screamed in agony with every movement, but he was determined not to let it slow him down. As he buckled the pack into place, he said, "My clan is out there, and my children need me. Would you stop at this point?"

"No, but I am a warrior." Gichyòbi straightened and squared his shoulders.

"As am I," came Kamanìo's response from where he sat.

Rutejìmo smiled as Tachìra approached the horizon. He gestured toward his home, across the familiar expanses of dunes and rocks. "I'm not a warrior. I'm not the fastest or the strongest. You have known it since the day we met."

Gichyòbi and Kamanìo both nodded.

He dug into his bag and pulled out the *Book of Ash*. Both men inhaled sharply as Rutejìmo set it on the ground at his feet. He hesitated for a moment, caressing the rough pages that had kept him company for five years. He knew that he wouldn't need it anymore. Mifúno would find a new owner.

He stood up. "But, I'm not going to stop. It doesn't matter how tired I am or how much they hurt me. If I must run, there is only one thing I can do—run. And if that means I die at the foot of the valley, then I will die among my clan."

And then the sun's power filled him, and the dépa raced past him.

Rutejìmo bowed once. "Shimusògo run. It's the only thing we can do."

And then he sprinted after his clan's spirit.

Chapter 27

A Longer Day

Clans declare domain over the oases of the desert, protecting each one as if they were the most precious of children.

—Nyochikomu Akómi, *Our Homes*

Rutejìmo ran because he was afraid to stop. The only thing holding back his exhaustion was Shimusògo's power flowing through his veins as he sprinted across the rocks. It didn't matter if his legs ached or his lungs burned. If he slowed to a walk, there was a chance he would pass out, and he couldn't risk even a minute of jogging, let alone walking, as there was a chance he would not be able to run again.

His feet had become a drum against the ground, a steady pounding that ate away the miles. No matter how fast he sprinted, he could feel the seconds slipping away. He wasn't fast enough. He wasn't strong enough. An endless litany of failures flashed through his mind and eroded the euphoria of the run.

Rutejìmo's destination was the Wind's Teeth where Pidòhu had fallen so many years ago. He considered trying to find a faster route, but he could not lose time to backtracking or risk ambush in unfamiliar terrain. He stuck to the path he knew.

He hoped Desòchu's plans included someone meeting him there. He desperately needed someone to run with and to share the night with. It was almost impossible to sleep at night with the fear looming over him. He couldn't rest as much as pass the time until the sun rose and he could run again.

With luck, Chimípu would be joining him for the last segment. As much as he would love to have his wife or Byochína along, having the warrior at his side would ease his fears. Chimípu could defeat anyone, he was sure of it, and she wouldn't stop until he was safe.

Guilt slashed through him. He should have wanted Mapábyo to be waiting for him. She was his wife, after all, and it would be better to race home to their children together. As he ran, he let his mind drift to reuniting with his boy and girl.

Kitòpi would be the excited one. He would pretend he was a warrior when he heard the story, and Desòchu's tale would only encourage him to fight harder and run faster. Already some of that spark lived inside him. If anyone was going to be a warrior, it would be Kitòpi.

In a stark contrast, there was Piróma. The rest of the clan didn't know what to do with her. She was quiet and curious, but with a strange way of speaking as if she was older than her body. Rutejìmo smiled and let the wind blow away his tears. She was destined to follow her own path, to forge a route of her own. She would probably end up one of the Tateshyúso, like Pidòhu. The shadow raptor clan made their home in the valley with the Shimusògo, but their powers were far different.

An unwanted picture flashed across his mind, Piróma wearing all white as she stood before a bonfire. A kojinōmi.

Rutejìmo stumbled and lost precious speed. He threw all his concentration on pushing past the flash of agony and regaining the steady beat of running. Tears burned in his eyes, but he bore the pain until he could run again.

He peered around the sands before him. It was easy to get lost on the endless sands, but there were landmarks and markers for those who knew where to look for them. To his left, he saw the dark blotches of a set of Wind's Teeth sticking out of the ground. The chain-high lengths were scattered throughout the desert, each one in a different arrangement, which made maps and navigating easier. The one he spotted was Five Fingers East, a popular location for traders despite the lack of water. He avoided heading toward that since it would be the most logical place for a larger group to stop. Or for an ambush.

His destination was a plume of colored smoke rising over the dunes. The thin smoke disappeared quickly in the winds, and he had to look toward it to find it. It marked a smaller oasis that the Shimusògo rarely used. When running to Wamifuko City, they used a much larger one to the south that had multiple clans protecting it.

He was avoiding the populated oases and stops. If the Kosòbyo could get word out, they would be waiting to ambush him on the known routes. That left him with the out of the way shelters. Which worked since he couldn't afford to stop for more than a few minutes while it was still light.

Rutejìmo bore down and continued to run. The dépa sailed before him, running always out of reach. He wanted to grab the feathers and let the spirit pull him along, but he couldn't run fast enough.

Concentrating on catching the dépa helped time pass. It felt like merely seconds later when he saw the oasis. Groaning, he started to slow as he approached.

Aches and burns prickled along his senses, increasing as the euphoria of speed ebbed. His broken nose throbbed as the wind and sand buffeted it, the whirls of pressure adding to his discomfort.

He almost stumbled but managed to keep running. Every moment of slowing down brought more pain across his senses: his cracked ribs burned, the arrow slashes throbbed, and his muscles ached.

Rutejìmo gasped at the onslaught of agony. A morning of running let him forget, but stopping would bring the full brunt of his injuries back. He could also add the ache in his thighs, the burn in his lungs, and his crippling exhaustion.

"No," he groaned and accelerated. If he stopped running, he may not be able to move again. Even a minute's respite was too much.

He raced past the oasis and accelerated back to his limits. With a shaking hand, he reached back and pulled out his water-skin. He would drink along the way.

As he finished drinking and secured the skin, he spotted something different. It looked like the dépa was a few feet closer than before. He frowned, trying to remember how far away the spirit ran. But, after fifteen years of racing across the desert, he no longer could remember the exact distance.

Pushing the thoughts aside, he bore down and kept running.

Chapter 28

Smoke and Honor

The desert promises someone in white will approach when needed.
—Desert proverb

After a night of barely sleeping in the dark, Rutejìmo had found a second wind. Or was it his third, or maybe fourth? The entire day passed with him able to run without stumbling or faltering, though he knew he would be paying for his sprint when he stopped again. At a mid-day oasis, he risked stopping for fresh water and ended up leaving a bloody smear near the water's edge when he slipped. When the clan protecting the oasis offered to give him shelter, he had respectfully turned them down and started running again.

Chasing Shimusògo also pushed away the fear and agony. He sank deeper into the run than he ever had before and lost himself in the euphoria of the wind rushing against his face, the peppering of sand and rock, and the steady drumming of his feet on solid ground.

His own worry focused on the end of the day, when his powers faded with sunlight. He had been staring at the sun for the last few hours, wishing that Tachìra would halt in his daily descent.

Rutejìmo's desire had no sway over the sun spirit, and it continued to sink toward the horizon. Even though it was bright outside, despair darkened his thoughts and the world behind him.

He scanned the horizon as he looked for a place to stop for the night. Avoiding landmarks made it easier, he could stop anywhere, but he wanted to find a low outcropping to hide against or a rocky valley where he could use the alchemical flame without lighting up the darkness. A warm meal and a place to shield his back were his only needs just now.

Rutejìmo was afraid of the dark, and nothing in his life had eased that pain. Terrible monsters crawled the desert when the sun was down. There were also the night clans. Even though he had served them as frequently as the day, his clan was of the sun and very few saw beyond the bright red and orange of the Shimusògo before drawing their weapons.

Coming up along one ridge, he spotted a low-rising rock in the distance, about six miles away in the middle of a large wash of sand snaking between two rocky plains.

Rutejìmo whispered a prayer of thanks to Shimusògo and Mifúno before sprinting forward.

Less than fifteen minutes later, he came to a sliding stop near the rocks. The wind of his passing blasted past him, continuing up the dune before raining sand down in a wide pattern. The hiss of his stop was almost comforting.

He straightened and stretched. The aches had already returned. His arms and legs burned from running, and his injuries prickled along his skin. Gingerly, he touched his nose and winced at the flash of pain.

Shaking his head, he inspected the rock and was happy to find it would suffice for the night. He unslung his bag and knelt to open it.

Movement caught the corner of his eye. Tensing, he gripped the hilt of his tazágu and turned to look.

Twin columns of smoke rose in the distance, maybe twenty miles away. His heart sank as he saw the yellow and white swirling around each other. He closed his eyes before opening them again, hoping his services weren't needed.

The smoke remained in the sky, lazily rising in two hazy lines that pointed down to where he saw a swirl of dust and a hint of movement.

Rutejìmo choked back a sob. He couldn't take another night of rituals. Staying up all night only wore down his reserves, and he didn't think he had much more. He had to get home and warn the others, to save his family from Kosòbyo's attack.

Groaning, he stood up. He was also a kojinōmi and one of the few in the area. There would be no one else to tend to the dead. This close to home, he probably knew the clan in need. It was his duty, despite his fear and exhaustion.

He struggled with his dread of another sleepless night as he switched into his whites. For a moment, he considered leaving his supplies by the rock, but it would have been foolish to risk it being stolen, destroyed by animals, or simply lost in the sand. He shook his head and packed his clothes and his tazágu into his travel bag and slung it and Kidóri's nearly empty one over his shoulder.

With a deep breath, he set off toward the smoke.

Less than an hour later, he came up the final ridge and looked out across a rocky plain. A crowd of warriors, all in yellows, whites, and bright colors, ringed the plain. He spotted bared weapons flashing in the rapidly fading light and the swirl of movement among runners and warriors.

They had surrounded a thick knot of black-clad folk, a clan of the night.

He froze as he stared at the scene. Even though he encountered an almost identical one near Kosobyo City, he had never seen it close to home. The clans in the western desert avoided each other or killed each other, not circled around like hounds waiting for someone to die. And when a fight did break out, the winner normally let the losing side escape and lick their wounds. He didn't get the impression from the crowd ahead of him that they were willing to let the fight end without a slaughter.

Rutejìmo frowned, disliking how the eastern ways were already seeping close to his more traditional home.

Clutching his straps tighter, he jogged down to the rocky plain and then accelerated into a sprint.

Only a few seconds later did Tachìra dip below the horizon, cutting off his power and leaving him stumbling forward. He grunted and awkwardly slowed into a fast walk.

He approached the crowd and lowered his eyes. The smell of sweat and oil wafted past him as he threaded through the crowd, moving forward as the living parted around him.

It felt right to move with the living, where everyone knew their place. He took a deep breath and shifted forward, working his way past the crowds and into the cleared space between the two groups.

Just as he stepped away, he saw a flash of embroidered cloth from one of the circling warriors. Only a fragment and not even a complete name, "—kikó—," but the cloth was the right color for the Kokikóru, one of the clans hunting him.

His heart began to beat faster, and his skin crawled. His footsteps faltered as he lifted his gaze slightly, trying to get some hint of the warriors surrounding him. He spotted red and green, Kokikóru's colors. He also saw blue and white flashing to his side. Tilting his head, he spotted a name engraved on one of the many bared weapons: Modashia Chitóru.

Most clans named their weapons and possessions as part of the clan. Rutejìmo's own weapon, his tazágu, had been named Shimusogo Migáryo after its original owner and his first shikāfu, Pabiunkue Mikáryo.

It was a trap, and his sense of duty had dragged him into it. He knew if he stopped, they would cut him down before he said a word. To give him a few seconds, he forced himself further into the knot of people and bridged the gap to the night clan. In his mind, he pictured the location of his weapon and prepared to draw it.

He continued to raise his eyes, focusing first on the black boots of the night clan before him but moving up as he fought years of tradition to look into the face of his ambusher.

It was a young man, in his early thirties, with pale skin and intense green eyes. They met Rutejìmo's. The man was a warrior, with a bow slung over his back and five throwing knives at his right side. On his left, a long blade danced in the light, reflecting the name of his clan: Demuchìbyo.

The warrior jerked and his eyes widened. "No," he said in a soft, lilting voice. He looked up and past Rutejìmo's shoulder. "You did not say you wished to trap Great Shimusogo Rutejìmo."

Rutejìmo inhaled sharply. He didn't know the man in front of him, but he knew of the clan. They were scouts who made no noise in darkness when they chose silence.

"Why," said a woman with a husky voice, "would one kojinōmi mean more than another?"

Rutejìmo shook as he turned around. The speaker was a Kosòbyo, a woman dressed in armored fabric striped with the serpent clan's colors. She had a feathered headdress on her head which looked out of place in the harsh desert. Rutejìmo assumed that it was a weapon or a defense, he wasn't sure.

The sanctity of the kojinōmi broken, he looked around at his opponents. There were easily seventy of them milling around. All their eyes were on him and they were smiling like a hound who had captured his prey.

The man near Rutejìmo spoke again, "For the kojinōmi of the day who slaughter my kind, I'm willing to sacrifice their lives to the desert. I'd risk the ire of the sands for that. But not Great Shimusogo Rutejìmo. He is one of the few who treat both night and day as allies and friends." The warrior stepped up to Rutejìmo, who flinched.

He looked over at Rutejìmo and bowed. "Forgive me, Great Shimusogo Rutejìmo," he whispered. "You were there when my father and my grandfather died of sickness, and I could do nothing. I will not ruin their honor by sacrificing you for the promise of money."

The warrior turned back and drew his sword. "I cannot do this, Kosobyo Tagéra."

Rutejìmo trembled and fumbled for his tazágu. The hilt was icy in his palm as he pulled it out of the pack. With a shrug, he let the straps slide off and the bag hit the ground.

Tagéra shook her head and tilted her head. Her eyes were a dark green, almost black with the pupils too large for Rutejìmo's taste. "You were willing to risk the sands when we negotiated two days ago."

More of the Demuchìbyo came up around Rutejìmo.

He flinched as they passed but then stared as they circled around him. They were all armed as warriors. The runes on their weapons flickered with a pale blue glow as they braced themselves.

Rutejìmo glanced past them to where the smoke came. Two pots sat on a rock. Typically, there would be a body next to the pots along with small trinkets or sacred wood. Instead, there was only a pile of shit on the rock. He closed his eyes for a long moment and then opened them.

Hefting his weapon, he looked back at the crowds. There were only seven of the Demuchìbyo and ten times that of the day clans.

"Feeling foolish, boy?" It was Kosobyo Tagéra. Her insulting voice added to the use of a label instead of his proper name.

Rutejìmo turned back to her. Years of needing to be silent while wearing white clothes kept him silent. Even betrayed and ambushed, he found it hard to say anything.

"Those rituals of yours are meaningless, but you are too weathered to pull yourself out of the groove you've grown into. I knew you'd fall for this because you have never turned down a single request. Even with the Nyochikōmu, you abandoned your own clan to serve."

Rutejìmo nodded, still unwilling to break his silence.

"You may be the first of the Shimusògo to reach this far, but you'll also be the last."

He flinched at her low, rasping words. He would have thought Chimípu would have passed him already. Mapábyo and Byochína were both faster runners than he would have ever been.

Tagéra smiled, her lips pulling back to reveal filed teeth. She straightened her head. "But, I wouldn't want to think I didn't respect that old desert spirit of yours." A tic fluttered in her neck as she shook her head.

The Demuchìbyo warrior jumped in front of the woman. There was a hiss of something flying through the air, and then the warrior staggered back.

Rutejìmo gasped as the younger man dropped to his knees, his chest and face hissing with acid. It burned away the skin, melting it to reveal stark bone. There was no time for him to scream before he fell to the ground, a gaping hole burning through his chest.

Gasping, Rutejìmo stared down at the fallen man and felt fear pulsing through his veins. The needle had struck and, in less than a second, the unnamed warrior was dead at his feet.

Rutejìmo looked up just as another tic ran along the woman's neck. With a cry, he brought his tazágu up to defend himself.

Four needles bounced off it, spinning into the air before landing to the ground. A heartbeat later, the rocks began to hiss and smoke.

She casually stepped forward, her cloth rippling around her with her movement. Ripples of golden energy flashed in the folds of her armor. She tilted her head again and then snapped it up.

Rutejìmo saw the flash of needles and brought his weapon to parry it.

But, the needles never hit as one of the other night warriors stepped into their path. He, like the first warrior, collapsed without a sound.

"How," she said, "did you earn this sacrifice? You are just a poor runner who blindly follows the sun. You don't deserve respect from anyone."

Another warrior stepped into the path as she flung another needle. He groaned as he collapsed to the ground, a throwing dagger slipping out of his hand to clatter against the rocks.

"They just throw themselves before you. Why?"

Rutejìmo couldn't answer, he didn't know himself. He clutched his tazágu and shook his head, trying to stop the other Demuchìbyo.

Another needle and another silent death.

Rutejìmo backed away from her, tears running down his cheeks. He tried to hold the next one back with his free hand, but the warrior said nothing as he forced his way in front of Rutejìmo a full second before she flung the needle.

"Our reports indicate you are slow—" She flicked her head and more needles shot across the short distance.

He started to close his eyes to avoid seeing another death, but didn't. The flash of black sank down, a woman this time, who closed her eyes as her face and throat began to hiss.

"—weak, and pathetic. You should have been the first to die but here you are, only a few days from home." She smiled and her eyes flickered to the side. "And only one warrior left to protect you."

Rutejìmo whimpered as he looked over at the last man.

It was a younger man, not even five years past his rite of passage. His skin was pale, and he sweated profusely. He looked at Rutejìmo as a tear ran down his cheek.

Rutejìmo could see the death in his eyes. He shook his head, praying the young warrior would run, not sacrifice himself.

"Let's see how powerful this love is."

Rutejìmo shook his head again. "No," he whispered to the young man.

A needle flashed past Rutejìmo, close enough he felt the wind of its passing.

The young man jerked, gripping his weapon tightly. He looked at the Kosòbyo warrior and then back to Rutejìmo.

"No," Rutejìmo said louder. "Don't do this."

Another needle and then a third.

"Die, Shimusògo," said Tagéra.

Rutejìmo closed his eyes as the young warrior jumped forward. There was nothing he could do as he heard the impact of a dozen poisoned needles piercing flesh. And then the high-pitched scream as the young man fell to the ground.

Turning back quickly, Rutejìmo looked down into the empty, smoking eyes of the young man who sacrificed himself.

Sorrow welled up inside Rutejìmo, bubbling up through his throat and out of his mouth. He inhaled sharply. He wanted to yell at the woman who killed the warriors, but he couldn't think past the flux of energy that burst out with his wordless scream. It rose to a high pitch, the screech of an injured bird desperately calling for help.

It ripped out of him and blasted away in all directions. He opened his eyes without realizing he had closed them to see a ripple of power radiating from him.

As quickly as the scream came, weakness crashed into him. Rutejìmo slumped forward, dropping to his knees. The sharp edge of a rock tore into his kneecap, ripping open fresh wounds as he slumped forward.

Snapping his hand out, Rutejìmo caught himself with the knuckles of his weapon hand. The hard hilt ground into his palm. He looked up at the Kosòbyo woman, and realized he was panting.

"The Call is exhausting, isn't it? But there aren't any warriors to protect you, are there? The nearest Shimusògo warrior is in your valley, a week away. No one can get to you in time."

Rutejìmo inhaled and tried to cause the scream to happen again, to see if a second could reach the Shimusògo, but he felt drained and almost fell again.

Tagéra chuckled, her teeth flashing in the golden light that clung to her body. "You can't call twice, even if there was someone to save you. And if you are hoping for Chimípu, she is just entering Wamifuko City tonight after failing to save the late Byochína."

Darkness draped over the ambush, but then golden flames grew around the warriors. It clung to weapons and the folds of their bodies, lighting up the rocks as bright as a bonfire. Heat rippled over him adding to the stench of death and acid.

Rutejìmo watched his shadow dancing around him. He panted and drew a breath, digging into his exhausted body to try one more time. He needed help. He couldn't survive without someone else.

Images of his body burning away from Tagéra's poisons, or the warrior's blades slicing through his skin, added to his fear. He felt it boiling inside him, tearing at his gut.

Blood oozed from where the wounds on his knuckles had reopened. He felt every one of his injuries tearing at his skin, reminding him that he had bled for this run, but he also survived.

Rutejìmo didn't give up. He had almost died in the desert more than once, but he never stopped running. He died and kept going, plodding through life until he found his place. He walked naked across the sands when most kojinōmi had given up the ancient ways.

He ground his teeth together, determined to call again. There was a chance someone could hear the second one. It would hurt, he could already feel it clawing into his reserves. Blood dripped from his nose as he tensed, preparing himself.

Taking a deep breath, he held it for a long count and then yelled. It wasn't the magical screech of a Shimusògo in danger, but a mortal voice ripping across his vocal cords.

Tagéra and the other warriors laughed, but Rutejìmo kept yelling.

His lungs burned and his throat tore, but he kept throwing everything into a yell.

And then, like a flame igniting inside him, he felt the energy burst up through his throat and his voice became a high-pitched scream once again. It burst out from around him, shaking the rocks and kicking up dust. It blasted out from him, pushing back the surrounding warriors and tugging on their clothes.

Rutejìmo felt the world growing dark, but he kept screeching. He clung to the ground beneath him, wrapping his fingers around the sharp rocks and squeezing down until fresh blood dripped through the gaps of his hands and pooled on the rocks.

And then more power was there, different but stronger. It was the voices of the desert whispering in his head, through his voice. He felt his vocal cords ripping, but the noise kept coming out, rising into the multitude of voices. He heard the children and mothers who died next to him, the cries of men sobbing without dignity. He heard a thousand dead echoing in his scream.

But, then the energy ran out. He slumped forward, crashing face-first into the rocks. He felt his broken nose cracking again, and flashes of pain danced across his vision.

He wanted to lie there and wait for the acid arrows. Every second, he waited for the attack but it never came.

Shaking, he planted his knuckles in the rock and pushed himself up.

No one was laughing. They stared back at him with pale faces and wide eyes.

Even Tagéra had paled and taken a step back. Her eyes were wide as she stared at Rutejìmo. The feathers of her headdress rippled with her movements.

Encouraged, Rutejìmo dragged his feet underneath him and pushed himself up. It took all his strength to stand, but he managed to do it in the stunned silence. He looked around at his opponents, as shocked as they were.

A single vulture's cry echoed out in the silence.

"W-What," gasped Tagéra, "was that?"

A moment later, a vulture landed on the ground between Rutejìmo and the Kosòbyo warrior.

Rutejìmo trembled as he stared at its sudden appearance. A breeze rippled around Rutejìmo from the bird's wings as it peered around at the warriors.

Icy wind blew past him, leaving a smear of hoarfrost on the ground. He blinked at the sudden cold, and a woman stood to his left. She wore black and blue clothes, and steam rose from her body. A long, black whip hung from her hand and Rutejìmo could see glass shards glistening along its length.

The vulture cried out again. Rutejìmo turned to it just as it finished blossoming into a full-grown man armed with a long sword.

Neither of the strangers said anything as they stood there, looking out at the warriors who surrounded Rutejìmo.

"Who are you?" demanded Tagéra.

The vulture warrior answered by charging toward the Ko-sòbyo woman.

The ice warrior, a clan that Rutejìmo had only heard of in stories, dissolved into ice and speared in the opposite direction. There were screams as the front ranks fell clutching their ice-caked faces.

Confused, Rutejìmo spun around just as a pack of pitch-black jackals drove into the back of the gathered warriors. On the ridge behind them, lit by the moon rising in the sky, a pair of older men directed them with whistles.

Rutejìmo felt a prickle of danger and spun around, bringing up his tazágu as three poisoned needles speared toward him. He deflected two of them and managed to avoid the third as it flashed past into the back of one of the Modashìa. The female warrior screamed as her flesh melted away.

"How did you do that?" yelled Tagéra as she parried her vulture attacker with the back of her hand. Her fingers dripped with acid and poison. She flicked it toward her opponent, but he jumped the blow and sailed over her to land in the melee that had sprung up among the surrounding warriors.

Rutejìmo saw two other clans, both of the night, fighting among the attacking day clans. There was only one of each, but they were giving no quarter as they attacked their brightly-clothed opponents.

"What did you do? How did you do that!? That wasn't a Call, only the Shimusògo would answer. What was that!?" Tagéra lunged for Rutejìmo and lashed out for his throat.

He parried her blow, wincing as the acid of her attack discolored his weapon. Twisting his wrist, he brought the tazágu down to block her foot which also glowed with magic. "I-I—" His voice cracked and he realized he couldn't speak louder than a whisper. "—don't know."

"Damn the sands, you did something. These aren't the Shi-musògo! These are night warriors. They will not save you, not —!"

An ice whip wrapped around Tagéra's throat, the shards of glass cutting into her skin. With a ripple of power, the runes along the whip flared a brilliant blue, and then Tagéra was sailing over the crowds. Rutejìmo heard her hit the ground with a muted thump.

The snow warrior stopped in front of him, her icy green eyes regarding him. "You called and I answer as if you were my clan. Day or night, I must protect you." And then she was gone, disappearing into the melee with a flash of her whip and a burst of cold.

Gichyòbi's words came back to Rutejìmo, about how the warrior felt the need to protect Rutejìmo as if he was one of his own clan. Rutejìmo had never questioned why, but hearing the dead calling out in his voice, he realized it was because of the desert. There was no Mifúno clan, because everyone was touched by death. All clans were hers, and all warriors would protect her champions. No, not all warriors. Gichyòbi had said it was a strong drive to help, not an absolute. Looking into the eyes of the attacking warriors, he could see them fighting the call with anger and greed.

There was no time to wonder as a Kokikóru warrior charged him, yelling at the top of his lungs, wielding a flaming sword.

Rutejìmo parried with his weapon and threw his weight into it to unbalance the man.

He failed, and the warrior slashed at him, the tip of his weapon slicing through Rutejìmo's skin. A splatter of blood painted the ground.

Rutejìmo staggered back and slammed into someone else. He flinched back, parrying two warriors' attacks as they came from both sides. He twisted between the two blows, using his tazágu to parry but not attacking on his own.

Even with his own life at risk, he couldn't suffer the thought of killing another person.

He heard a scream as the vulture warrior fell under flashing blades. A heartbeat later, he heard a jackal cry out before ending sharply.

Rutejìmo fought for his life, parrying and balancing. He hoped that more would come to help him, and he knew if he just held on, he would survive.

The night warriors thinned out his opponents. He stepped over ice-rimed corpses and bodies torn apart by the jackals. Blood flowed across the rocks, but it was still lit up by the glow from dozens of warriors still standing.

His attackers, now three of them, were pressing him further back. He flinched from opportunistic attacks by passing warriors. Blood dripped down his face and side. He could feel hundreds of cuts, all near misses, burning along his skin.

Grunting, he hammered his weapon against them, parrying frantically as he tried to find some shelter or place to protect himself. Even one side would be better than standing in a crowd of enemies.

A needle flew past him. He spun to avoid it, bouncing off the burning blade of an attacker. He cried out as he felt the sharp edge drawn across his back, sliding clear to his spine but thankfully deflecting off the bone instead of cutting further.

Agony tore through him as he staggered forward, spinning awkwardly as he tried to regain his senses. He saw a golden light in the distance, coming along the edge of the plains, and let out a moan of despair. Allies of his opponents were approaching and he could barely hold off the few in front of him. Only warriors could retain their powers after the sun disappeared.

A blast of ice raced through the fight, buffeting Rutejìmo. He tensed against it, ducking his head as if it was the wind coming from his passing. He felt the ice plucking at his lungs and freezing the blood dripping from his nose.

As soon as it passed, he looked up to see the ice warrior falling. The surrounding men who killed her were nothing but shattered chunks of blood-flecked ice.

Rutejìmo panted in the silence. He looked around the fight. There were no more warriors of the night. The six strangers had taken out half of the other clans. Blood steamed off the ground and there were cries and the moans of the dying. He saw cut throats, broken bones, and disembowelings that turned the ground into a hellish world of ichor and gore.

"All that and you are still going to die," gasped Tagéra as she staggered up. Blood covered the side of her face and dripped from her armored cloth. Gouges scored her neck and shoulders, and there was a shard of glass stuck against her collar. Her headdress had been ripped off leaving only a few feathers still clinging to her black hair. She clenched her hand and a fresh burst of energy gathered around her knuckles.

He gripped his weapon tighter and tried not to think about the point shaking violently. He couldn't calm it down, nor could he stop the pulsing in his head as he fought dizziness and his injuries.

With a gulp, he held his weapon before him.

"You won't give up, will you?"

"No." His voice wavered slightly.

A translucent dépa blasted past Tagéra and disappeared into the darkness.

Rutejìmo gasped, the weapon almost slipping from his hand. Only one person could run that fast.

Tagéra opened her mouth to say something but before she could produce a sound, she exploded in a shower of blood that was sucked out of sight in a straight line following the dépa.

Pressure built around him, and Rutejìmo dropped to his knees. He abandoned his weapon and clapped his hands over his head.

A crack of thunder exploded around him, picking up rocks and dust and sucking it past. He planted his feet as the world screamed around him, crushing his ribs as the rumble rose to a deafening roar.

Silence.

Rutejìmo staggered as he stood up.

Around him, the other warriors were doing the same. Many of them bled from their eyes, ears, and noses. The golden flames around their bodies rose in response, glittering off their injuries.

In the darkness, a burning dépa blossomed into existence, towering over everyone, translucent and brilliant. It sank down, shrinking into a lone woman walking back. It was Chimípu.

The light of her passing lit up the blood smear of Tagéra's body. There wasn't a piece larger than Rutejìmo's hand remaining.

Chimípu stormed closer, her eyes burning as bright as the sun. Sweat dripped off her body, pouring down her face and chest to soak into her shirt. Rutejìmo could see her limbs shaking, and he felt a new fear building.

In fifteen years, he had never seen Chimípu winded. She had never been exhausted from a run, ever since she gained power. And now, she was soaked as though she had run from one end of the desert to the other. If Tagéra's words were true, she was just entering Wamifuko City that night. His call must have reached her, but that meant she had just covered two days of Rutejìmo's running in less than an hour.

The ground hissed under her feet as she stopped two chains away from Rutejìmo. "That's my little brother you attacked," she panted as she lifted her hand. She had a short knife, no longer than a foot, and her clothes. She had somehow abandoned her pack and all her supplies. She looked at the gathered warriors and took a ragged breath. "I'm going to kill all of you."

Rutejìmo sobbed with relief. He didn't know how she got there, but he was thankful.

One of the warriors, a Kokikóru, managed to step forward. "There is only one—"

His words ended when his head thumped against the ground. Chimípu stood a rod past him, her knife still clean but a howling trail of wind dying around her. Blood hissed as it splattered against the ground, mixing with the shattered rocks and sand.

A murmur rippled through the remaining warriors.

"Jìmo."

Rutejìmo jumped at Chimípu's voice.

She wiped her brow with the back of her hand and it came away dripping. "Are you seriously injured?"

"C-Cuts and burns. I-I'll live. Thank you, Great—"

"Good. Go to sleep."

Another warrior snorted.

Rutejìmo stared at her in shock. "W-What?"

Chimípu looked at him, and there was sadness in her eyes. "You need to rest, and I don't want you to see this."

The warrior who snorted spoke up. "Just like that? Go to sleep in the middle of—" His torso thumped on the ground. "—a fight?" He looked up to where she had cut through him, severing his spine right below the ribs. He gaped as his organs began to spill out of his chest before his legs fell.

"Jìmo, go to sleep. I promise you will wake up in the morning."

Rutejìmo shuddered as he obeyed, sinking to his knees and then curling up. It didn't matter that he was in a pool of blood or there was a corpse a foot away from his head. He closed his eyes tightly, clamped his hands over his ears, and prayed he wouldn't hear what would come next.

There was a blast of air and a scream. A splatter of blood splashed across him and he shuddered at the touch.

Sobbing, he curled up in a tighter ball.

More screams. He heard crunching of someone running toward him, but it ended with a crack of air and the thud of a body hitting the ground in too many pieces.

The stench of death surrounded him. But, despite the horror happening around him, he felt exhaustion yanking him down. Days of running and sleeping with one eye open clawed at his consciousness. Somehow, he felt more peace knowing Chimípu would save him from the warriors dying around him.

One of his eyes fluttered open just as Chimípu grabbed a warrior by the head with both hands. She grunted as she spun around. The man's feet were kicked off the ground as she became a vortex of power and the warrior's body became the disk of glowing light.

With a wet sound, he saw the man's body ripped from his skull and fly off. There was a flash of a spine moments before Chimípu launched the man's skull in the opposite direction.

Rutejìmo clamped his eyes shut and plastered his hands over his ears. Even through his fingers, he heard the thump of the body impacting another and the wet explosion of a skull fracturing against yet another body.

Shuddering, he prayed for sleep and, for once, Mifúno granted his request. Darkness yanked him down into unconsciousness.

Chapter 29

Shimusogo Chimípu

A promise given from the heart can overcome death.
—Fenrik de Kasin da Golver, *Three Errant Kids*

Rutejìmo wasn't surprised when he woke up. He was surprised that as he regained consciousness, he was still sobbing. Tears soaked his cheeks and dripped to the ground, mixing in with the rivers of blood that soaked the rocks. He blinked at the effort to crawl to his knees and looked around.

In the pale light of dawn, he saw nothing but death. Warriors had been slaughtered, their limbs sticking up at obscene angles, and thick rivers of gore ran along the waves formed by the rocks. He saw bones piercing rocks and the smeared remains of the warriors who fought through the night.

The two pots that held the smoke that summoned him had been shattered but a few wisps of yellow smoke still bubbled out from one broken bottom.

He planted his hand down for balance but encountered hard flesh instead. Gasping, he lifted up and turned to see that he was sleeping on Chimípu's lap.

She looked up at him, her eyes rimmed in darkness and her face smeared with blood. Golden flames, only the faintest wisp, ran along her body. She had long cuts scoring across her breasts and hips. Her shirt, once a brilliant red, had been smeared black and hung on her body in tatters. Her skin was coated in crimson, thick bubbles rolling down her chest.

"No," gasped Chimípu, "It's okay."

"I… I didn't mean for this."

"I know, little brother." Her voice was a rasp. He saw that she had been cut across the throat and collar. Blood poured from the cut, running in rivers.

She should have been dead. He had seen a thousand people die with less serious injuries but, somehow, she was still breathing.

"Mípu? H-How?"

She smiled as a tear formed in her eye. "I promised… my little brother would wake up."

"No!" Rutejìmo crawled forward, heedless of the rocks that dug into his knees. He grabbed her shoulders. "No, you are the warrior! You are supposed to save us. You were the one who was going to make it!"

She slumped forward, her chin striking his shoulder.

He froze, terrified she had just died. When he felt her mouth moving, he shook his head as the tears rolled down his cheeks. "No, Mípu, no. You can't die! No, not for me!"

"Prom…"

"Mípu!?" Rutejìmo pushed her back to look into her fading eyes.

"P-Promise me."

"What? Anything!"

"Don't stay for me."

"B-But," he sobbed, "you are my friend. My best friend. My big sister."

"I'm… also a warrior. Tachìra will take… me."

She lifted her hand. It was dripping blood, and she was missing a finger. She pressed it against his chest and pushed weakly. "Shimusògo... run."

Rutejìmo shook his head violently. "No, I can't. I can't leave you. I left Desòchu when I should have—"

A dépa flashed past him. She gasped. "Shimusògo—"

She drew her hand back.

"—run!" Her punch was surprisingly strong but it was nothing compared to the blast of wind that slammed into him.

Rutejìmo was thrown back and off the ground. He landed only a few feet away, tumbling over his shoulders and onto his face. Fresh blood splattered against the back of his head. He gasped and pushed himself up. "Mípu!?"

Chimípu pressed a hand against the ground, groaning as she started to stand up. "Shimusògo... run," she gasped.

Rutejìmo staggered to his feet. "No... no, I'll run. I promise. I'll run, Mípu."

She slumped back. Her shoulders shook as she panted for breath. "You better, J-Jìmo. I know about Sòchu... and Nèku... and Ríshi. You will make it. If you... run."

Shaking, Rutejìmo looked around for his pack, but only found pieces of it. His tazágu had been bent in half. Molten metal had pooled where the hilt used to be. It looked like Chimípu had used it to skewer someone's skull.

Rutejìmo glanced back at her. She was watching him, her intense eyes peering through her blood-soaked hair. He knew she would force him to run if he didn't leave soon.

His foot thumped against Chimípu's messenger case. He trembled and picked it up. A few rods away, he spotted his own battered bone one. He quickly jammed her portion into his own, not caring if he tore the pages. Seconds later, he sealed his and set hers down.

Looking at her, fresh tears rolled down his cheeks. "I... I'm sorry."

She coughed, and a fresh dribble of blood ran from the corner of her mouth. "I'm not. Not... for a single moment. I love you... little... brother..."

The light of the sun gathered around her and the flames that traced her body grew brighter until the flames were as white as his cloth. It wavered in the air as the heat beat against his face.

Rutejìmo gasped as he watched the ends of her reddish hair crinkle and darken before it caught on fire. Her clothes burned away almost instantly, the brief yellow and blue only a flash in the whitest flame Rutejìmo had ever seen.

"Shimusògo... run." Her voice was hoarse and wavering, her body burning from the inside as the sun claimed his warrior for himself.

Rutejìmo could only stare as the flames consumed her, burning cleanly and rapidly. In a matter of seconds, there was only a skeleton and even that burned away before he could blink again. The rocks beneath her had melted in puddles of white liquid that quickly faded to red.

There were legends of Tachìra taking a warrior for some great deed, but it had not happened since before his grandmother's time. He shook as he felt the flames of the sun licking at his skin. The great spirit had honored Chimípu as one of the greatest warriors of the desert, but Rutejìmo only felt the grief of losing his sister, his warrior, his friend.

Rutejìmo backed away as he hoisted the messenger case over his shoulder. He didn't have a weapon or any other supplies. He didn't know how he would survive the night, but he didn't have a choice.

Shimusògo raced past him, and he turned to follow the spirit. There were no more words he could say or thoughts he could dwell on. He did the only thing he could do at that moment.

He ran.

Chapter 30

Keep Moving

No mortal voice can ever produce the full extent of one's sorrow.
—Gamas Tikin Runor

Rutejìmo's wail ran along the pitch-black dunes, but he no longer cared if anyone found him. Night or day, it didn't matter if they were allies or enemies. He couldn't stop the clawing that tore at his heart.

He had lost almost everyone in the last week: Byochína, Nifùni, his brother, Chimípu. Warriors of unknown clans had come to save him and died. He had seen the people he loved and strangers alike—slaughtered because of him, the weakest of the Shimusògo.

Even though it was night, he didn't stop walking. His feet shuffled in the sand, and he trudged up one dune and over the other. It was exhausting, but he didn't care, and he couldn't stop. He had no food, no water, no weapon. He had left everything behind besides the clothes on his body and the case over his shoulder.

His stomach rumbled and a high-pitched whine followed him everywhere he went. He managed to crush a few scorpions and some insects for food, but that was the extent of what he had eaten for days.

Rutejìmo inhaled and wailed again. His throat was raw, and it came out as a high-pitched keening. He wished he could call for others, to summon warriors to defend him. But, when he tried, there was nothing. No energy, no power, no need.

He was alone and terrified.

He couldn't stop anymore. He had to keep walking.

— Chapter 31 —

Wind's Teeth

The Winds Teeth are mysterious rock formations scattered throughout the
Mifuno Desert. The type of rock is unknown, as is the purpose
—if there is one. — Tosomi Kadokíchyu, *Stories of Sand*

By the time Rutejìmo arrived at the Wind's Teeth he could no
longer remember how long he had been running. The three
jagged rocks had been there from the beginning of his adulthood. His eyes automatically rose to the one that Pidòhu had
fallen from, breaking his leg, and setting off the chain of
events that led to him becoming a man despite all the odds.

He came to a halt, his feet digging a long furrow into the
sand. When he stopped, the wind blowing behind him died
and grains rained downed on him. He stepped forward and headed straight for where Pidòhu had fallen many years ago.

There was a small poem carved into the rock. Pidòhu had
ventured out of the valley to follow Rutejìmo as Rutejìmo gave
one last apology. He knelt by it, rubbing his fingers on the faded letters that sand and wind struggled to erase.

He smiled to himself and leaned his head against a nick in
the rock that he had made the day Mapábyo became his wife.
While against Shimusògo tradition to hold the ceremony away

from the shrine, Desòchu had insisted Rutejìmo choose his own way.

Remembering his brother brought tears to his eyes, but the sorrow quickly faded. His brother had died saving the clan. Chimípu had done the same. He was poised to follow in their footsteps unless he could survive the last segment home.

He thumped his head against the mark on the rock. Five years ago, he had tripped during the ceremony and cut his hand on the Tooth. Later, Chimípu had returned and cut a line along the rock to memorialize the occasion. Now, it was just a quiet reminder of his life. A good life. A happy one until recently. He ran his hand down the rock. He hoped that Kitòpi and Piróma would add their own marks when they became members of the clan.

Realizing he was falling asleep, he pushed himself from the rock and started around the other Teeth, looking for signs of anyone else. The Shimusògo frequently camped among these rocks, as did a number of other clans, but it was far enough away from the normal routes that only a few knew about it. It didn't stop him from looking, just in case yet another ambush waited for him.

He yawned as he circled the rocks a second time. He didn't want to stop, fearing he would fall and never get up. Every second that he wasn't running was one second longer that he struggled to remain standing.

Two days of running with no sleep, food, or water had ruined his body. His lips were swollen and bleeding. When he touched the rock, he could feel tremors coursing along his muscles and a searing ache that refused to subside. Dehydration and starvation gnawed at his insides and a piercing headache burned in his skull.

He looked out to the horizon and listened to the gentle hiss of sand rolling across the dunes. It was a clear day with blue skies stretching out in all directions. In three days, he would be home, maybe a little less if he once again walked through the night.

Rutejìmo circled back to the poem and hesitated. It was hot and windy, but he didn't dare stop. He yawned and started another lap around the rocks. He didn't know how long to wait. There was only one person who could be waiting for him, Mapábyo. Desòchu may have not planned on anyone meeting him at the Wind's Teeth like Nifùni had met him earlier. Or, even if he did, it could have been Byochína or Chimípu.

He closed his eyes and continued to pace around the rocks. He prayed Mapábyo had already made it to the valley. Their children were going to need them both in the coming war. Fights among the clans were bloody enough, but going against the most powerful clan of the desert would be suicide for the Shimusògo.

"Jìmo?"

Rutejìmo jumped at Mapábyo's voice as it came past the rocks. He turned on his heels just as she came around the far end. Her black skin shone in the sunlight, almost drinking it in.

She wore one of her favorite running outfits: red trousers with an orange top cut low enough he could just barely see the black dépa tattoo on her shoulder. Her bare feet crunched through the sand as she stood away from the rock and looked at him.

"Pábyo," he whispered hoarsely.

She took a hesitant step toward him. "Is it you? Really you?"

He nodded, but then hesitated. It felt like he was about to fall off a cliff, a sense of vertigo tugging him forward. He stepped forward, and the sensation passed. Stumbling, he opened his arms and pulled her into a tight hug.

Her body pressed against his, just as it always had. He could feel the heat of her skin and the familiar way her curves caressed his skin. She pulled back to kiss him, her lips almost as cracked as his own.

She looked him over and then gasped. "What happened?"

"I was attacked... a few times."

"A few times? You? How?"

"The last time," he said bowing his head, "was two days ago. Chimípu came, but she... she..."

Mapábyo sniffed and pulled him back into a hug. "I'm sorry, love. It isn't fair."

Rutejìmo's skin crawled for a moment but he pushed it aside. He held her tight. "Just like Desòchu and Nifùni. They are taking us one by one."

"But they didn't get us."

And then it hit him. Mapábyo always said the same thing in the quiet moments of their lives. A single phrase that came when the rest of the world had refused to look at him, a greeting passed her lips every morning they woke together and every time they parted. There was only one reason she wouldn't have said it.

He held her against his chest, knowing it was already too late. "I see you."

"I'm right here."

And then a pause.

Rutejìmo closed his eyes.

The knife slid into Rutejìmo's side but somehow missed his lungs. He felt the burn of it as it pierced deep into his body, cutting through organs before the hilt smacked against his skin and the point broke through the far side. A flash of black washed over his vision.

She whispered in his ear. "How did you know? I said the right things." It was his wife's voice and her face, but the tone was wrong.

He shook his head and pulled back.

She withdrew the dagger and let it drop to the ground.

Rutejìmo clutched his side as blood seeped from the wound. The dagger had cut deep and left a very small opening. He squeezed down on it to hold it shut.

He started to say something, but then the taste of acid rose in his mouth. He coughed and blood coated the back of his throat. Trembling, he lifted his hand to his gaze and saw it waver.

"It's poisoned. You have minutes, maybe an hour at most." The woman sounded almost sad.

"Why?"

"Because I defend my clan against all enemies."

"Even if they are betraying Tachìra?"

She nodded and then held out her hands. "You are an enemy, Great... Shimusogo... Rutejìmo."

The pause and the unfamiliar cadence of his name identified the speaker. "Great Kosobyo Dimóryo."

She gave a short bow. She didn't smile.

"I thought you were just a guard," he groaned.

"I am. Just not second rank."

"What are you?"

"Champion. One of the four greatest warriors of Kosòbyo."

Rutejìmo felt a trickle coming from his nose. He swayed as he tried to reach for it, but the blood dripped down into his palm. He stared at the crimson splatter and gulped. "M-Mistress of the Streets?" Gichyòbi had a similar title.

Her smile broadened. "Yes, actually."

"What happened to Mapábyo?"

"Your wife?"

He nodded and then stumbled back from the effort. The burning in his stomach spread out into his guts and he could feel them twisting as the taste of acid bubbled up to tickle the back of his nose.

Dimóryo sighed and stuck her hands in Mapábyo's pockets. "We caught her outside of an oasis. She was in a hurry to get there and failed to notice our trap."

He took a step back from her. When she didn't follow, he took another. "D-Did she know about her parents?"

"Yes, we needed information from her and a fear for family makes it easier to get it. She was told you died also. That finally broke her."

Rutejìmo's eyes blurred and he shook his head. He started to stumble, but caught himself. He kept backing slowly away from the Kosòbyo warrior. "H-How do you... have her—"

"Face? Body?"

"Y-Yes," he slurred.

"I needed information and thought her skin would be useful."

He froze at the hard words. "Y-You tortured her?"

"Less than a day, but she told me enough to pretend to be her. And that's all we need. Though I obviously missed something. The people around here trust Shimusogo Mapábyo, which we will need in the coming days."

Anger grew inside Rutejìmo. He dug his hands into his side to hold his wound. "You killed her?"

Another bow. "Very few people live long after being skinned. It would have been cruel to make her one of them. I ended it before the pain grew too much."

A wave of darkness crushed Rutejìmo, and blood dribbled out of his nose. He swayed as he tried to find some way of lashing out at the warrior. He had nothing but speed and the desert. He could outrun her, but he didn't know how she had reached the rocks. She may have some way of moving quickly through rocks or sand.

Except for in that moment, Rutejìmo had never wanted to kill anyone in his life. He reached out for the desert, desperate for some weapon.

The wind rose around him, peppering his skin. He glanced down for the patterns. There were lines he had never seen before on his skin, but they were as familiar as the sand around him. The desert had marked him for death, but there would be no kojinōmi to tend to his soul when he died.

Gulping at the blood staining his throat, he whispered to the sand around him. "Please?"

"Please what?" asked Dimóryo.

Rutejìmo shook his head and knelt down. "Please, give me something," he whispered to the desert.

Wind buffeted his back, and he felt a prickling of power. The patterns clinging to his body were clear, he was going to die.

"Please, let me fight."

"You aren't a fighter, Rutejìmo. The only thing you can do is die."

Rutejìmo looked up sharply. "Yes, but so can you."

Dimóryo snorted. She shook her head as her hands began to glow. "Choosing the sacrifice. A good way to die."

Groaning, Rutejìmo pushed himself into a standing position. "No... I can do this." He tried to speak for Mifúno, but he couldn't. The energy wouldn't rise inside him, as if the desert resisted him.

He pulled with all his mental might, knowing he might die before he finished.

The wind grew stronger, ripping at his clothes. He felt all the aches and pains slam into him, but he continued to pull harder, drawing on the might of the endless desert.

And then there was no more resistance. In a single moment, he became one with the desert, an endless expanse that was too large and too powerful for his mind to comprehend. Sadness and joy crashed into him, a million people fighting and loving on the sands, rocks, and stones. The intensity burned him from the inside, withering his organs as if he had jumped into some endless pit of fire and ice.

The wind rose to a howl and then stopped instantly. In the silence, he found his voice. "I am Rutejìmo, and I speak for Mifúno."

"You aren't dressed as a kojinōmi right now."

"No, but in this moment, I will gladly trade my life to kill the one who harms my family and broke the laws of this desert. You are dead to me, Kosobyo Dimóryo."

"Like I—"

"You are dead to the desert and the sands." Power burst along his body, and his voice took on a strange echoing tone, like the voices of the dead speaking through him once again. "You are dead to Mifúno until the end of time."

Around her feet, the sand began to blow away, forming a depression. She looked down at her feet and then clenched both of her fists. Golden power exploded around her fingers and then dripped down. Acid burned at the sand crawling away from her.

With a snarl, she jumped out of the pit and over to Rutejìmo, bringing both hands together to crush him. The fire in her hands left a wave of poison trailing behind her.

Rutejìmo prayed that the words rising in his throat would have the power needed. "You are dead to Tachìra!"

The flames surrounding Dimóryo's hands snuffed out instantly, and she plummeted to the ground. Her impact shook the earth. The sands instantly crawled away from her, digging a hole around her body.

Rutejìmo coughed and blood dribbled from the corner of his mouth. He fought against the urge to curl up and die. He could feel Mifúno waiting for his death, the looming of the spirit ready to claim him as her own. But, he fought against it. Gasping, he forced the words out. "You... are dead to Chobìre and the wind and the spirits of the desert."

The hole grew faster, and she sank rapidly. She clawed at it, but the sides peeled away from her hands, and she clutched air. He could see her trying to scream out, but no sound came from her throat.

She clawed at her face, and it peeled away to reveal the woman Rutejìmo saw before. Bloody strips fell to the ground only to dissolve into mist as they struck the sand. She lashed out at the hole around her, but the shifting rock slid away once again.

Rutejìmo's hands shook as he held them up to the sun. "You are dead to all the spirits of land and air and you will never," he screamed through a torn throat, "never find peace again!"

Dimóryo looked up, her eyes wide with fear, and then the earth collapsed around her, filling the hole instantly.

He expected to feel her life fade, but it didn't. Instead, it sank deep into the ground as more of the sand and rock boiled away from her. In his mind, he felt as she fell to solid rock far beneath the surface and then stopped. But, even there, far away from the sky and air, her life continued to pulse, trapped in some grave far beneath the Wind's Teeth.

He dropped to the ground as the power, memories, and senses fled him. He sobbed bloody tears as he thought about Mapábyo being tortured. In the rapidly fading memories from the desert, he saw his wife's last breath well up. It was a single terrified scream as she begged for Rutejìmo to save her, a single phrase he never thought he'd hear. "I can't see you!"

Icy claws gripped his heart, squeezing down until he could feel every pulse beating through his body. It burned along his left arm and he couldn't breathe. Everything shook around him as he stared at the sand marking the Kosòbyo warrior's living grave.

He had lost everything.

His stomach heaved, and he vomited. Black ichor poured out of his mouth followed by crimson blood. He clutched his heart as he started to topple forward.

"No!"

Finding strength, Rutejìmo caught himself. The desert had his heart, but he couldn't give up. Not yet.

He pushed himself to his feet and turned away from the rocks. He had to warn the others. He shoved one foot forward but dropped to his knees. More blood ran from his nose and mouth, splashing on the ground.

Rutejìmo still had family. He had a boy who called him a coward and a daughter who walked her own way. A clan unaware that the Kosòbyo was poised to slaughter them. They were in the valley, and they were helpless if he couldn't run fast enough.

He jammed one foot into the sand and staggered forward, barely keeping his balance until Shimusògo ran past. Then, he reached out for the clan spirit and threw everything he could into running. A heartbeat later, he felt the burn of the poison fade under the euphoria of running.

It would come back, he knew that, but only when he stopped.

As long as he kept running, no more of his family would die.

Chapter 32

Limits

Despite the vast expanses of the ocean, love and hatred will always meet.
—*Perils of the Sea Queen's Son* (Act 1)

Rutejìmo sprinted as fast as he could, gasping with the effort to cover every mile before the sun dipped below the horizon. He didn't dare stop or even slow down. If he did, the poison could take hold, and he may not survive another step.

He focused on the dépa before him, ignoring everything else in the world except for his endless attempts to catch up with the translucent bird. So long as he did, he could ignore anything else, including the overwhelming need for food, water, or the blood in his veins.

The sun was almost below the horizon. Every passing second brought him a chain closer to his destination. He wasn't going to make it. He knew there was no force in the universe that would let him reach home before the sun set.

Despair hung over him, a dark cloud of death that chased after him. It was Mifúno, he could feel whispers echoing in his mind. There was no anger or excitement, only a calling to slow down and let oblivion take him.

The temptation was powerful, but the fear for his family was stronger.

Foot after foot, mile after mile, he ran at his limit and kept pushing against the restrictions of his own spirit. Rutejìmo couldn't channel power fast enough, even knowing that Mifúno chased after him. He may have cheated death but only for a day.

The dépa took a sharp turn to the left.

Surprised, Rutejìmo dug into the sand and ripped a deep furrow in the ground before he slowed down enough to turn. He surged forward and shot after Shimusògo.

Arrows slammed into the ground behind him. He didn't know if they would explode like before but he was already past them before the next ones caught up with him. He felt one graze his ribs, but it was nothing compared to the searing agony already eating him from the inside.

The dépa jerked to the side and he followed, leaving a long gouge in the sands before shooting out. More arrows flashed past him. One of them caught the wind and fluttered away, zooming past his ear as he raced by.

He wished he could grab one and throw it back, but he didn't dare. He needed to run. He followed the dépa, ducking and weaving the arrows until they no longer sailed past him. The bird straightened and so did he, accelerating back up to full speed in a matter of seconds.

Rutejìmo held his breath and waited for the one last lucky shot, but it never came. Wind howled past him, ripping at his skin and drying the blood and vomit on his chest. He didn't care, so long as he kept moving.

The left side of his face ached, and his vision clouded over with crimson. He tried to wipe it off his face. He pulled back a stained hand from where his nose was bleeding and his eyes were dripping black.

Between one footstep and another, the dépa and the sunlight disappeared. Rutejìmo let out a cry as he fell forward. He curled his shoulders as he hit the hard ground and rolled forward. He dug into the rocks with his hands, cracking his fingernails but finding purchase to regain his feet.

No longer able to pull on the power of Shimusògo, Rutejìmo ran with only his physical body. Bare feet slipped and smacked against the smooth rock. He tripped and clawed at the ground, using hands and feet to keep moving forward.

He reached the edge of the smooth rock and stumbled on rough gravel beyond. Thankful for the sharp rocks that sliced at his palms and feet, he staggered forward without looking back. As soon as he did, Mifúno would catch him.

Whimpering, he reached a ridge along the gravel and ran along it. He hated that he cried out with every step, and the ragged, wet gasps escaping his throat, but he couldn't stop. He had to tell his clan.

Rutejìmo kept running even when the sun's light faded. Soon, he was blindly crawling in the dark, unsure if he was heading in the right direction or racing toward a cliff. In his mind, he could imagine a thousand deaths that would take him in the night. He had seen giant snakes, men falling off cliffs, or even a sharp rock that cut an artery or sliced into a groin. A million ways to die and he was still racing in the pitch darkness.

Blood poured down his chest and soaked his thighs. The poison continued to burn his insides, but he had nothing left to throw up. He wanted to curl up and die, to find a bed, to find peace, or even a sharp rock that would end the agony in a flash. Anything other than running through the horrid darkness and praying that the spirits would guide him.

A wave of nausea crashed into him, and weakness took him out at the knees. He pitched forward and slammed into rocks, his head striking something that left bright sparks floating across his vision.

"No!" he gasped and dug his hands into the ground, pulling himself forward without a clue where he was going. He sobbed and dug his cracked nails into the rock.

His legs refused to work. He sobbed as the rocks scraped against his belly and chest, cutting at his flesh. He gripped rocks further along and pulled himself harder, inching across the black desert as he tried to reach home.

And then his hand caught nothing. He pawed at the air, trying to find purchase, but nothing came to his grip. He sobbed as he clawed down, batting at the ground as he clutched to the side of the sharp edge. He had found his cliff.

"No... no, this can't be it."

Footsteps crunched before him. He felt a blast of hot breath against his back.

Crying out, he tried to pull back but lost his balance. With a scream, he fell forward only to land on sharp rocks. He rolled against his side until sharp rocks digging into his back stopped him. They were short, but it felt like a thousand knives digging into his skin.

Someone coughed, a man.

And then a woman's voice spoke close to him. "You really are pathetic, aren't you?" It was a voice that plucked memories from beneath the veil of pain and exhaustion. His first shikāfu, his obsession for ten years that almost destroyed Rutejìmo's love for Mapábyo. It was Pabinkue Mikáryo.

Chapter 33

Pabinkue Mikáryo

There are no words shared between horse and human, but I can hear them as close as any lover's whisper.

—Pabinkue Tsubàyo

There was no wind on Rutejìmo's face, and his feet weren't touching the ground. He gasped as he tore himself out of unconsciousness. His broken fingernails scraped against the rocks as he tried to push himself to his feet and start running again.

"Keep him down," snapped Mikáryo.

A strong hand caught Rutejìmo in the chest and shoved him back down into the softness of a sleeping roll.

"N-No, I have..." He coughed, wincing at the hoarseness of his breath and the burn of acid in the back his throat. "... can't stop. I can't!" He pawed at the hand, not seeing the man who held him down but feeling the muscular grip that held him down.

"Stay down, Jìmo." It was the man speaking. The pressure on his chest increased, but Rutejìmo continued to flail. And then he felt a knee drive into his thigh, pinning him down as the other hand caught his shoulder. "Down!"

Rutejìmo sobbed. "P-Poison, I can't—"

"You aren't going to die tonight, I promise," said Mikáryo as she knelt next to him.

Between his gasping, he could hear the crunch of sand as it compacted under her weight. He clutched for her, his hands pawing against her until he realized he was touching bare thigh close to her hip. She was warm compared to the cool air around her.

She chuckled. "No, hold on. Just grip there."

He obeyed, fingers digging into her flesh until he felt her hip bone. Moments later, his strength faded and his hand slumped down.

"There you go. You aren't going die."

"Tonight at least," amended the other man. It sounded like Tsubàyo, a former member of the Shimusògo clan who tried to sacrifice Rutejìmo to Mikáryo. But that was over fifteen years ago, and both of their lives had gone separate ways.

"B-Bàyo?"

"Yeah, Jìmo. It's me."

"W-Why can't I see?"

Mikáryo leaned into him, and he felt the rim of a cup pressed to his lip. "Here, drink this. It's going to taste horrid."

Rutejìmo opened his cracked lips and hot liquid flowed into his mouth. It was coppery and sharp. He choked on it, sputtering as it overflowed his mouth.

"Sit him up," commanded Mikáryo.

Tsubàyo got off Rutejìmo and pulled him into a sitting position.

Rutejìmo saw movement in his right eye as the vision started to clear. In his stomach, the heat pooled with a comforting warmth.

"Here, drink some more. Your vision will come back a little."

"W-What about—" He gulped and then gasped as the liquid coated his aching throat on its way down. "—the poison?"

"It's still there, but Bàpo will hold it at bay for the night. It will still be there in the morning, but by then you'll be running and you won't feel it."

"B-Bàpo? Who is Bàpo?"

"Her horse," said Tsubàyo as his grip on Rutejìmo's shoulder increased. "Now shut up and drink the sun-damned blood."

Rutejìmo felt his stomach clench. "B-Blood?"

"Bàyo," said Mikáryo in a sharp voice, "he didn't have to know that."

"He's just going to whimper as soon as he sees it. He is pathetic that way."

Rutejìmo's vision came back slowly. He looked up to see Tsubàyo kneeling next to him. He was older than Rutejìmo but only by a few years. As a child, burning oil had scarred his face and right shoulder. Over a decade of riding in the desert had deepened the disfigurements with sharp edges and deep furrows.

Tsubàyo looked down at Rutejìmo. "Drink, Jìmo, it's the only thing keeping you alive. I'd rather Bàpo's sacrifice didn't go unheeded."

Rutejìmo nodded and opened his mouth, still staring at Tsubàyo. When he felt the rim of the cup pressed against his lips, he gulped deeply and tried not to think about the source of the heat or the comfort he gained from a creature's blood.

Tsubàyo had stripped down to his loin cloth. Hard muscles defined his body but Rutejìmo saw scores of fading scars along his arms and shoulders. One of them bisected his scar tissue, creating a ridge between the bottom and upper half. A discoloration remained at the end of the cut, it looked like a blade had been left in the wound.

Rutejìmo drank deeply as he focused on Tsubàyo's scars.

"There you go," said Mikáryo as she drained the last of the cup into Rutejìmo. "That should keep you with us for another hour." There was a scuff of the cup being set down and then strong fingers caught Rutejìmo's chin.

Mikáryo tilted his head toward her, and Rutejìmo let her. The vision in one eye scanned along the ground, pausing when he saw Mikáryo's massive black horse on his side, sides heaving with labored breath. He felt a pang of sadness, and then he was looking at her.

She looked just like he remembered from five years ago, except for more wrinkles and gray strands in her black hair. Her skin was dark brown with black horse tattoos covering every inch except for a few bare areas. Like Tsubàyo, she had stripped down to her breast strap and a loin cloth, but Rutejìmo knew what she looked like underneath even the thin fabric covering her. She was his first in many ways.

Mikáryo cupped Rutejìmo's chin with both hands, peering at him with her green eyes. "One eye is ruined, isn't it?"

"I-I can't see out of it."

"The poison has filled it. Can you run with one eye?"

He nodded. "I-I have been for almost a day now."

"Good. I hope whoever did this got what they deserved."

Rutejìmo remembered the look of horror on Dimóryo's face as the sand swallowed her. "I... I think I killed her."

Tsubàyo snorted back a laugh.

Mikáryo glanced at him and then back. "I have trouble believing that."

"S-She killed—" He sobbed at the memory. Tears burned his eyes as he inhaled sharply, his shoulders shaking as he tried to hold in his sorrow.

Mikáryo pulled him to her chest, her hard body somehow giving comfort to him as much as her breasts.

He shook as he wrapped his arms around her and sobbed. "She killed Pábyo. Tort... tortured her. And... I... was so angry, and I couldn't do anything." The words came out in bursts, punctuated by wet gasping. He was weak, and it was his only hope.

"And you killed her?"

"I... asked the desert to declare her dead."

Mikáryo stiffened under his grip.

"And the sun... and the moon." He sobbed and closed his eyes. "And the wind. And then she lost her powers... and then the ground swallowed her up."

Tsubàyo groaned. "Oh, sun fuck me in the eye."

Mikáryo took a deep breath and wrapped her arms around Rutejìmo. "You killed her, Rutejìmo."

"He didn't kill her!" Tsubàyo snapped, "He created a ni-bonyāchu. A demon. How—"

"Bàyo!" Mikáryo rested her head on Rutejìmo's shoulder. "It's okay. You killed her, and she is going to suffer for the rest of time for what she did."

Rutejìmo let out a long gasp and slumped against Mikáryo, the strength flooding out of him.

"Jìmo?"

"I..." He thought about what he did. "I didn't know what else to do."

"No, for a murdered wife, that was appropriate," said Mikáryo. "Though most husbands just stab the killer, not doom them to endless suffering and torture."

Tsubàyo grunted.

Mikáryo lifted her head. "You would have done the same thing, Bàyo."

"She wasn't murdered."

Rutejìmo stiffened. He tried to remember Tsubàyo's wife's name. He did, though he was drunk when Mikáryo told him. Lifting his head, he turned to look at Tsubàyo. "Rojikinomi Fi-múchi? You lost her?"

Tsubàyo's eyes widened and then he looked at Mikáryo. "You know her?"

"Káryo," he remembered that Mikáryo insisted on familiar names, "told me about her. And you had three children."

Tsubàyo's expression softened. "She died last year, in child-birth. For our sixth." He ducked his head. "We lost the girl too."

Rutejìmo sniffed. "I'm sorry." He held out his hand. "It hurts."

The expression hardened. "What would you know?"

"I lost my first child, a boy, the day Gemènyo died."

Tsubàyo froze, his face paling. "Mènyo? How? He was... the only one nice to me."

Rutejìmo choked on the memories. "I..."

Mikáryo squeezed him. "Go on, it's going to be a long night, and you can't sleep."

He looked back at her. When she shook her head, he re-signed himself to a long night and turned back to Tsubàyo. Closing his eyes, he dredged up the painful memories and started his tale at the point Mikáryo rejected him for the last time.

It took him hours to speak, punctuated only by Mikáryo go-ing to the horse's body to draw more blood. Rutejìmo wanted to ask what she was doing to the creature, but she pushed him to keep speaking about his life and the subtle way she changed the topic told him the question would never be answered.

He told the two more about his life than anyone besides Mapábyo knew. Of the loss of his child, what he did when cast out of his clan, and even the struggles to learn and perform the purification rituals. With her prodding, he even went into the details of the deaths he had seen and the growing realization that he was connected to Mifúno long before this journey.

When he finished, he felt drained—but also relieved. A weight had been removed from his shoulders. He took a deep breath, thankful that whatever Mikáryo gave him had eased his throat, and looked up at Tsubàyo who sat across from him while Mikáryo cradled him with her body.

Rutejìmo sighed. "I... I don't know what else to say."

"Do you think," asked Tsubàyo, "that being a kojinōmi is really like being a warrior? That you're going to die serving her?"

Rutejìmo nodded.

"And yet you never gave up."

"I... couldn't. Now, I'm trying to save my children and my clan."

"But, you're going to die." Tsubàyo's eyes glittered in the light of a small fire.

Behind Rutejìmo, Mikáryo's grip on his side tightened.

Rutejìmo nodded again.

"Well, that makes things difficult." Tsubàyo stood up and walked into the darkness.

Rutejìmo watched him leave, a prickle of discomfort rising. He felt it gathering in his shoulders and his stomach.

Mikáryo pulled him down against her chest. "Don't mind him. He's just struggling with something we were told to do."

He leaned into her and drank from the offered cup. It was stallion blood, but there were herbs and powders that Mikáryo added to it. It didn't stop the poison, but it halted its ravaging of his body.

Mikáryo set down the cup and wrapped her arms around Rutejìmo. "It's easy to accept a command to kill a man you know when you're still angry."

Rutejìmo's body tensed.

"It's harder when you've walked a mile in his footsteps. Your story reminded Bàyo that you aren't much different than him."

"You were told to kill me?"

Mikáryo squeezed him as an answer.

"Not the Shimusògo? Not the others?"

"No, the elders of Pabinkúe were quite specific. Shimusogo Rutejìmo. You are the first, last, and only one to make it this far. The others have already been killed, so Kosòbyo thinks that if they stop you here, their secret will be safe."

Rutejìmo closed his eyes.

"I'm not going to kill you, Jìmo."

"Why not? Your clan demanded it."

She squeezed him again and leaned forward to rest her head against his. "I care more about my shit than I do about my clan. They are my family and my elders, but that doesn't mean I agree with them."

"Won't they be angry?"

"Yes. They may even kill me for this, but I'm still going to do it."

"Why?"

"Because you are..." She smiled. "... pathetic. Helpless. I still see that little boy peeing his trousers as he tried so hard to be brave."

Rutejìmo blushed.

"And then again when Bàyo tried to sacrifice you to save his own life. But, even then, I saw a strength in you. It went beyond the whimpering—"

Rutejìmo grimaced.

"—and the peeing—"

Rutejìmo squirmed in discomfort.

"—and the whining—"

"I get the point."

She smirked. "—there was just something that I saw in you. Maybe it was the thing Chyòbi told you about."

It took Rutejìmo a heartbeat to realized she was talking about Wamifuko Gichyòbi.

She chuckled. "I think it is something else. You had spirit and determination. You made a lot of mistakes, but you also kept trying."

Rutejìmo settled back down. He took a deep breath and winced at the ache in his body. He was going to die soon, but it only tempered the gift of having one more night to live. "I'm a coward."

"Says the man who walked into a plague valley, risked his brother killing him to save his clan, or even kept running into danger because his boy and girl needed him. I don't know where you got the idea that you're a coward, Jìmo, because you aren't. You are just as strong as the rest of us, maybe stronger since most people would let their weakness define them."

"I am weak."

"And yet you aren't known as the weakest Shimusògo. Around here, you are Rutejìmo, the kojinōmi who treats the day and night as allies. The one who somehow bridged the gap between Tachìra and Chobìre and became one of the few Mifúno to ever exist."

"I really am Mifúno?"

She chuckled. "Mifúno is a wonderful but vengeful mother. If you spoke for her without her permission, you would have died before the words left your lips. I couldn't even joke about it, but you did. The Pabinkúe heard rumors of you speaking for Mifúno long before the Kosòbyo came to us with an offer of power and money."

Rutejìmo took a deep breath. He felt warm in her grasp and dreaded the moment he would have to run.

"Why did they take it?"

"Because of... Bàyo, I think."

"Bàyo?"

"He didn't tell you this, but when his wife was dying, he asked me to find you."

Rutejìmo tensed.

"But, Múchi's father fought against that. And as elder of the Rojikinòmi, his weight held much more sway than Bàyo's. It came to blows and Bàyo lost. He was chained in the caves when Múchi and the girl died. Her father released him when it became grim, but it was too late. Both of them knew, though, that I could have found you before they lost her. And," Mikáryo sighed and wrapped her arms around Rutejìmo's chest for a long moment, "I think they both blame you for not being there."

"H... How could I?"

"It doesn't matter. Losing a daughter or a wife poisons the heart. Neither could stab the other, so they used you as the safe target for her loss."

"But, why did Bàyo ask?"

Tsubàyo approached and sat down heavily. "Because, despite what was between us, I respect you above all other koji-nōmi. You spoke with your heart, and you never gave up. And, just like Káryo, I kept looking for you—"

"Bàyo!" snapped Mikáryo.

"—every time we entered Wamifuko City, because we both ended up caring about you."

"He didn't have to know that."

Tsubàyo raised an eyebrow at her.

"Horse-thief," muttered Mikáryo as she leaned back.

"Outcast," replied Tsubàyo with a grin.

Rutejìmo stared at them both, then lifted his head to look at her. "But, you cast me aside. I wanted to go with you and you... threw me away."

Mikáryo sighed, and her eyes sparkled in the light. "Because you couldn't go where I needed to go. But that doesn't mean I didn't love you."

"But...."

"Jìmo, you had to find your own path. And you did. Look at where you are, at what you've done. You wouldn't have found that among the Pabinkúe, and I knew it."

Rutejìmo bowed his head.

"I do love you. And I still do, which is why I'm here and not bringing your head to the Kosòbyo like they demanded."

The back of his throat tickled, and he coughed. And then again. When he pulled his hand back, there was fresh blood on it.

Mikáryo stood up and hurried toward her horse. Rutejìmo watched as she knelt by her favorite stallion's throat and he felt a pang of sadness. The horse shuddered and then slumped down.

Rutejìmo bowed his head, mouthing a prayer to Mifúno for the horse's sacrifice.

She came back with tears in her eyes and a fresh cup. "Come, drink this, and I will tell you some stories. We still have a long night, and we have to keep you up."

Chapter 34

One Last Time

Even the most insignificant person is a lead in their own play.
—Stomker Disan

Mikáryo chuckled. "After that, Hūni refuses to talk to Bàyo a-gain." She drank from a wine bottle.

Rutejìmo was cradled by the same arm and the movement ground his cheek against her breast. He took a deep breath of the faint perfume of oil and dust that permeated her clothing. His eyes fluttered close with his exhaustion and the ache in his sockets.

She relaxed and released him. A second later, she tapped his thigh with the bottom of the bottle. If it wasn't for the poison, it was a light touch but it felt like she was punching his leg.

Forcing his eyes open, he looked up at her. A sad longing filled him. For ten years, he had a shikāfu for her, a flame for the only woman in his life. Only when Mikáryo cast him out in his moment of need had he found his true love, Mapábyo.

Sorrow bubbled up, and he leaned back against her. She wasn't holding him like a lover this time, but as an anchor. He needed something to keep him going on through the night.

With each passing hour, he could feel Mifúno rising in the darkness, the force that avenged his wife's and his clan's death expected her due.

He closed his eyes.

"No," whispered Mikáryo in his ear. Her warm breath tickled along his lobe. "You can't sleep."

He forced his eyes open. "I'm not."

"And don't think about that either."

"They all died."

"Yes, but you are still here. You will see them soon enough; don't rush to her breasts. Focus on today and your run, nothing else." She squeezed him tight.

"And then what?"

"Just run. It will—" Her whispers stopped sharply.

Fear prickled Rutejìmo's skin. "Káryo?"

Mikáryo lifted her head. "Bàyo?"

Tsubàyo was standing up. "It's time."

"Time?" Rutejìmo looked around and then stood up as Mikáryo pushed him to his feet. "Time for what?"

Standing up, he saw a sliver of brightness along the eastern horizon. The sun would not rise for another half hour. He swayed from hours of inactivity and the burn of the poison began to creep back into his senses. It burned at his nostrils. He pressed one finger to his nose, but the bleeding had not yet begun. "Káryo?"

Mikáryo hurried over to her horse. The black stallion no longer breathed, but she still circled to kneel in front of it. Her dark skin, covered in tattoos, seemed to crawl as she rested her hand on the dead animal. "Thank you, Great Pabinkue Datobàpo."

Standing up, she sniffed once. "Rutejìmo, the rest of the Pabinkúe know you're here. They come from all directions and will be here in less than ten minutes."

Rutejìmo gasped and then grabbed his only belonging, the message case. Slinging it over his shoulder, he looked around. "I... I need sunlight to run."

She gathered up her own clothes and quickly dressed in less than a minute. He focused on her two weapons. Both were tazágu, one was unnamed and the other glowed brightly. "No, you only need feet to run. Bàyo?"

Tsubàyo tugged his shirt over his head. He reached backwards just as one of the black horses stepped out of the darkness, seemingly out of solid stone. Rutejìmo knew that the Pabinkúe's magic was to move through darkness, but it always terrified him when he saw a horse appearing from nowhere. Without a noise, Tsubàyo turned and swung onto the horse's back.

Mikáryo clicked her tongue. "Who is out there?"

Tsubàyo lifted his head. He nodded and the horse silently tapped its foot against the rocks. "I feel Fín's, Gìbi's, Óchi's, Pòja's, and Káki's herds. Just under a thousand head. They are all coming in at my limits. Hūni is out there, but she's just riding Dāpa."

Rutejìmo frowned at the unfamiliar names. He had heard some of them in Mikáryo's and Tsubàyo's stories. None of them were there to save him.

Mikáryo shook her head. "I can stop Hūni, how many can you handle if you start with Fín?"

Tsubàyo looked at her, the scar on his face dark in the pale light of their dying flame. "All of them." He smiled grimly.

A smile stretched across Mikáryo's face. "My little horse thief. I always said you could steal Pabinkúe herself."

Turning to Rutejìmo, she grabbed his shoulders and looked at him. "Jìmo... Great Shimusogo Rutejìmo."

Rutejìmo swallowed and trembled. Mikáryo had never used his full name before.

She opened her mouth and then closed it. Shaking her head, she let out a short, bitter snort. "I've been spending all night trying to figure out how to say this. And everything I can think of just comes off as insulting. I'm sorry, I just don't have the words."

Rutejìmo glanced away to avoid showing his tears. He wished he could say something himself, to thank for her risking her own life to save him from the night.

The burning in his nose increased and he felt blood trickling down his lip. Sniffing, he wiped it away and caught sight of Mikáryo's horse. An idea blossomed and he dug down to see if he had the energy to thank her properly. After a moment, he decided he would simply try. Slipping from her hand, he headed for the corpse.

"Jìmo," said Mikáryo, "what are you doing? You don't have time to do anything for Bàpo."

As he approached, he prayed to Mifúno. The wind rose around him, peppering him with sand but also giving him strength. She would help him, he knew it, even though she demanded his death. With a trembling hand, he pressed his palm against the cool body of Mikáryo's companion.

The horse didn't move, but suddenly ash poured out of its body. The corpse dissolved underneath his hand, flesh becoming a fire's ash with no flame to create it. It swirled around him in a black cloud before the wind blew it away.

Weakness drove into him as the power faded. He struggled to remain standing as the burn of poison and the ache of his injuries ignited. Turning around, he struggled to walk back.

Tsubàyo and Mikáryo stared in shock, their eyes focused beyond Rutejìmo. He could feel the wind blowing behind him, and knew the desert took the ash away. He didn't have to look back to know Mifúno had accepted the horse's spirit.

Mikáryo's jaw dropped as she turned her head to him.

Rutejìmo fought a wave of dizziness and struggled to keep it from his face. He wanted to thank her, and passing out wouldn't let him do it. "You're right. I am a Mifúno."

A tear welled in her eye. She stepped into him and hugged him tight. Her lips caressed his and drew back bloody. "I was wrong, Jìmo. You aren't pathetic."

There was a brief pause, and then she nodded.

Rutejìmo bowed to her, but said nothing.

A black horse stepped out of the darkness. It was a stallion but one Rutejìmo had never seen. Mikáryo grabbed his mane and pulled herself up. She nodded once to Tsubàyo and then clicked her tongue.

The horse jumped forward, diving into the shadow Rutejìmo cast on solid rock. Even as Rutejìmo winced, she disappeared from what was left of his sight and out of what remained of his short life.

Gulping, Rutejìmo shivered and then turned.

Tsubàyo motioned for him to follow and turned his horse, not diving into darkness but walking to the southwest, toward Shimusogo Valley.

Rutejìmo followed, jogging to keep up. Every step was a struggle, with the poison coming back in sharp waves of agony.

The minutes stretched toward the moment when the sun rose above the horizon. Rutejìmo could feel the anticipation growing.

"You're going to die."

He looked up at Tsubàyo who continued to stare forward.

"No matter what happens, you're going to die as soon as you stop running."

Rutejìmo nodded. "I-I know."

"They have a word for that, don't they? The Shimusògo?"

"Ryodifūne. The final run." Rutejìmo shivered at the name. It was the noble death of the Shimusògo, to die serving the clan. "But I can't do the ryodifūne. I don't have the power... or the ability."

Tsubàyo finally looked at him. "Are you really that stupid? Of course you do."

"I don't, Bàyo. I don't know how they do it. They talk about the death at the end, not how they started their run."

"Jìmo. I've hated you most of my life. But, as the years went on, I realized I could never amount to what you've done and what you've become. You've earned your ashes on that damn bird's statue. You, of all the Shimusògo, belong in the shrine in a place of honor."

Rutejìmo sniffed and struggled to keep up. He had to turn his head to watch Tsubàyo from his one good eye.

"And today is a good time to find out exactly how fast you can run. Because you have almost a thousand miles to go before you die. If you don't make it, the setting sun will steal your powers and your family is going to die."

Rutejìmo ducked his head and mulled over the words. He didn't understand the ryodifūne. It was supposed to be the climax of a runner's life, the point where all their magic comes down to a single run. It also took their life at the end. He glanced behind him.

The wind was already gathering, and he could feel the desert spirit's hand reaching for him. He already had death following him.

He shivered and focused on the horses around him. When they started the run, there were a few dozen black horses, but in a matter of minutes their numbers swelled. As he watched, more horses burst out of the shadows of the ones already there, adding to the black mass of silent horses surrounding him.

Rutejìmo turned back and concentrated on moving. Tsubàyo had sped up and Rutejìmo had to shift into a run to keep up with the herd.

"Look over there." Tsubàyo gestured but Rutejìmo could only see movement. He turned to look where Tsubàyo pointed. In the distance, he spotted black dots moving around fires. "There is a speed clan up there and most of the Pabinkúe. The Pabinkúe will be panicking because they just lost their herds," he smirked as he spoke. "The speed clan is riding giant lizards and I couldn't steal their mounts."

He gestured ahead of him. "I was listening through the horses while you rested. The Kosòbyo said that they've hired at least four other speed clans to ambush you further along, mostly around the home valley. If you get there, be ready for an ambush. I suspect one of them hides underneath the sand."

Tsubàyo pointed further to the west. "Up there, past that ridge are the Madashikóme. They are snipers from the south. Not exactly allies of the Pabinkúe, but a small band of them were in the valley when the Kosòbyo hired us."

Rutejìmo shivered.

"They specialize against speedsters and fliers. And the moon will be above the horizon for about an hour after Tachìra breaches. Which means that for an hour you have to find some way of outrunning them."

Rutejìmo gulped. "H-How? I can't run that fast. I never could."

Tsubàyo swept his hands forward, and the black horses charged. Hundreds of them galloped past and moved to the side, forming a thick wall of darkness.

Lowering his hands, Tsubàyo clutched his mount's mane and leaned over to him. "You have a quarter mile to figure that out. And then if you don't, your clan is going to die."

Rutejìmo glared at him.

Tsubàyo favored him with a sad smile. "Shimusògo run, right?"

Rutejìmo nodded, and a splatter of blood from his nose splashed on his thigh. His vision blurred and he felt the acid tickling the back of his throat.

"Then run."

Rutejìmo nodded.

"And one more thing..." started Tsubàyo.

When Rutejìmo looked at him, he gave him a deep bow from on top of his horse. There were tears glistening in Tsubàyo's eyes. "I... see you, Great Mifuno Rutejìmo."

The sun burst over the horizon, and Rutejìmo felt energy pour into him. The translucent bird shot forward, and he burst into movement after it, throwing himself into running fast e- nough to keep the poison from killing him.

One of the horses stumbled. A splatter of blood burst out of the side of its body just as Rutejìmo raced past it. He spotted the flash of an arrow, but then the blood sprayed against his face.

He winced as more cracks followed, piercing through the shield of horses as he raced along with them. He couldn't see his opponents, but he could feel their arrows as they slaugh- tered the horses obscuring him.

He shuddered with every scream as they dropped.

Rutejìmo concentrated on the dépa, trying to push himself, but he knew his limits. He glanced up and saw the horses thin- ning. It had been less than twenty seconds, and he was almost at the end of his shelter.

Memories of Desòchu's and Chimípu's death burst into his mind. He remembered the sorrow of losing his wife and seeing Nifùni's decapitated corpse rotting in the sun. More memories came, of the deaths that he had witnessed over the years. They flashed past him, and he imagined himself in their position.

And then a single moment, frozen at the beginning of his nightmares: Karawàbi. He was one of the boys who failed the rite of passage. Rutejìmo and the others had found him at a campsite, his throat cut and his body abandoned. The worst way to die, rotting in the sands with no one to care for him.

Unless he could run faster, that would be Rutejìmo's fate.

Rutejìmo sobbed and screamed. He had to run faster, but his body wouldn't move.

He thought about his children, Kitòpi and Piróma. Their bodies would rot in the sun if Kosòbyo invaded the valley. The snake clan wouldn't give them peace or a proper burial. There would be no kojinōmi to guide them and their spirits would be abandoned to the winds.

"No!" His voice cracked.

An arrow pierced his arm but then snapped as he brought it down to his hip. The pain flashed through him. He saw a cloud of more arrows rise out of the horizon, sailing in a wave of darkness he knew he couldn't avoid.

With a scream, he pushed with all his might.

"Shimusògo!" He heard the voices of the dead echoing in his throat. Energy flared around him, and there was a crack of thunder.

The world blurred around him, the sands turning to haze as they whipped by.

The arrows never struck.

He gasped, but he couldn't turn away. He couldn't do anything but run. The world blurred around him, moving faster than he thought possible. He could feel the ground solidifying underneath his feet, but he was no longer riding in the plume of Shimusògo but leading it.

The translucent bird, a constant companion for fifteen years was no longer in front of him.

It was beside him.

He had caught Shimusògo.

Sadness bubbled up but was burned away by an intense rush of power that poured through him. It tore at his senses and his body, destroying him as fast as the poison would have. But Shimusògo wouldn't let him die while running.

If he stopped, it was over.

But he would make it home.

Chapter 35

Shimusogo Valley

The Ryayusúki are horse riders with the ability to pass through sand as easily as most run across the ground. They are fast, but not the fastest.

—Shimusogo Tokimòshi

At just past noon, Rutejìmo first saw Shimusogo Valley, just a dark blur along the horizon, a hundred miles away, but the shape of the carved-out valley was distinctive to those who approached it for most of their lives.

He didn't feel hunger or agony or thirst anymore, only the overpowering need to reach the valley before he stopped.

His feet slammed across the rocky plains for less than a heartbeat, and then he was past. He heard the wind howling behind him and knew a plume would mark his passing, but there was nothing he could do to hide his presence.

Ahead to both sides, he saw other plumes racing toward him. Flashes of power and lightning were visible even from this distance, and he knew they weren't Shimusògo. They were the clans the Kosòbyo hired to kill him.

Mouthing a prayer to Shimusògo and Mifúno, Rutejìmo continued to race straight ahead. He didn't think he could turn while running, at this speed he didn't have any choice. He wished he had his tazágu, in the hopes of parrying at least one blow.

He tried to shift to the side, but the power coursing through him drove him forward. He was going to charge straight into the valley or die.

Minutes stretched out into a tight ball of tension. He could do nothing but watch as the ambush approached him. They aimed for the path ahead of him, a perfect ambush with his inability to move to the side or dodge.

Then he saw a shadow of a massive bird sailing over the sands toward him. It was Tateshyúso, the spiritual ally of Shimusògo and the guardians of the valley. The bird spirit's wings spread over a quarter mile on sand as she approached. One moment, he was racing in the brilliance of Tachìra and then, in the next, he was in the darkness of the bird's shadow. Despite his speed, he didn't come out the other side; the shadow followed after him.

The air wavered before him, hazy as a figure appeared. It was Pidòhu. His body rippled with his movement, a translucent form that did little to obscure the ground behind him. The thin man wore only a loin cloth but he had a wiry build and his brown skin shimmered like the wind. His thin hair fluttered.

"Great Shimusogo Rutejìmo. Did your brother give you a head start to give you a chance to beat him?" Pidòhu smirked as he gestured back to the valley.

Rutejìmo opened his mouth to warn him, but the only noise that came out was a screech. He tried again, but his voice refused to make any other sound.

Pidòhu's smile dropped instantly. Rutejìmo watched as he took a second look at Rutejìmo, his eyes gazing down as the wind blew through his ethereal body. When he looked up, determination replaced the amusement on his face.

Turning around, Pidòhu let out a sharp screech of his own. It was deeper in pitch but just as insistent as any warrior's call.

A heartbeat later, two more shadows of Tateshyúso burst out of the valley and sailed toward them. They slammed into the darkness hovering over Rutejìmo, and two more figures, a man and a woman, appeared in the eye before him. They were both dressed like Pidòhu, with the woman wearing an additional white breast strap. All three of them hovered in front of Rutejìmo, their translucent bodies rippling with his speed.

Pidòhu turned sharply to the other Tateshyúso. "Rutejìmo is in danger. Tikói, check out the movement to the south. Menodàka, you—"

Both disappeared as their shadows burst out.

Pidòhu turned to Rutejìmo. He nodded curtly before he faded away, and then Rutejìmo was running in sunlight again.

He watched as the two shadow spirits covered the distance in a matter of seconds and then sailed back. The massive shadows swallowed dunes before they settled over Rutejìmo.

All three appeared before him. Pidòhu's back was to Rutejìmo but his voice was clear. "There are fliers coming up behind him. They are armed with arrows."

Tikói shook her head. "Speed riders, lizard and bird. They are also armed and I don't know the clans."

Menodàka said, "Archers and fast horses. I also saw disturbances in the sand in front of him, someone is hiding, and I don't think they are friendly."

Rutejìmo gasped and tried to say something, but only a screech came out.

Pidòhu glanced at him and there was sadness in his green eyes. "I'm sorry, Jìmo. Keep running. I promise you'll make it home."

"What about Desòchu and the others?" It was Tikói, the female in front of him.

Rutejìmo shook his head, unable to say anything.

"Damn the sands," snapped Pidòhu. He pointed to her. "Summon the Ryayusúki in the next valley. Tell them we are in danger."

"What about that?" asked Menodàka as he pointed to the message case around Rutejìmo's neck.

Pidòhu shook his head. "We can't carry that, it's too heavy. If you grab it, you'll lose the wind. No, Rutejìmo must deliver it. Now, you go get the Karāchi and remind them that we have a pact to defend each other. And there is no time."

"Yes, Great Tateshyuso Pidòhu." The other two disappeared as their shadows sailed off. One headed toward a valley just barely visible with Rutejìmo's good eye. He knew it was the Ryayusúki clan's valley, horse riders that had sworn to protect the Shimusògo as they swore to protect them in turn. The other spirit headed toward a mountain much further away, but it was the home to a bird rider clan who had the same pact.

"Rutejìmo, I will tell the Shimusògo. Can you run straight and fast?"

Rutejìmo nodded sharply, his vision blurring.

"Shimusògo run. Don't you dare stop," whispered Rutejìmo's friend, and then he raced toward the valley.

Rutejìmo watched the spirit disappear into the valley and then focused on the approaching clans. They were going to intercept him in less than ten minutes, and he still needed twice that to make it home. He didn't know how he could stop before slamming into the cliff, his body refused to do anything but run.

A ripple of power exploded from the valley entrance. He watched as it expanded in a wide circle that flowed across the sands. At the same time, light shone as one of the Shimusògo warriors ignited into flames. It streaked toward him, racing in a straight line that kicked up a burning plume of dust and feathers.

As the ripple washed over the sands, and all through the valley Shimusògo dropped what they were doing and raced back to the cliffs. Small plumes of sand and dust followed their trails as parents and grandparents brought the children back to the shelter.

The ripple faded before it reached Rutejìmo, a screech to call the others. It was his turn to need help, but he knew they would be too late.

Tateshyúso's shadow raced ahead of the warrior and settled over Rutejìmo. Pidòhu appeared. "Great Shimusogo Rutejìmo."

Rutejìmo opened his mouth, but then closed it.

"Run straight, run fast. Don't slow, no matter what. I promise that you will make it." Pidòhu turned and then threw his hands into the air. Energy crackled but didn't burn Rutejìmo like the time in Gichyòbi's room. The two clans had compatible energies that let them use powers without feedback.

The sand around Rutejìmo exploded straight up in a mile-long wave of darkness. Only a rod-wide path remained clear, the same path that Rutejìmo raced along.

Pidòhu disappeared as his body was yanked back past Rutejìmo.

Rutejìmo plunged into darkness. He felt the power beginning to ebb around him. Biting down, he dug deep and prayed he could keep running.

More sand burst before him, carving out both sides of the path.

Tornadoes of golden energy rose from the ridge above the valley entrance. At first, there was one, and then two, and then more. A dozen swirling vortexes of power. And near the bottom, bright discs of energy appeared before shots rocketed out from valley and sailed toward him.

The side of the storm cloud burst open as a runner, a dark-skinned woman with a curved knife, burst out in a swirl of sand. She snarled and snapped forward, charging toward Rutejìmo as her body blurred into the shape of a snake. Not Kosòbyo, but another snake clan that Rutejìmo didn't know.

He wanted to move to the side. But turning was fighting a storm. Both Shimusògo's power and the wind kept him along a straight line. He let out a scream as he prepared to break off his path.

Then the golden flame of the Shimusògo warrior caught up with the snake. A burst of black and gold flared as the two bodies impacted and disappeared into the storm cloud.

Rutejìmo gasped and stopped trying to move from his path. He had lost speed and tried to regain it, but the power was beginning to falter. He gasped as he realized he had slowed himself down. And death came if he stopped.

The burning shots from the valley reached him, disappearing into the sandstorm. Flames exploded inside the violent maelstrom, and he saw bodies of warriors and creatures shadowed by the bursts of light.

More shots rocketed out from the valley.

Suddenly, the ground burst open as a golden figure rose and slashed at Rutejìmo as he passed. The sparkling weapon caught Rutejìmo's arm and sliced through it. The blade caught bone, and he heard a crack as he sprinted past.

Agony snapped through his body, and he lost his rhythm. His foot caught against a dune, and he was pitched forward. With a scream, he held his hands before him as the ground came rushing up.

He caught the impact with both hands, and he saw his right arm snap in half and tear off when he slammed into the ridge. Before he could scream, he was flying through the air, flipping helplessly as blood sprayed out behind him. He barely registered that his arm had ripped off before he hit the ground and bounced again.

The fireballs shooting out from the valley rained down on his position. He knew they avoided the narrow path he raced along, but he had bounced out of it when he tripped.

Screaming, he saw one of the glowing shots streaking toward him just as he reached the apex of his bounce.

Wind blasted around him, and darkness surrounded him. Pidòhu appeared as Rutejìmo threw his remaining hand forward. Howling winds shot forward in a spear that knocked the shot away, tearing a chain-long path out of the sand.

Rutejìmo flew through Pidòhu, bouncing again. He felt his bones crack and ribs shatter, but his speed shielded him from the agony.

More warriors burst out of the sand before him, weapons drawn.

Half-blinded by the sand in his good eye, Rutejìmo saw the ground coming up again. With a grunt, he concentrated on running as soon as he hit the ground.

The dépa burst past, and the ground solidified into rock. Curling his body, he hit with his shoulder and felt his collarbone crack, but then he was on his feet and chasing the dépa. He accelerated, outpacing Shimusògo as he sprinted forward.

He approached the ambushers in their pits with a strange sense of calm. He couldn't take more punishment, but he wasn't going to stop.

The ground behind the ambushers swelled up and then two blood-red horses burst out of the ground. The Ryayusúki had come in their heavy armor. Both warriors held long spears in their hands, and they plunged their weapons into the backs of the closest men poised to attack Rutejìmo.

Grateful, Rutejìmo blasted past, outracing the screams.

Almost to the valley, he saw that most of the clan stood on either side of his path, hands outstretched as if they were going to catch him. In their other hands were slings with rocks swinging from the bottom.

At the end of the impromptu corridor was Tejíko, his grand-mother and the eldest of the clan. She stood straight, her braid whipping back and forth as she yelled something.

Rutejìmo whimpered. He couldn't stop without hurting his grandmother. Pidòhu also said to not stop. He bore down and charged forward straight for his grandmother.

He reached the first ranks of the Shimusògo before he could blink. He felt two hands smack him, and then his body shud-dered as part of his speed poured out of him, into the hands, and then into the slings. Transferring momentum was one of the Shimusògo powers, but he had never seen someone go from standing still to instant movement before.

In a burst of light, two shots fired back the way he had come, cracking the air.

More hands smacked against him, bleeding off his speed as they used it to create vortexes of spinning power. The cracks of the flaming shots burst behind him as his speed was turned into weapons for those who chased him.

He slammed into his grandmother weakly. She staggered back as he collapsed into her, dropping to his knees as blood splattered against her. More of it poured out the ragged end of his right arm, soaking into her dress.

The three Tateshyúso appeared next to him and threw their hands up. Wind screamed as it tore down the front of the cliff and then away from the valley. There was a rumble of power and then a crack of thunder.

"Jìmo!" cried his grandmother as she dropped to her knees.

The stench of blood and acid filled the air around him. He glanced at the stump of his arm and then looked away as na-usea threatened to overwhelm him.

"What happened?" snapped Tejíko.

Hands were on him, holding him down as more people wrapped his arm to staunch the blood.

Rutejìmo ignored them as he looked at his grandmother. His mouth opened, and he tried to say words, terrified that only screeches would come out. "K-Kos..." Gasping with relief, he realized he could talk. "Kosòbyo are... coming to kill... us."

He fumbled for the case, hoping that she could understand it.

Tejíko snapped the strap off his neck and tossed it to another Shimusògo. She gripped Rutejìmo. "Where are the others?"

"Dead. Kiríshi... also dead. They are hunting us. Ambushed. Hyonèku is hurt... with the Wamifūko." He was desperate to speak before the poison killed him. He could already feel it burning the back of his throat.

Tejíko's lips pressed into a line. She looked up. "That merchant who showed up yesterday without warning?"

"Yes, Great Shimusogo Tejíko," said one of the Shimusògo warriors.

"Kill him."

There was a blast of air as the woman disappeared.

Pidòhu knelt next to Tejíko. "Great Shimusogo Tejíko. There are siege weapons coming in from the south. Metal scorpions and snakes. Fast clans come from the side, and they are armed for war."

Tears sparkled in Tejíko's eyes as she shook her head. "Why?"

Rutejìmo clutched her with his hand, sobbing as he felt the poison tearing at his insides. "Kosòbyo... is going to Chobìre."

A stunned silence.

"Please, Grandmother... I promise, it's true."

Tejíko clutched him. "I trust you, Jìmo." She lifted her head. "They obviously are trying to stop the message before it goes out. And we never fail to deliver our message."

There was a blast of air as the warrior who had left for the merchant came back, her hand dripping with blood. "Done."

Rutejìmo gasped for air.

"Papa!"

"Jìmo!"

He jerked when he heard his children. He looked up as they raced toward him, but then Tejíko held up her hand. They didn't slow until two elderly Shimusògo caught them and picked them off the ground.

Kitòpi screamed. "That's my papa!"

Tejíko snapped at him. "Not now!" She turned around. "We need to save the children. They can't be in this war. Where can we take them?"

"The Ryayusúki will take them," said an older man. He was the elder of the horse clan. Rutejìmo had tended to his second wife when she died of a rotted wound.

Rutejìmo groaned as flecks of crimson began to dance in his good eye. He watched his son struggling to free himself from the elder. Two others joined in to hold him.

Piróma stood still, her eyes locked on his.

A heavily armored man knelt next to Tejíko, bowing. "The Ryayusúki will protect them with our lives."

Tejíko nodded. "We have to deliver this message."

"I heard."

"As did the Karāchi." It was a woman. She landed on the ground. Her cloak of feathers settled down as she bowed deeply, her forehead touching the ground. Rutejìmo saw a mark on her forehead, but didn't recognize the symbol. "Who will you deliver it to?"

"Everyone," growled Tejíko before she spoke up, "If you can run, run. Ràchyo and Záji, we were waiting for Desòchu to return for your rites of passage. Decide now if you are a child or an adult. If you stay with us, you'll find Shimusògo in battle or die."

The two teenagers gasped.

"Shimusògo!" Her voice echoed against the walls. "We are abandoning the valley. Children go with our allies. Warriors go out to protect the ones on courier runs. All contracts are burned as of this point! The rest of you, take what you need and run. Find shelter but deliver this message: Kosòbyo is abandoning Tachìra."

Air exploded around them as the Shimusògo raced back into the valley, leaving the children and teenagers standing behind. The girl about to become a woman ran after them, not using magic but racing on her bare feet.

The other, the boy, shook his head. "I-I can't. I'm not ready."

Tejíko bowed her head. "Then protect the children. They'll need you."

"H-How?"

"Shimusògo will lead."

"Papa!" Kitòpi ran toward Rutejìmo, but stopped at the widening puddle of blood. "Papa? What happened?"

"Boy," snapped Tejíko, "turn around!"

"No, he's my papa! Where's Mama!? What happened to Mama?"

Rutejìmo opened his mouth, but the words wouldn't come out. Blood bubbled out of his mouth and he slumped forward as he vomited on his grandmother's dress. It came out black and foul, hissing in the air.

"Ràchyo," yelled Tejíko, "turn him around!"

The teenager ran over, tears on his face and grabbed Kitòpi. The younger boy screamed and fought, but he was forced to turn around.

Rutejìmo saw the others doing the same. He was dying, and even in that moment of his greatest need, they couldn't look at him.

Tejíko leaned into him. "I never thought it would come to this, Great Shimusogo Rutejìmo. You have become something I never expected, and I'm so proud of you."

Rutejìmo sobbed and covered his mouth, trying to stop his insides from pouring out. It bubbled out of his mouth, nose, and ears. His stomach and insides twisted violently as the poison reached for his heart.

"And I pray that we will have a home to return to. But somewhere, sometime, I promise your vase will be Shimusògo's finest. I only wish there was someone to tend to your—"

"Tejíko."

She lifted her head at the armored man's voice.

Rutejìmo looked to the valley entrance, drawn by sudden whispers in his head.

Piróma stood at the entrance, bare-footed and wearing one of Rutejìmo's white shirts. It hung over her shoulders, the loose cloth barely catching on her neck. The end of it dragged through the dust with only her toes visible.

"Oh, Tachìra," whispered Tejíko sharply.

Rutejìmo gasped as his daughter stepped forward, bowing her head as she walked along the ground. The gathered children stepped aside as she made her way toward him.

There were blasts of air as the Shimusògo returned from the caves. Seconds later, gasps filled the air as they grabbed the children and yanked them around once again. Tejíko let out a soft sob as she stood up. Tears splashed on the ground as she turned away herself.

Rutejìmo sobbed as he reached for Piróma.

Piróma didn't stop at the puddle of blood. She padded through it, splashing as she came to his side and knelt.

Rutejìmo smiled and pulled her into a tight hug. "Great Mifuno Piróma."

She clutched him tight. "I... I don't know what to do. What do I say now?" Her voice was a whisper, felt more than heard.

Rutejìmo closed his eyes as his vision faded. "Listen, just listen to me."

He held her tight as he began to whisper into her ear. He didn't have a *Book of Ash* to give her, but he could tell her about the patterns of the sand, the feel of the desert, and the path she had just stumbled on.

When he realized that he couldn't feel her anymore, he kept on whispering everything he could, giving her the things he'd learned and the rituals to follow. He didn't know if she could hear him, but he wasn't going to give up until the last breath left him. He kept speaking until there was only darkness.

And then Great Mifuno Shimusogo Rutejìmo was gone.

About D. Moonfire

D. Moonfire is the remarkable intersection of a computer nerd and a scientist. He inherited a desire for learning, endless curiosity, and a talent for being a polymath from both of his parents. Instead of focusing on a single genre, he writes stories and novels in many different settings ranging from fantasy to science fiction. He also throws in the occasional romance or forensics murder mystery to mix things up.

In addition to having a borderline unhealthy obsession with the written word, he is also a developer who loves to code as much as he loves writing.

He lives near Cedar Rapids, Iowa with his wife, numerous pet computers, and a pair of highly mobile things of the male variety.

You can see more work by D. Moonfire at his website. His stories and novels can be found on the Fedran website.

- https://d.moonfire.us/
- https://fedran.com/

Fedran

Fedran is a world caught on the cusp of two great ages.

For centuries, the Crystal Age shaped society through the exploration of magic. Every creature had the ability to affect the world using talents and spells. The only limitation was imagination, will, and the inescapable rules of resonance. But as society grew more civilized, magic became less reliable and weaker.

When an unexpected epiphany seemingly breaks the laws of resonance, everything changed. Artifacts no longer exploded when exposed to spells, but only if they were wrapped in cocoons of steel and brass. The humble fire rune becomes the fuel for new devices, ones powered by steam and pressure. These machines herald the birth of a new age, the Industrial Age.

Now, the powers of the old age struggle against the onslaught of new technologies and an alien way of approaching magic. Either the world will adapt or it will be washed away in the relentless march of innovation.

To explore the world of Fedran, check out https:// fedran.com/. There you'll find stories, novels, character write-ups and more.

License

This book is distributed under a Creative Commons Attribution-NonCommercial-ShareAlike 4.0 International license. More info can be found at https://creativecommons.org/licenses/by-nc-sa/4.0/. This means:

You are free to:

- Share — copy and redistribute the material in any medium or format
- Adapt — remix, transform, and build upon the material

The licensor cannot revoke these freedoms as long as you follow the license terms.

Under the following terms:

- Attribution — You must give appropriate credit, provide a link to the license, and indicate if changes were made. You may do so in any reasonable manner, but not in any way that suggests the licensor endorses you or your use.

- NonCommercial — You may not use the material for commercial purposes.
- ShareAlike — If you remix, transform, or build upon the material, you must distribute your contributions under the same license as the original.

No additional restrictions — You may not apply legal terms or technological measures that legally restrict others from doing anything the license permits.

Preferred Attribution

The preferred attribution for this novel is:

"Sand and Bone" by D. Moonfire is licensed under CC BY-NC-SA 4.0

In the above attribution, use the following links:

- Sand and Bone: https://fedran.com/sand-and-bone/
- D. Moonfire: https://d.moonfire.us/
- CC BY-NC-SA 4.0: https://creativecommons.org/licenses/by-nc-sa/4.0/

Patrons

This book is freely available on the Fedran website. It can be reformatted for any device, shared, and even reposted on other websites (with attribution and a link to the original). If someone wants to write a fanfic or create art inspired by the book, they are allowed to do so with relatively few limitations, which are set down by the license described in the previous section.

- https://fedran.com/sand-and-bone/

It is hard to compete with "free" in this day and age. Releasing a book under a Creative Commons license is one way of doing that, but there are still costs associated with producing the results. There are hundreds of hours put into writing it, hiring editors to go through it, and even hosting it on a website. As economics will tell you, there is no such thing as a free lunch. Most of the time, you pay for a book before reading it. Sometimes you have a sample of a few chapters to give you a hint, other times just a blurb. Here, you get the entire piece. If you like it, please consider supporting my writing.

The cheapest way of helping is simply to talk about the book. Post opinions on social networks, write a review and put it up on Amazon or Goodreads, or give a copy to someone who might like it.

The second way of helping is to donate money. Even a dollar helps. There are quite a few ways of doing this: you can buy a print copy; the tip jar at Broken Typewriter Press; or even consider becoming a patron. Patronage provides advance access to works-in-progress, votes on new stories and titles, and input into the world and my writing. You can read more about patrons at:

- https://broken.typewriter.press/dmoonfire/
- https://fedran.com/patrons/

I can only hope that if you like it, you'll help me write the next one.

Thank you.

Credits

There are a wide variety of people who were involved with making this book.

Alpha Readers

- Bill H.
- Ciuin
- Tyree C.
- Cindy M.
- Aimee K.

Beta Readers

- Chandrakumar M.
- Laura W.
- Marta B.
- Mike K.

Editors

- Blurb Bitch
- Ronda Swolley
- Shannon Ryan

Patrons

- Ashish P.

Family

- Susan
- Eli
- Bruce

Colophon

Each chapter of this book was written and edited using Atom, a Javascript-based editor. The files for the novel were managed in a Git repository on a private GitLab instance. Each chapter was an individual file formatted using Markdown. Information and working notes about the chapters were placed into a YAML header at the top of each chapter.

These individual chapters were combined together using a Typescript-based framework (mfgames-writing-js) which produces the EPUB, MOBI, and PDF (via WeasyPrint) versions of the novel. These are built using GitLab's Continuous Integration runners.

The cover was created using Inkscape. The color scheme uses eight colors of a monochromatic scale. These colors are shared among all of the Rutejìmo novels. Likewise, the "100-02" along the spine indicates this is the third published book ("02") with Rutejìmo as the main character ("100").

The font used on the cover and interior is Corda in various weights and styles.